Marbal House

A novel by

Sue Rilstone

With ~~best~~ wishes

Sue Rilstone

To my dear friend

Hilary

Marbal House

Sue Rilstone is a Cornish writer living in Bodmin, who has had a play and a series of co-written monologues broadcast on Radio 4. Marbal House, set in Cornwall, is her first novel.

Published in 2012

ISBN 978-0-9569189-1-8

Cover illustrated by Rosie Kennett

Published by: CB Productions SW

Printed by: TJ International

Padstow, Cornwall

Thank you Richard for your support, and thank you Sarah and Kate for patiently leading me through I.T. technicalities. Thank you Sophie for your marketing advice and enthusiasm, and thank you Rosie for spurring me on from the early days of Marbal House right through to the end.

Many thanks also to Chris and Jill Batters for being always available with their publishing help and invaluable publishing advice.

Chapter 1

Marbal House, as Sister Bernadette knew, had been built towards the end of the 19th century. A solid, granite stone house with bay windows either side of a porch that still retained the terracotta, cream and black tiles once vigorously scrubbed by a succession of housemaids. Now, as Sister Bernadette could not fail to notice, the tiles were streaked with dry mud and strewn with equally dry leaves blown from the cherry trees at the front of the garden. Sister Bernadette briefly wondered why Agnes hadn't set to on the porch. Agnes usually and fervently set to on anything in need of a brush or a cloth. Sister Bernadette unlocked the front door with one of the keys Agnes had given her, and went inside.

From the hallway Sister Bernadette could hear the soft hum of a dentist's drill as it delved into some unfortunate's cavity. The sound came from what was once the front parlour reserved in days long past for special guests and Christmas gatherings. Now the whole of the downstairs on the left was partitioned off, with entry via the old kitchen to the Bright Smile Dental Surgery, specialists in intra-oral camera technology and phobia alleviation. In front of Sister Bernadette was the original late Victorian staircase, its chunky banister now sinfully painted in Brilliant White gloss. The front room to the right of the stairs had been turned into a bed-sit. 'Murder On the Dance Floor' flowed out of it, competing with the dentist's drill, and winning.

Everywhere, it seemed, had been covered in white gloss, even the anaglyptic wallpaper. They'll have a devil of a job getting this lot off, Sister Bernadette thought as she climbed the stairs to Agnes' room. Lush red flock, the wallpaper should surely be. Sister Bernadette, who had long been fascinated by social history and the changing décor of houses, envisaged the walls cheerily red. At the stair turn, an oblong window with borders of red and blue stained glass spilt colourful patches on the stark walls. The window at least had been saved, not replaced by PVC, knocked out, blocked in or indeed smothered in white paint. Sister

1

Bernadette was grateful for the miracle. The rooms on the first floor were converted into flats. The original doors, mahogany and panelled, had been replaced by regulation fire doors fitted with security locks. At the end of the landing Sister Bernadette needed the second key Agnes had given her. Behind this door, a short flight of steps led to what was once the servant's room, but was now Agnes' bed-sit.

Agnes, who was expecting Sister Bernadette, had prepared a tray with two mugs and an unopened packet of Ginger Nuts. She greeted her guest with a wan smile and cursory nod, and set about pouring hot water over tea bags while Sister Bernadette openly enthused. "Well now Agnes, isn't this a grand little place you have here? Everything you need and so – so compact and tidy." Her eye swept over the neat single bed with a crucifix above, the chairs, one each side of a single bar electric fire, the tiny area for cooking slotted in under sloping beams. "And you'll have your own lavatory up here, will you?" She turned a small semi-circle, wondering where, in this confined space, ablutions could take place.
"If you need to go, it's in there." Agnes pointed the teaspoon she was holding towards a door beside the bed.
"Ah no, Agnes I don't need to go, I was just wondering where it might be. May I take a peep in there?"
Had Sister Bernadette needed to go, she doubted she would be able to squeeze even side-ways into the little room that had not only a lavatory but somehow a shower cubicle as well. Fortunately Agnes was thin. Ramrod thin.
"Well, well, isn't this just the thing? And all your bits and pieces fitting in so well." Sister Bernadette took the mug of tea Agnes was offering and sat down by the fire wondering if Agnes would think to switch it on. "And your cleaning job at the hospital Agnes – you're still enjoying that?"
Agnes nodded solemnly. "Yeah. Yeah it's alright."
"Bit of a trek for you though, isn't it? It must be a good four miles either way. Have you not managed to get hold of a bus timetable yet? Surely there is no need for you to be walking there and back,

not now the weather has turned so cold." Sister Bernadette eyed the electric fire, hoping Agnes would take the hint. The room needed cheering up. There was a definite chill to the place.

"I'm not wasting money on buses. It don't take long and I've got a brolly if I need it."

Sister Bernadette pictured Agnes flying Mary Poppins style, her umbrella aloft, carrying her through the town and out of it, up the hill to St Luke's Hospital. She thought of sharing her foolishness with Agnes and then thought better of it. Agnes wouldn't see the humour in it.

"Of course Sister Mary keeps me informed. She said you were doing a grand job at the cleaning." Sister Mary had indeed said that. She said Agnes squirted her antiseptic and buffed away with a zest never before known in Women's Surgical. Sister Bernadette pondered, not for the first time that perhaps Sister Margaret had intoned a mite too much into Agnes that cleanliness was next to godliness. After all was said and done, the way Agnes had turned out was down to the nuns who had brought her up – and genetics of course. The nuns couldn't be held wholly responsible, and as for the genes, God only knew where they came from.

Thirty-four years ago, on one blistering day in July, Sister Bernadette had returned to the Sacred Heart Convent hot and flustered. Her pupils at the convent school had also been hot and flustered. Their attention was low, their irritability level high. The day had been an unhappy mix of lethargy and sly retorts. Quite a normal summer's day at the convent school in fact. But the day wasn't to stay normal for much longer.

Sister Margaret was eagerly waiting for Sister Bernadette's return, bursting to tell her. "Reverend Mother wants to see you right away. She has something for you." Sister Bernadette's cheeks turned even pinker. She wiped her steamed up glasses on the sleeve of her habit. Reverend Mother had something for *her?*

"Now it wouldn't be a cool glass of lemonade, would it Sister Margaret? Because there's nothing I'd like more right now than a cool glass of lemonade," Sister Bernadette said with forced cheerfulness.

"If I were you sister, I wouldn't stand around making feeble jokes. I'd hurry along to Reverend Mother," Sister Margaret said severely. "She's in her study waiting for you."

Sister Bernadette entered Reverend Mother's study after knocking on the door and receiving a rather quieter "Come" than usual. Reverend Mother was standing behind her desk. On the desk top, apart from the usual oddments of stationery, was a navy blue carrycot.

Reverend Mother had a finger to her tight lips. "Ssh. Come in quietly sister and don't raise your voice. This child has at last decided to sleep."

"Do you mean there's a baby in that carrycot, Mother?" Sister Bernadette whispered, bemused and curious. A baby at the convent was more than a novelty, it was unheard of. "Would it be alright if I took a peep at the little mite?"

"Oh I think you should, sister." Reverend Mother replied tartly. "You should also take a look at this." She held out a scrap of paper, torn from a note-pad. Sister Bernadette looked at the baby, then at the note. DEAR AUNTIE BERNADETTE, PLEASE LOOK AFTER AGNES FOR ME. I'LL BE BACK FOR HER LATER. X X

Then she looked at the baby again. "What do you know about this sister?" Reverend Mother asked. "Were you aware that your niece was going to leave her child while she went off on – on a shopping spree, or where-ever?" Sister Bernadette shook her head. "I'm completely baffled, Mother."

"You do have a niece, don't you?"

"Indeed I do, Mother. I have six nieces."

"Then take another look at the child. Which one of your nieces does she look like?"

A baby looks like a baby, thought Sister Bernadette. Some are bigger than others, some more handsome. But at just weeks old as this baby surely was, she hadn't had time to grow into her own features, let alone anyone else. To humour Reverend Mother,

4

she looked again. The baby had no hair, and a turned down mouth, grimacing with wind. No, Sister Bernadette could honestly say none of her nieces looked like that. "Even if the baby – Agnes, did belong to one of my nieces, what would she be doing here, in Cornwall, when they all live in Dublin?" Sister Bernadette mused. "At least, as far as I am aware, all of my nieces are still in Ireland."

"One of them obviously is not." Reverend Mother snapped. "This really is most tire-some, sister. You'd better take the child down to the kitchen and take care of her until your niece returns. She has at least put a feeding bottle in the carrycot, and a tin of milk." Reverend Mother lifted the cellular blanket covering the foot of the carrycot. "And there are nappies here and a change of clothes." Reverend Mother folded her hands together, tucked in her chin and looked at Sister Bernadette sharply. "She obviously intends to be gone some hours, sister. When she does return, the *moment* she returns, send her to me."

"I will Mother." Sister Bernadette grabbed the handles of the carrycot. It was heavier that she expected and lurched and swayed as she lifted it from the table. Agnes opened her eyes and mouth and bellowed. "Sorry Agnes, but I'm not used to this." Sister Bernadette murmured. "Don't cry now. Your mummy will soon be here." Even as she said it, Sister Bernadette had a sinking feeling that it wasn't true. If Agnes' mummy ever came back it would not be soon.

"Would you like another cup of tea?" Agnes asked.

"Ah – no. No thank you Agnes." Sister Bernadette already feared she might have taken more bleach into her system than was healthy. It was one thing for Agnes to wash her mugs with bleach, but had she rinsed them thoroughly? From the strong smell and taste of it, Sister Bernadette was doubtful. "I must be going shortly – now that I know you have settled in alright."

"Yeah, I have." Agnes looked around her with a contented sigh. "I like it here. It feels like home, some'ow."

"Home." Sister Bernadette echoed. The convent had been Agnes' home. She looked at Agnes, sitting in the chair opposite. She was plain, it had to be said. She wore her short, prone to greasy hair parted in the middle and gripped back above the ears. Her face usually had a somewhat blank expression, not puzzled even, because that would require thinking. Just blank.

When Agnes was a child, Sister Bernadette had sometimes wondered whether she had lacked oxygen at birth. On particularly trying occasions Sister Bernadette assumed Agnes was just plain stupid. Recently though, she had read an article on autism; some of the listed characteristics seemed to fit Agnes, particularly difficulty with social relationships, communication and imagination. All things considered, Sister Bernadette concluded that Agnes veered towards the Asperger's Syndrome end of the autistic spectrum. She had to discount the 'often have specialised interests, usually highly academic' bit because that didn't fit Agnes at all, unless obsessive cleaning counted as a specialist interest. Sister Bernadette smiled, "You've always liked cleaning haven't you Agnes? Ever since you were a little girl. Do you remember the first dustpan and brush you had?"

Agnes shook her head.

"Your fourth birthday present from Miss Trellis, God bless her. Pink plastic it was, with yellow nylon bristles. You loved that present."

Agnes shrugged." I don't even remember Miss Trellis," she said.

"Ah now surely you remember Miss Trellis, Agnes." Sister Bernadette said, with a hint of exasperation. "She was the convent's benefactor. If it hadn't been for Miss Trellis, you would have been sent to the orphanage. You must remember me taking you to the convent cemetery to where –" "Yeah, I know *who* she is," Agnes said, sounding irritable herself. "I said, I don't *remember* her. Like what she looked like and stuff."

"No. Well it was a long time ago that she died, sure enough. You would have been about six I suppose. Do you never wonder about -" Sister Bernadette hesitated for a second, wondering if it was wise to continue, then decided to plough on. "Do you never wonder who it was who left you at the convent, Agnes? Do you never wonder who your real mother was?"

6

Agnes shook her head. "Not much point in that, is there? You tried to find out and couldn't. I'm not bothered. She don't need me and I don't need her."

"Now isn't that strange," Sister Bernadette murmured, "when I've never stopped wondering about it. A day never passes when I don't wonder about it. But you're the sensible one, sure you are." She gave Agnes a bright smile. "You're quite right. There's no point to it at all. And now I really must be going". Sister Bernadette stood up and wagged her finger playfully at Agnes. "You could do with a little dustpan and brush on the porch downstairs, couldn't you now?"

Agnes frowned. "What?"

"The front porch could do with a bit of a clean, by your standards. Doesn't it drive you crazy passing it in the state it's in?"

"Nothing to do with me, I come round the back and use the fire escape, that way I don't need to speak to no-one." Agnes swivelled round towards the curtained door by the cooking area. She pulled back the curtain to show a flight of metal stairs winding to the ground. "You can go that way yourself if you want. It's quicker."

Sister Agnes declined. "It looks hazardous to me. Surely you don't use the fire escape in the dark? Wouldn't you rather risk meeting someone on the landing than breaking your neck on those stairs?"

"No. I've got me torch if it's dark."

Sister Bernadette turned slowly. "Ah, well you want for nothing then, what with your brolly, your torch – and your faith. Will we say a little prayer together Agnes, before I go?"

Agnes shook her head. "No it's alright thanks. I said one earlier. Thanks for comin' then," she added, and quickly opened the door ajar to speed up Sister Bernadette's exit.

"You'll come and visit us at the convent now, won't you Agnes?" Sister Bernadette asked. She patted Agnes briefly on the arm as she passed. "You know we'd love to see you."

"Yeah, when I've got time. Mind how you go then." Agnes watched as Sister Bernadette descended the stairs to the landing, then she shut the door, switched on the electric fire and opened the packet of Ginger Nuts.

Tomorrow was Thursday, post op. day. That meant Agnes would be able to give the wards a good seeing to. It also meant the patients would be rallying round a bit, talking and asking for things. Agnes hoped no one would ask her to touch their backrests. Patients didn't seem to realise that she wasn't supposed to touch anything on the beds. Under the beds was fine, but not on the beds. Somebody was bound to ask her, somebody always did ask her to do something, and somebody always got upset when she said no.

That night Sister Bernadette found it difficult to sleep. Her thoughts swirled around Agnes up in the attic at Marbal House. Still, it was as well she had left the convent at long last. Miss Trellis had set up a fund allowing Agnes to stay at the convent for as long as she wished, but as Agnes had stayed until she was thirty two and not sixteen as Miss Trellis had anticipated, the fund had long since dried up. It was not that Agnes hadn't earned her keep cleaning and cooking for the nuns, it was the fact that she hadn't become a nun herself that was irksome. Poor Miss Trellis. She was convinced Agnes had been sent to the convent through some divine intervention. "She was sent to us for a purpose," Miss Trellis would say, and with her money and sharp tongue she took on everyone from social services to the bishop, insisting that Agnes stayed at the convent. And stay she did. Agnes grew from a noisy baby into a quiet child with no time for other children, or anyone else for that matter. Miss Trellis was convinced that Agnes' social detachment stemmed from her budding saintliness. She didn't need mortals the way other children did. As time went on it became apparent that Agnes wasn't like other children in many ways. It wasn't only her social skills that were poor, so were her attempts at reading and writing which naturally led to difficulty in other subjects. Sister Bernadette considered it was fortunate Miss Trellis died before Agnes' ineptness became too obvious. Miss Trellis had only to ponder over Agnes' apparent lack of interest in her religious instruction. Prayers, catechism and stories of saints washed over Agnes without leaving a mark. She remembered nothing. Even Miss Trellis sometimes harboured doubts that Agnes was a saint after all, but never mind, if not a saint, someone very special – and at worst she would become a good Christian nun.

If Miss Trellis had no concern as to whose baby Agnes was, Reverend Mother certainly did. Her only lead was the note left in the carrycot and the unfortunate fact for Sister Bernadette, that it was addressed to her. It was Sister Bernadette's duty therefore to rout out the errant mother and her first job was to go to Dublin and interrogate her family.

At first her sisters and brother in Dublin were pleased at her rare visit. It was only after Sister Bernadette brought up the topic of Agnes, that things turned hostile and indignant. "What is it that you're saying Bernadette? Do you think my Catherine's had a baby without me, her own mother, knowing it? And then she's supposed to have gone all the way over to England is she, and deposit the baby at your convent – all that without stopping for a cup of tea with you before she went on her way? Well I call that pretty insulting Bernadette. And if I stopped to take into account the fact that my Catherine has barely turned sixteen and is as good a Catholic girl as you'd wish to find, I'd be more than insulted, I'd be bloody murderous, so I would."
"I'm not accusing anyone Mary – particularly not your Catherine." Sister Bernadette said hastily. "She's a fine girl, I know that. But if I could just have a sample of her handwriting, to compare with this note- look, wait 'til I show you -."
Mary had turned so nasty at this suggestion that Sister Bernadette decided it would be safer to conduct further investigations without bringing calligraphy into it. Her sister Kathleen proved to be more cooperative, mainly due to the fact that amongst her seven offspring only the twins were girls and they were just nine years old. From this righteous position Kathleen felt free to be judgemental and able to cast aspersions. "What kind of a selfish

9

cow would do such a thing? And isn't it a wonder no-one saw the poor baby's mother leaving her? Sure a carrycot's big enough to be carting up a drive in broad daylight. A right dozy lot of buggers the nuns at your convent must be not to have seen anything." Kathleen shook her head sadly as she stirred her coffee. "I just can't imagine who would do such a thing – abandon their baby to a load of sour faced nuns like that. No offence to you Bernadette." Sister Bernadette forced a smile to prove none was taken. "Fortunately we have Miss Trellis to take care of Agnes' needs," she said, adding after a moment's thought, "Mainly that means paying for the day nursery." Kathleen shook her head in commiseration for Agnes once again. "Whoever it was left the poor mite deserves a good horse whipping. And to think it could be one of the family." Her eyes suddenly narrowed. "Have you spoken to Patrick yet? His eldest Jacqui would be capable of anything. Mind you calling the girl Jacqui was enough to turn her into a Jezebel. Not that I want to speak ill of my own brother's daughter but that girl has a reputation Bernadette that you wouldn't want to know about."

"I have spoken to Patrick," Sister Bernadette said. "He showed me a photo of Jacqui. She grew up to be a big girl didn't she?" Sister Bernadette stopped to conjure up the photograph. Jacqui in a low cut frilly blouse, showing plenty of freckled bosom, her plump arm around some man who had apparently whisked her off to Australia and her red hair reaching down and settling on her shoulders in a scribbled mass of curls. Now baby Agnes didn't have any hair at all on the top of her head, but at the base, just above her neck was a thick band of jet black, straight fluff. Not that colour alone could eliminate Jacqui from suspicion, but the fact that she was in Australia when Agnes was abandoned, did.

"Jacqui wasn't in Ireland let alone Cornwall." Sister Bernadette said with a sigh. "She'd been in Australia a good month before Agnes came to us."

"Ah that's right. Patrick did tell me she was goin' abroad with that good for nothin' fella of hers." Kathleen snorted. "Last in a long line of fellas I can tell you. And she's probably dumped him for another by now. Well now, it wasn't our Catherine's Mary who did the dirty deed, and it wasn't Patrick's Jacqui, nor could it be my two little ones. That only leaves our Maureen's two. And one of them's had the calling and the other no man would look at."

Sister Bernadette sighed a second time. "I know – that is I know none of my nieces could be the mother, not that that Bernice couldn't get a man if she'd a mind to. Sure she's pretty enough in her own homely way. But that's it Kathleen, she's homely. According to Maureen, Bernice only leaves the house of an evening to go to confession or a service."

"That would be right, sure it would. Tied to her mammy's apron strings that Bernice is and her nearer to thirty than twenty.

So there it all is Bernadette," Kathleen concluded, folding her arms across her chest. "You can go back and tell that Mother Superior of yours that there is no dirt to be dug up in our family – disregardin' that hussy Jacqui of course. The cheek of the ol' fool. That note in the carrycot was nothin' but a red herrin' sure it wasn't." Kathleen squinted at her sister's crestfallen face. "You're looking disappointed Bernadette. Did you expect that one of your nieces was capable of having an illegitimate baby and dumpin' it three hundred miles away in a convent of all places?"

Sister Bernadette felt she should defend the choice of convents for dumping babies if they were to be dumped anywhere, but couldn't quite work up the enthusiasm. "Naturally I didn't for one minute consider any niece of mine would be so sinful," she said, and prayed God would forgive her lie. "I'm only disappointed Kathleen, because I want to know who poor Agnes' mother is. And I 'm no further forward."

That was thirty-two years ago, and still Sister Bernadette was no further forward. She took a sip of water from the glass on her bedside table and resolved not to give Agnes another thought. She lay back on her pillow anticipating sleep. The rain was lashing against the window and the wind was getting rough. The fire escape steps would be slippery when Agnes set off to work in the morning. It would be dark too, to be going down those wet steps. There now, what was that blessed girl doing creeping back into her thoughts again?

11

The house, Marbal House, was grand enough though. At least it had been, before it was turned into a dental surgery and bedsits. Sister Bernadette pondered over Marbal House, and thought about when it had belonged to one family and hadn't been divided and doused in white paint. A grand family it would have been, leading a grand life.

When Sister Bernadette visited Agnes' flat several months later, she knew differently. She knew about the Marbals now. Sister Bernadette opened the half glazed door leading to the fire escape. She stood on the first gleaming step and looked down to the foot of the stairs. Not a sign of algae, no small piles of black dirt packed into corners, not so much as a cobweb – just stark cleanliness and the lingering smell of bleach.

"It was an accident," Agnes said from behind her.

"You didn't like him though, did you?" Sister Bernadette asked.

"He shouldn't have come," Agnes said.

"I told him not to," Sister Bernadette said.

Chapter 2

Clara Marbal felt decidedly unwell. The pains in her back and stomach that had been niggling away all day, were now quite intense. She sat forward in her chair, letting the small, white lawn nightdress she had been working on slip to the floor. The tight spasm that had been gripping her began to ease slightly, but Clara knew it would return. She knew it had something to do with the baby; everything about having a baby was dreadful. Conceiving had been dreadful. Clara, who had never seen a naked man before her wedding night, and made sure she hadn't seen once since, had been shocked by the whole degrading business. Her mother should have warned her, and then she could have broken off her engagement to Albert and gone to Africa and worked amongst lepers or something; anything would have been preferably to the pain and the indignity she had to suffer as a married woman. It was nearly four o'clock. Clara had decided to wait until Ruby came in with the afternoon tea, and then she would casually tell her about the painful spasms. Ruby was quite common, so she would probably know what was happening. In fact Ruby was so common, Clara wouldn't have been at all surprised if Ruby knew about men's' dangling bits and what they did with them, even though she wasn't married. The pain was coming back. Clara suddenly decided against waiting and being casual and heaving herself from her chair, waddled gasping, to the bell pull by the fireplace. "Ruby!" She bellowed, in case her maid should dawdle, not realising the urgency of the situation. "Ruby – get here now!" As it happened, Ruby was at that moment crossing the landing to Mrs Marbal's sitting room. Ruby held the tea tray aloft with one hand and opened the door with the other. Mrs Marbal was standing at the back of her chair, clutching at the brown velvet so tightly that her knuckles had turned as white as her face.

"Are you alright madam?" Ruby asked, although she could see perfectly well that madam was far from alright. Before Clara had chance to answer, a gush of water escaped from her body, drenching her legs and splashing her shoes before ending

13

in a puddle around her feet. Clara gave a surprised gasp and looked down in horror.

"My word," Ruby said calmly, placing the tray on the table by Clara's chair. "Looks like that baby is on its way then."

"What's happening? Why have I – why am I wet?" Clara groaned. She clutched the base of her protruding stomach feeling its rock hardness and preparing herself for the next onslaught of pain.

"Your waters have broke, Madam that's all. I've twice seen my sister give birth and she didn't have too long to go neither times once her waters broke, so I think madam it would be just as well to get you out of they wet clothes and into yer nightdress before the baby pops out."

"Pops out? Where will it pop out from?" Clara squeezed her eyes shut and curled her toes against the pain that was wrapping around her. "Where ever it is, I hope it pops out soon." Ruby looked at Clara standing there wet and groaning in pain, and felt as close to pity towards her as she ever would; at the same time, she couldn't wait to divulge to everyone that her high and mighty mistress didn't have a clue where babies came from. She wanted to tell her that it would pop out the same way it popped in, but knew that Clara, even in her hour of agony would be mortified by such crudeness.

"The baby will come out where – where all that there water came from," she said "Now madam would you like a cup of tea to keep body and soul together or shall we get you sorted out first?" The only reply Ruby had was a long, low moan of pain. "Best we forget the tea then," she murmured. "You'll 'ave ter try and walk to yer bedroom madam. Here, hang on to me and we'll take it slow." The walk across the landing to Clara's bedroom seemed interminably long. Once inside, Ruby guided Clara to the bed, and then knelt down to remove her wet shoes and stockings. Although she would never lower herself to say so, Clara couldn't help think that Ruby was wrong. It was physically impossible for a baby to appear the same way the water had. All the same she had to concede it was a comfort to have Ruby with her, because Clara felt scared, very scared. She could only give herself up to what- ever was happening to her body; she had no control over it

14

and no knowledge of what was taking place or why. Ruby had knowledge; she would know what to do. Clara lifted and lowered her arms as Ruby removed her day clothes and dressed her in a loose, white, cotton nightgown. She at least felt more comfortable now, but the pain continued, so strong that beads of sweat covered her face and trickled down her neck.

"Now we got you sorted, best we send for Dr. Pinner, 'cos the way yer contractions are comin' you won't 'ave much longer to go," Ruby was saying. Clara gripped her arm in panic. "No – no Ruby you mustn't leave me, you mustn't go anywhere." Ruby was unused to having power over her mistress and acknowledged a feeling of satisfaction in seeing Clara's face pleading up at her instead of her usual dismissive, arrogant expression. "I'm only goin' downstairs to ask cook to send Millie," Ruby said. "I weren't intending to go running up and down that hill to Dr Pinner's meself." She decided to drop the 'madam' at the end of her sentence. Clara was hardly likely to pick up on it the state she was in. Clara tried to tell her to use the bell pull to summon someone instead of going down to the kitchen, but a wave of pain made it impossible to speak. Ruby took her chance to escape for a few minutes. "If I was you, I would try walking around a bit. My sister Demelza, has 'ad four babies and she swears walkin' is better than lying," she said, as she headed for the door. "Won't be more than a minute or two, madam." The 'madam' had slipped out. Force of habit. Part of Ruby would have liked to dawdle down the stairs to the kitchen but her feet hurried her along. After all was said and done, Clara was a woman same as herself, and a woman in distress. At times like this women had to stick together even if one of them was a stuck up bitch.

Mrs Grundy the cook was sitting at the kitchen table trying to work out a discrepancy in the butcher's bill before handing it over to Mrs Marbal who picked up on every penny. Millie, the skivvy, was at the sink, peeling vegetables for the evening meal. "The baby's on its way," Ruby announced with importance. "So Millie 'ad better get herself round to Dr. Pinner's smartish." Millie stiffened, a knife in one hand, a half peeled potato in the other. Mrs Grundy looked up from the butcher's bills and murmured, "Never, that baby hasn't started to come has it?"

Ruby sighed. "I jus' told you didn't I? I should know, I was there when madam's waters broke all over the drawing room floor."

"Never," Mrs Grundy said again, "not all over that lovely bit of Turkish carpet. Well I hope you've cleaned it up my girl or t'will be ruined else."

"Millie'll have to do it. I've got my hands full with 'er contracting all the time, and not wanting me out of 'er sight 'cos of the awful pain." Ruby said, jerking her head in the general direction of upstairs.

"That poor soul'll be going through it," Mrs Grundy wiped the corners of her eyes with her apron. She always became uncharacteristically sentimental and shed a few tears when she knew someone, anyone, was in labour. "Well you heard what was said Millie, so what are 'e waiting for? Get yerself off to Dr Pinner's and tell him to come quick." Mrs Grundy snapped, her last tear and all sentimentality spent as quickly as it came. "Tell him Mrs Marbal's in terrible pain."

"I can't," Millie wailed, "I 'aven't finished the spuds yet." Millie was scared of men, particularly men in authority like doctors and teachers. The last thing she wanted to do was order a man to come to Marbal House. "And anyway," she added desperately, "I've got that carpet to sort out."

"Are you daft as well as insolent?" Mrs Grundy twisted around in her chair to face the back of Millie's head. "That dear baby in' goin' wait for you to do yer chores first, is it? So don't you tell me what you can or can't do my girl, 'cos you're goin' an' if you don't hurry it up, you'll have my boot on yer backside to help you on yer way."

"I'll have to get me coat," Millie said sulkily, taking off her hessian apron and flinging down her knife.

"Don't you bother with no coat," Ruby ordered. "You run all the way there, then you won't need no coat." As soon as Millie was out the back door, which was swiftly as Mrs Grundy had hurled a wooden spoon at her, Ruby said, "You'll never believe it, but Mrs Marbal hasn't got a clue where this baby is comin' from." Mrs

16

Grundy put her hand to her mouth and couldn't decide whether to shed a few more tears or smile. "Never," she said dry-eyed. "Well 'tis for certain sure she'll soon find out poor soul." Placing both hands on the scrubbed kitchen table, she levered herself up, and fetched a bundle of newspapers from under the Welsh dresser. "Here, you'd best take these to cover the mattress with. I've bin savin' up Mr Marbal's old dailies ready for madam goin' into labour," she said, sounding pleased with herself, even though it was the butcher's wife who had suggested it.

"I wonder if she wants Mr Marbal fetched home," Ruby mused as she took the newspapers. "You'd best ask her," Mrs Grundy said, then flapped her hand at Ruby. "And you'd best get back up those stairs right away. That poor woman will be wonderin' where you are."

Clara was still rooted to the spot where Ruby had left her. The sweat from her hands left dark patches on the polished mahogany bedstead. "Where have you been?" she gasped, as Ruby walked into the bedroom. Ruby chose to ignore the question and smiled brightly. "Millie's gone to fetch the doctor, and cook's sent these up," she said, taking the newspapers over to the bed. Clara stared at the newspapers, waited for a contraction to subside and then snapped, "Is the woman mad? The last thing I want to do is read!"

"Oh no madam, they're not for readin', they're to protect the mattress. T'would be a shame to get the mattress all blood – messed up." Ruby stripped back the peach satin eiderdown, the blankets and embroidered sheets as Clara watched in horror. It would get worse – worse than this? "I'll find an old bit of cotton sheeting to put over these papers." Ruby said, surveying her neat handiwork of latticed broadsheets. She looked up at Clara, now doubled over at the end of the bed, clutching on the bedstead for all she was worth. Her blonde hair straggled down over her face and her groaning became steadily louder. Ruby straightened up and tentatively put out her hand, wondering for a moment if she should perhaps comfort her mistress, pat her shoulder, or something. Mrs Marbal wasn't built for childbearing. She didn't

17

have big hips and stamina like Ruby's sister Demelza. Demelza swore a good deal when she was in labour, groaned when she had a contraction and joked when it subsided. She paced about, stopping every now and then when the pain was really bad gripping anything in sight – usually Ruby. Then, just before the baby was born, she'd crawl onto the bed, pull on a piece of tied sheet, strain and groan until she was red in the face, and whoosh. She made it look easy really, giving birth. Ruby's hand dropped down to her side. It was one thing to rub your sister's back, but she was only Mrs Marbal's servant after all, so it wasn't really her place to make physical contact. A kind word then, perhaps. "Cook was wonderin' if you'd like Mille to fetch the master when she gets back," were the kindest words she could think of. Unfortunately the last person on earth that Clara wanted to think about mid contraction was her husband. At the mention of him, she forced herself upright, threw back her head and screamed so loudly that even Ruby jumped.

Mrs Grundy, hearing the scream, decided she would wash the Turkish carpet herself. She cut off a sliver of Sunlight soap, heaved out a bucket and cloth from under the sink poured in hot water from an ever simmering kettle on the black leaded stove, and headed for the hall passage. Mrs Grundy had never had children or sisters. The truth, although she would never admit it, was that she knew little more about the mysteries of childbirth than Mrs Marbal. The upstairs sitting room then, being opposite Mrs Marbal's bedroom, would be a good vantage point to listen and learn, particularly if she left the sitting room door wide open.

Millie meanwhile, had hurried as fast as her flat feet would allow, down the hill and into the town. With eyes downcast she scuttled passed Oats Photographic Shop, Harvey's Drapery, and Pollard's General Groceries. With her head bent and her thoughts busily rehearsing what she would say to Dr Pinner when he opened the door to her she nearly walked headlong into a coal merchant. It was only a shout of, "Watch where y'um goin' yer silly bugger," that made her look up and step aside as he heaved a sack of coal off his horse drawn cart and onto his back before depositing it down a coal chute. Millie hurried on. I've been sent to fetch the doctor for Mrs Marbal, she would say. The baby's on its way so could you come quick…..please.

Passed the public water pump that had been the cause of typhus twelve years earlier, contaminated as it was with pollution from three privy-pits, across the bridge and there it was; a row of four smart houses, each with an iron railing, white lace curtains and a black front door with a coloured glass fanlight above. There was a gleaming brass plate on the wall of Dr Pinner's house, and a brass doorknocker in the shape of a lion's head. Millie's heart thumped as she grabbed the lion's head and knocked it loudly against the door. She heard the sound of footsteps clicking along the corridor. I've come for – she rehearsed again, then the door flung open, not by the doctor, but his wife. Mrs Pinner was tall, straight and thin. Her grey streaked hair was plaited and wound onto the top of her head. She had a no nonsense expression and a voice that had struck fear in many a nurse and patient during her time as a ward sister. "Well?" she demanded of Millie. Millie took a step backwards. The whiff of disinfectant coming from the black and white tiled hallway combined with being under the scrutiny of Mrs Pinner, made Millie's nerves crumble.

"I – the mistress is havin' a baby", she blurted, wincing as soon as the words left her mouth. No, that wasn't right – she'd said it all wrong. Mrs Pinner raised an eyebrow, and looked at Millie with measured coldness. Millie tried again. "I've been sent for the doctor, please 'cos the mistress is in labour."

"And who might your mistress be?"

"Mrs Marbal from -"

"Yes, I know where Mrs Marbal lives. Not that it makes any difference. The doctor isn't here." Millie gulped. Although Mrs Pinner was almost as frightening as a man, she couldn't go back and tell cook the doctor was out. Cook would kill her.

"But 'er waters've broke and she's in terrible pain." Millie persisted. She bit her lip and waited for Mrs Pinner's stinging response.

19

"Naturally she's in pain." Mrs Pinner snapped. "Having a baby is a painful business and you'd do well to remember it." Millie felt confused and frustrated and close to tears. None of these emotions were new to her; in fact she experienced them on a daily basis. Fortunately however, Mrs Pinner softened a touch, seeing Millie shivering on the door- step, a film of tears over her squint eyes.

"If the doctor hasn't come back in half an hour, I'll visit Mrs Marbal myself," she said sighing as if it would be a great inconvenience, but secretly looking forward to the chance of being present at a birth again. Millie inwardly brightened until Mrs Pinner added. "Have you thought to inform Mr Marbal that his wife is in labour? No I thought not. Well you'd better hurry along to his office then hadn't you? And for heaven's sake, next time you come out in a biting wind like this, wrap yourself up – otherwise you'll be the next one wanting to see the doctor." The door slammed shut and Millie trundled slowly along the pavement.

Mr Marbal was a solicitor. He had a big office in the town with gold lettering on a frosted glass window 'Albert Marbal & Company, Solicitors, Conveyance, Wills and Probate.' Millie had never been inside the building, and she didn't want to go there now. Besides, she had scarcely ever seen Mr Marbal and had certainly never spoken to him; now she was expected to tell him his wife was in labour, which was quite a personal thing to tell a man in Millie's view. Still, she'd just have to do it somehow, or she'd be in for it.

Luck however, was on Millie's side for once. As she trudged along the cobbled road towards her master's office, she saw him standing outside talking to none other than Dr Pinner seated in his pony drawn trap. Millie nearly smiled. Now everything would be alright. Both Dr Pinner and Mr Marbal could know about Mrs Marbal, with Millie only having to explain it once; the only problem, which was quite a big one for Millie, was having to butt in on their conversation. She hovered at the rear end of the pony waiting for a chance to speak.

"The chap got down off his cart", Dr Pinner was saying, "took one look at her lying in the road covered in sticky red goo, thought he'd killed her and had a heart attack."

"And he hadn't killed her?" Mr Marbal asked.

Dr Pinner gave a hearty laugh. "No – bit of concussion that was all. Thing was she'd been carrying baskets of strawberries. Course they'd got crushed and that's what the chap thought was blood and guts."

Mr Marbal laughed, and then saw Millie. Her head had been swivelling from him to Dr Pinner, as she tried to work out how someone having a heart attack was funny. Mr Marbal frowned, recognising her. "Mary isn't it? Why are you hanging around that pony, girl?" Millie blushed, and stepped forward, bobbing a little curtsey. "The mistress's baby is comin' and I've been sent to fetch you and the doctor, sir", she said in such a low voice that Mr Marbal had to lean over to catch the words. Dr Pinner turned in his seat to scowl at Millie. "What's the matter, girl?" he asked in his cut glass voice, making Millie tremble.

"It's Clara," Mr Marbal answered calmly. "Apparently she's in labour and Mary here has been sent to fetch us."

Dr Pinner was about to question Millie further, then sensing it wouldn't be worth his bother, invited Mr Marbal to climb up beside him. With a flick of his whip, Dr Pinner's pony and trap headed out of the road and up the hill. Millie trudged along behind, her head once more bent down and her arms hugging her body trying to keep out the chill March wind. Her feet were heavy, but her heart was light. She had completed her mission.

Ruby was more than delighted to see Dr Pinner. She was tired of asking Clara if she wanted to push yet, and getting no response other than groaning and wailing. She was also beginning to feel uneasy. For one thing, this was a labour such as she was unaccustomed to, and on £20 a year didn't think she should have to put up with. There was a limit to the amount of pain a maid should have to witness. When she'd taken the job she hadn't imagined for one minute that she would be expected to deliver her mistress's baby. And things were not proceeding, as they should

21

with this labour, at least not from Ruby's limited experience. When Dr Pinner made his entrance, Ruby rushed over to him as if he were a lost friend. "Dr Pinner – I'm some glad you've come!" she gasped.

"Now then, what's going on here?" he asked with forced joviality as he sidestepped Ruby. "Pour me some water into a bowl, if you please so I can wash my hands." Within no time, he was pulling back the bed covers and parting Clara's legs in a way that would have mortified her hours earlier. Now she was beyond caring. All that mattered to her was that her body should rid itself of the baby and with it her unspeakable pain. Failing that, imminent death seemed like a welcome option. His examination complete, Dr Pinner gave Clara a cursory pat on the hand. "There, there, m'dear, chin up. Everything is progressing nicely." Ruby looked at him doubtfully, "But int there somethin' you could do for her pain doctor?" she asked. "Her screams are terrible at times."

Dr Pinner, a religious man, turned his attention to Ruby. "No need for medical interference m'girl. Bring forth in pain, that's what the bible says. Bring forth in pain. Childbirth is a natural process, it requires -" at which point his voice was drowned by an animal- like cry from Clara. "Besides," he added hurriedly, "it should all be over in an hour or two." Dr Pinner was a bones man. Give him a limb to amputate or straighten and he would be happy. For him, being with a woman in labour held no such appeal. He was therefore more than relieved if a little surprised, when at that moment his wife Hester entered the room. With a cursory nod towards her husband, she closed the door quietly behind her, and placed her little black bag on the dressing table. "I assume you were summoned as well, m'dear," Dr Pinner said, picking up his own medical bag. "Excellent. Mrs Marbal is not quite fully dilated yet, so I'm sure she'll find your presence very reassuring while we wait, and – er, well there's nothing more I can do for the moment. Nature must take its course." Hester Pinner nodded and removed her leather gloves. "No, indeed – there is nothing more you can do. I'll take care of Mrs Marbal now," she said.

Dr Pinner turned and swiftly left. Albert who had been pacing the corridor outside his wife's room met him mid stride. "Look," he

22

said to Dr Pinner, "Do you think I should go in there or something? The poor thing's making a frightful row." Dr Pinner put his hand on Albert's shoulder and led him towards the stairs. "Your wife is doing well, believe me- and in very capable hands, I might add. Hester trained under Mrs Bedford Fenwick at Barts y'know. Formidable woman, but by Jove she knows her nursing."

Albert wasn't sure whether the doctor was referring to his wife Hester, or the Fenwick woman whom he'd never heard of. "Well that's good," he said brightly, pleased to have been given an excuse, if not an order to keep out of the way. "Look, why don't you join me for dinner? Mrs Grundy will have prepared something and as Clara's not up to eating…she's not is she?" Dr Pinner shook his head. "No, well in that case, what do you say? I could do with the company to tell you the truth – and you'd be on hand, should anything go wrong up there." He jerked his head towards Clara's bedroom. Dr Pinner could smell something good coming from the kitchen and as Hester obviously wouldn't be cooking for him that evening, he was eager to accept Albert's invitation. "Be delighted dear chap," he said. "Be delighted."

"You can leave now," Hester told Ruby. "I'll ring down for you later." Ruby didn't need to be told twice. Her stomach rumbled with hunger and she desperately needed a pee. Clara made a feeble attempt to make her stay, but Ruby rushed unheeding from the room. Hester opened her bag and put on a white apron over the nurse's uniform she always wore when helping out at her husband's surgeries. "Now then," she said, holding Clara's clammy hand between her own cool palms, "when the next contraction comes, grip me as hard as you like. Try to relax. I'm here now my dear, I'll see you through." Clara opened her eyes. "I can't go on," she said gritting her teeth, "The pain is beyond enduring." Hester Pinner looked towards the door and then said something that would make Clara love her in varying degrees for the rest of her life. "Don't despair. I can give you something for the pain." Hester moved across the room and took a facemask and a small bottle of chloroform from her bag. Covering her nose and mouth with the mask she said, "If this was good enough for Queen Victoria, I'm sure it will be good enough for you."

Tipping a teaspoonful of chloroform onto a cloth she added, "I'm afraid the doctor doesn't agree with pain relief during labour, so let this be our little secret. Just a small whiff now. We need you to push when the time comes."

It was nearly five hours later when Ruby was summoned to her mistress's bedroom. She stood at the foot of the bed while Clara yelled and heaved and pushed for all she was worth. Then suddenly the baby's head appeared, and with the help of Hester, the shoulders soon followed. Then there he was, propelled onto the bed, warm and wet and protesting loudly. Despite the fact that his lungs were obviously clear, Hester picked him up by his ankles and gave him a sound whack. Clara, who would have liked to give him another whack for the pain he had caused her flopped back on to the bed exhausted. "Congratulations. You have a fine healthy boy." Hester announced. After severing the umbilical cord, she wrapped a towel around the baby and held him out to his mother. Clara closed her eyes and turned her head to one side. "Take him away," she murmured. "I'm far too tired to hold him."

"You've done well Clara. We'll let you rest just as soon–" Hester suddenly and sharply called out to Ruby and thrust the baby into her arms. "I need to attend to her. She's bleeding. Fetch the doctor – quick."

With the baby warm and snuggled against her chest, Ruby sped down the stairs and into the drawing room where Dr Pinner and Albert sat by the fireplace. They looked up, surprised by Ruby's sudden entrance. "You're wanted upstairs sir," she said to Dr Pinner. "The mistress is losing a lot of blood." Both men leapt to their feet. "She's alright, isn't she?" Albert said, looking from Ruby to Dr. Pinner then back to Ruby. Dr Pinner gestured for Albert to sit down and assured him that he would be able to see his wife in a short while. As soon as he had left, Albert walked over to Ruby and peered cautiously at the baby. "Do I have a son or daughter?" he asked.

"It's a boy sir," Ruby looked down lovingly at the baby's plump red face. His unfocused eyes blinked back at her, making her smile. "Mrs Pinner said he was good an' healthy and I mus' say he feels a fair ol' weight." Albert pulled back the towel to get a closer look at his son.

"Would you like to hold him sir?"

Albert seeing dried blood and white, waxy vernix around the baby's head declined. "I'll wait until he's cleaned up. Bit of a mess at the moment, isn't he?" He gave Ruby an earnest look. "How is my wife, Ruby? She will be alright won't she?" Ruby wanted to say, how the hell should I know? Instead she smiled reassuringly. "She'll be fine sir." Albert nodded limply then poured himself a whisky and soda. He looked over his shoulder at Ruby who still standing in the middle of the room, smiling at the baby and gently stroking his cheek. "Well you'd better put the child in his cot Ruby," he said, "and then return to your mistress." Ruby bobbed a curtsy, and took the baby upstairs to his nursery.

With the baby in his crib, she lit the gas mantle and drew the curtains against the black night. It was chilly in the room, and the baby started to wail in protest against his alien surroundings. "There, there now, little 'un, don't you cry. There's enough of 'em in there lookin' after your mother, so I reckon you and me should 'ave a cuddle." Ruby scooped the baby up again and held him close. "Fine welcome into the world you've 'ad, I must say," she murmured and kissed his matted blonde head. And so the first loving caress Agnes' grandfather had was from a family servant and as fate would prove, so would be his last.

Much to Clara's surprise she did recover from childbirth, but it was two days before she would even look at her child .She made it clear that breast-feeding was definitely out of the question, so Hester had a Dr Soxhlet milk steriliser fetched from the chemist, and gave Ruby instructions on how to use it. Albert had Clara's mother, Mrs Treverton, fetched from Truro, and calm was replaced by chaos at Marbal House. Mrs Treverton had no regard for the sanctity of Mrs Grundy's kitchen, and no faith in any of the servant's ability to cater properly for her daughter's needs. And her needs were many. Port wine jelly, mutton broth, beef tea, junket and tapioca cream soup were part of the nutritious menu Mrs Treverton flounced downstairs to demand on a daily basis. Mrs Grundy could have coped if only Mrs Treverton hadn't stood over her as she gave her instructions, ready to watch her every move. And then there was Ruby, fussing in the kitchen, getting in the way, muttering over the steriliser, `water must boil briskly for three quarters of an hour, steam escaping from the edge of the lid' repeating it over and over like a mantra in case she would make a mistake and somehow harm the baby. The baby was hers to care for.

Mrs Treverton and Hester Pinner devoted themselves to Clara. A nursemaid had not been arranged, mainly because Albert considered three servants to be a big enough expense, and also the thought of having six women, (seven if he counted Hester Pinner who seemed to care for Clara beyond her call of duty,) in his house, was more than he could tolerate. Ruby, who had a trundle bed in the nursery, appeared bleary eyed in the kitchen every morning. After tackling the Soxhlet, she washed nappies and baby clothes, had her breakfast and returned to her charge. Mrs Grundy prepared breakfast for Albert and his mother-in-law, which a terrified Millie clad in one of Ruby's aprons, was made to serve. Mrs Treverton personally collected Clara's breakfast tray, Albert escaped to the office, and another day of frayed nerves and shot tempers would begin.

The baby was two weeks old before his parents decided to give him a name. Albert wanted to call him Jesse, after his hero Jesse James. Clara would have preferred something British and masculine, Howard or George she suggested half-heartedly. Albert frowned. "But I'd rather like a little Jesse," he said, with a touch of petulance. Clara, who lay back on her pillows pretending to feel sleepy, opened one eye and squinted at him. She

26

wondered how she could ever have imagined herself in love with the man. True, with his fair hair and neat moustache, his blue eyes and tall stature, he was attractive enough when he had his clothes on. Attractive to some maybe, yet Clara increasingly found his tone and mannerism irritating and just the thought of his body close to hers was repugnant. She closed her eyes tightly to blot him from sight. Why, she speculated would a professional lawyer want to name his child after a vicious murderer with a sissy name? It was ludicrous. *He* was ludicrous. She sighed impatiently. "Let him be named Jesse then," she said, "If that is what you want."

"Is it true," Millie asked, "that the master is goin' away to war?"
"And where did you hear that from?" Mrs Grundy, who was spreading a flapjack mix onto a baking tray, looked up at Millie and frowned. "From that shifty lad at the grocer's, I'll be bound." Millie, now seventeen, had grown in size and confidence over the years since Jesse was born; even so, the thought of Jake made her blush. "Well actually, it weren't me he told. I just over'eard him saying as how Mr Marbal 'ad enlisted." Mrs Grundy sniffed.
"You spend a mite too much time in that there grocer's hanging around with that Jake boy."
"T'was you who sent me there. You wanted treacle and stuff for they flapjacks and was lucky to get it, with the shortage. Any'ow," Millie went on, suddenly looking crestfallen, "Jake says he's goin' to war, an' all. Tis all them Kitchener posters what's swayed him. He's goin' down the Town Hall to sign up first chance he gets."
"That Jake's not old enough, is he?" Ruby asked. She tolerated Millie far more these days, particularly as Millie had taken on most of Ruby's chores as well as her own, leaving Ruby time to look after Jesse.
"He says he's gonna lie about his age so 'e can be a soldier."
"My daddy's going to be a soldier." Jesse, now three years old, stood on a chair at the kitchen table. Over his clothes he wore an apron that covered him from neck to shoes. His hands were smeared with flour and dough as he diligently cut out shapes with a fluted biscuit cutter. Ruby smiled at him. "You'm doin' a lovely

job with they there biscuits Jesse. Reckon your daddy will want to take some of 'em with him when he goes off to France."

"So he is goin' then," Millie said. "Fine thing when you 'ave to hear it off someone else first. I never get told nothin' in this 'ouse."

"That's 'cause nothing' concerns you my girl." Mrs Grundy said. "You young maids are all the same these days, full of cheek and above your station. You just get on with layin' up Mrs Marbal's tea tray."

"I only found out meself today Millie." Ruby ruffled Jesse's hair. "You told me didn't you, Jesse? You said daddy was goin' to be a soldier. An' mummy said, yes you was right. You're some clever boy."

"Well I hope your clever boy is gonna clear up his mess." Mrs Grundy pretending to be peeved shook her head at the flour on Jesse's chair and on the flagstones around it. "Looks like we've 'ad a snow storm right 'ere in the kitchen with all this white stuff about." Jesse giggled, grabbed a handful of flour from the jar and threw it up in the air.

"Here now, that'll do – that's enough of that Master Jesse. Take him upstairs for heaven's sake Ruby. The boy's getting over excited." Mrs Grundy now genuinely aggrieved whipped the flour jar from Jesse's hands. "There now, look at that. There's flour all over me flapjacks!"

Millie and Ruby tried to keep straight faces. Stifled spluttering sounds emitted from their mouths; then they caught each other's eye and could contain themselves no longer. Jesse joined in the shrill laughter. "Tis no laughing' matter," Mrs Grundy scolded. "That boy's bein' spoilt rotten. Go and get his 'ands washed Ruby and take 'im back upstairs where he belongs." Ruby, still grinning, whisked Jesse to the sink and wiped the dough from his chubby fingers. "Let me put 'is biscuits in to bake, then I'll help clear up 'is mess, he don't mean no harm, do you my bird?" Jesse entwined his arms around Ruby's neck and wrapped his legs round her waist, snuggling close against her. "He loves bein' down here and who can blame 'im? Them upstairs have got no time for 'im.

She's always off out with Mrs Pinner and he – well he does his best when he's about which isn't very often."

"Now then Ruby, you shouldn't go talkin' about Mr and Mrs Marbal like that, 'specially not in front of the boy." Mr Grundy sat down heavily and sighed. "I didn' mean to snap. It's just what with this 'ol war an' all the young men rushin' off to get killed and what are they fighting for? That's what I'd like to know." Ruby sat Jesse on Mrs Grundy's chair by the kitchen range. "They're fighting for victory of course," she said. More than that, she didn't know, besides that seemed reason enough. If your country said you were needed to fight only a coward would refuse.

"Anyway," she added brightly, "they say 'twill all be over by Christmas."

Millie pinned on her white cap, ready to take Mrs Marbal's afternoon tea upstairs.

"I hope they're right, then" she said, thinking of Jake's safety. He was the only boy who had ever spoken kindly to her, and spotty and spindly though he was, Millie's heart pounded at the thought of him.

The night before Albert left to do his bit for King and Country, he quietly entered his wife's bedroom, and stood with his back against the door, taking in the scene, wanting to remember everything so that in the difficult times ahead he could conjure the picture and get comfort from it. The room was mellow with soft lighting from candles under their opalescent pink glass mantles. Wispy flames licked around red coals in the grate and the air was sweet with rose water. The smell of Clara.

She was seated at her dressing table a silver backed nail buffer in one hand, the fingers of the other arched as she swept the velvet padded buffer across her pale fingernails. At the sound of Albert entering the room, she looked up into the dressing table mirror and silently watched him. He moved towards her, keeping his gaze on her mirrored image; her beautiful impassive face, her neck circled with the white lace of her nightgown, the emerald earrings he had bought her dangling from her small lobes. He

29

noticed their sparkle, droplets of suspended green, as he moved closer still and laid his hands gently on her shoulders. She stiffened at his touch and slowly placed the nail buffer onto the dressing table. "You've come to say goodnight." It was not so much a statement as an expressed hope, although she sensed he had come for more than that. "I want to stay tonight," he answered confirming her fears. "This after all is my last night Clara, naturally I want to spend it with you."

His fingers were already unfastening the top buttons of her nightgown, cool mother of pearl buttons, one, two, three undone, and the nightgown pushed slowly apart, four, five undone. He looked in the mirror, tantalised by the sight of Clara's exposed throat and the glimpse of her partially uncovered breasts; so white, so soft, yet firm under the touch of his fanned out fingers as he pressed first across them, and then down inside her gown to cup one breast in each hand. "Albert, you must stop." Clara tried to keep her voice steady, even so the words sounded unnaturally high pitched. She managed without difficulty to break free of his grasp and rise from her chair.

"I must *stop?*" Albert looked at her quizzically. "You forget you promised to love, honour and obey me Clara. You promised before God." He was desperate this time and determined. He slowly shook his head at her. "No Clara, you have a duty as a wife."

Albert was not surprised by Clara's reaction to his advances. It had been apparent to him since their wedding night that Clara was a frigid creature. It had come as an unpleasant surprise to him that she had turned out to be so cold, disdainful even, particularly as many a young lady of his acquaintance in his bachelor days had seized every un-chaperoned moment to kiss, grope and cuddle and one or two demure little things had been only too willing to go further than that. Yet, he admitted, Clara's impeccable behaviour before their marriage had excited him. She was like a beautifully wrapped parcel, a concealed present that he could only gaze at longingly and fantasise about what might lie beneath. He became increasingly intrigued, allured, mystified.

30

The moment when he could strip away the wrappings, see and feel her limbs entwined with his penetrate her, erase her virginal chastity, was a delight worth waiting for. Unfortunately, the reality, as with most prettily wrapped gifts turned out to be a disappointment. Her body was just as wonderful as he had imagined it to be. Only it didn't work properly. When it came to sex, Clara didn't function. Albert had confided this to his friend Dr. Pinner and Dr. Pinner had confided back to Albert that his own wife Hester was a cold fish too. He had only ever tried making love to Hester once, and that had proved so disastrous for them both that they never tried again. But Dr. Pinner was a good forty years older than Albert and twenty years older than Hester. Hester and Dr. Pinner had married for mutual convenience; neither love nor sexual gratification had been a requisite to the arrangement. Hester had married for the financial security Dr. Pinner could give. Dr. Pinner had needed a housekeeper and a trained nurse who would be useful in the surgery. Hester fitted both roles perfectly. The fact that she had turned out to be as uninviting as she looked, didn't bother him unduly. He wasn't that interested in sex himself, if the truth were told. Albert however was, and as he could not get it willingly from his wife, he found it elsewhere. Tonight was different. Tonight he wanted Clara, for in spite of her being passionless, he still loved her. She was the most beautiful woman had ever seen, and he still lived in the hope that one day, or rather night she would melt a little and begin to welcome his advances towards her.

"You throw my wedding vows back at me, but you made promises too." Clara was saying, in rather a whinging way that made Albert suspect that tonight would not be the night she began to thaw. "You promised to look after me in sickness and in health, so how can you expect this of me Albert – how can you be so cruel?"

"Frankly Clara, you are not so much sick, as unwilling."

"Yes – yes I am sick," Clara said, beginning to realize that this would be one of the times that Albert did not defer to her, no matter how she protested. Nevertheless, with as much drama as she could muster added, "I have not yet recovered from the terrible trauma of having your child."

31

"That was over three years ago Clara. You will forgive me my love, if my patience begins to grow a little thin."

Albert smiled in spite of himself. Good God, was she going to use that excuse again? It hadn't worked on their rare couplings in the past, although admittedly he had stopped short of ejaculating into her, which was not his intention tonight. Tonight he would be abandoned in his passion.

"But each time you force yourself upon me I'm scared of becoming pregnant. You know how I suffered. I would rather die than go through that again." Clara wailed.

"And I have always been careful not to get you pregnant. Oh, my dearest Clara," Albert bent over her, and pushed back her hair to kiss her neck. "I love you, I *need* you. This night spent with you will mean more to me than you could ever know," he murmured the words into her neck, indulging in a dramatic moment of his own. "It will carry me through the darkest times and the bloodiest of battles. Now come to bed Clara." Clara blanched knowing she was trapped. There was nothing left for her to say without telling the truth, that the thought of intimate contact with him made her cringe; and even she acknowledged the words were too brutal to speak before he left for war. Besides, something in his tone and manner told her he might well be brutal back. He was, she realised, ardent with desire and her only recourse was to succumb and get it over with. She was done for – or soon would be.

Albert took her hand and led her towards the bed. She was not as willing as he would have hoped for yet he had known her less compliant and by now he was too aroused to care. She was about to climb, resigned, between the sheets when Albert pulled her back. "No not yet, my love. Take off your nightgown. Let me carry the image of you, all of you, with me."

"You want me to…?"

"Yes. I want to feast my eyes on your naked body. I want to devour you first with my eyes, then with my tongue, then-"

"Stop Albert," Clara said quickly. She had already heard too much and wondered whether she might be fortunate enough to faint before he was through. Closing her eyes and biting her lip, she

32

grasped the hem of her gown, hauled it over her head and felt it drop beside her feet. Her green earrings glittered, the red coals shifted in the grate. A candle inside a pink, opalescent glass mantle flickered and trembled as Albert held it aloft and came to stand in front of her.

When he was done, which was quicker than he would have liked and much longer than Clara could bear, Albert rolled away from her and turned onto his side. "One last request, my love."
Clara, her eyes staring ahead seeing but not registering, her mind numb, her body bruised, inwardly groaned. No, no more.
"You will see me off at the railway station tomorrow, won't you? I should like you and Jesse to be there when I leave." Clara's body began to relax. A soft sigh of relief escaped her. "But of course. There is nothing Albert," she said with feeling, "that I would like more, than to see you off at the station."

They made a handsome couple, he in his smart khaki uniform, she in a blue swirling skirt and matching jacket trimmed with velvet; and a pretty hat with tiny iridescent feathers and wings of black net perched jauntily over her upswept curls. Their little boy in his best knickerbockers and white kid boots trotted between them, holding their hands and looking every so often behind him, to make sure Ruby was still there. She walked along with Millie. This was a rare treat for them both to be excused from their household tasks. Instead they were allowed down to the railway station to wave off the local lads who had enlisted in the Duke of Cornwall light infantry.

Ruby smiled at Jesse as he turned to grin at her. If it hadn't been for Jesse's tantrum and refusing to go with his parents unless Ruby came too, she'd be sweeping carpets right now. Mrs Marbal had not been too pleased at Jesse's outburst, neither had she approved of Mr Marbal swiftly agreeing that Ruby could walk with them. "Why not make this a household outing and invite all the servants along?" Clara had asked with sarcasm. Millie, who along with Mrs Grundy had been waiting dutifully in the hall to say their

33

goodbyes, seized her chance. "Oh thank you, madam," she squealed and ran to fetch her coat. Mrs Grundy said thank you, but the sight of seeing all those young men going off to their death was more than she could stomach. Besides, her veins were playing up and she'd never make it back up that steep hill.

There were about twenty young men at the station when the Marbal household arrived. A heavy old train billowing smoke and spitting steam was standing ready to transport its innocently brave cargo. The men were in jubilant spirit. It was a crisp, late autumn morning with frost lacing the ground in defiance of a pale lemon sun. Breath turned to steam as young men and their families called to each other, laughed and hugged and cried. Millie, who had been covertly looking for Jake, suddenly spotted him being embraced by his mother. Millie hung back too embarrassed and shy to intrude, until Ruby gave her a small shove. "Go on, yer drip. Look, he's seen you – he's smilin' at you. What yer waitin' for?"

"I don't know 'im that well," Millie mumbled, but another shove from Ruby pushed her forward, so blushing fiercely, she walked down the platform towards him. Jake stepped onto the train, slammed the door shut and had just stuck his head out of the window when Millie reached the spot where he had been standing. "Have 'e come to see me off Millie?" He called. Millie took a few paces forward. "I've come to see the master off – but, well good luck an' that." Jake grinned at her. "An' I thought you'd come 'ere special to see me." Millie smiled back. And then Jake's mother dabbing her eyes with a handkerchief, stepped in front of Millie, entreating her son to write at first chance, and not to eat his crib before the train reached Bodmin. Millie ambled back to Ruby.

Albert kissed his wife on the cheek, and then bent down and swooped Jesse up in his arms. Jesse was surprised at this unusual show of affection and wriggled slightly as he felt his father's bristly moustache on his face as he kissed him. Jesse dutifully returned the kiss and was set back on the ground, where

34

once more he was absorbed, by the noise and smell of the steam engine. "Well, I had better embark," Albert said, feeling as he had the first time he went off to boarding school, a mixture of apprehension and excitement. Then on impulse he held out his hand to Ruby and asked her to take care of his son. Surprised, Ruby shook his hand, bobbed a curtsy, ensured him that she would look after Jesse and wished him good luck. Clara gritted her teeth. Who did the girl think she was? Albert looked at Millie and decided he had better shake her hand too, after all the poor girl's squint eyes were misted over with tears for him, and then he turned back to his wife and hugged her.

"Albert, you had better board the train now." Clara broke free from his embrace, straightened her hat and forced a smile. "Good luck," she whispered back to his mouthed, "I love you."

Albert waved to his wife and son from the carriage window until the train began to move out of the station, then he settled into his seat surveying the other four occupants. They were very young, and laughed loudly when one of them said, "We'm bloody done it now boys. We'm off to war!" Albert guessed they were lads from local farms; they looked rough and coarse, despite their new uniforms of the 1st Battalion. He hoped they would show him some respect; he had after all been selected as officer material at his training unit. He looked out of the window at disinterested cattle in fields, at the river beyond and there, on the far side of the grey ribbon of road, he could see the church where he had scarcely missed a Sunday service, the church where he and Clara had wed, and where Jesse had been baptised. A feeling of panic suddenly gripped him. What if he never saw his family again? What if he never held Clara in his arms again, or lived to see his son grow? He'd been too hasty in joining this war. He wanted the train to stop so that he could run back down the track and return to the safety of his office and the comfort of his home. Or did he? He leaned back in his seat.

"Would 'e like one, sir?" One of the farm boys was offering him a cigarette. Albert leaned forward to accept. The boy struck a match and held it out. Albert noticed the boy's hand was shaking

35

and briefly steadied it with his own hand as he lit the cigarette and inhaled deeply.

Clara dutifully waved her lace handkerchief until the train pulled clear of the station. Her eyes were quite dry and she smirked at the thought of Albert being safely out of her way, until Christmas at least. Jesse started to cry. She thought at first he was crying for his father until he began to wail that he wanted to ride on the train too.

"There, there, my bird," Ruby soothed, "We'll come and see the train another day." Clara stiffened. "I hope you do not habitually refer to my son as a bird," she said crisply. "You will at all times address him as master Jesse. Is that clear?"

"Yes madam." The insolence in Ruby's voice did not escape Clara. She would like to be rid of her. Since Jesse's birth, the girl's mere presence had caused her embarrassment. She had witnessed the whole degrading business and had an air of arrogance because of it. It was too bad of Albert to let the girl think she was even more important than she already did. Take care of my son, indeed. "Take Jesse home, and get on with your chores." Clara said, with irritation. "And for goodness sake Ruby make sure he keeps his shoes clean or the cost of a new pair will come out of your wages." She swept passed them, walking at a hurried pace. As soon as it was convenient she would dismiss Ruby now that Albert would not be around to interfere; for the time being however, Ruby had her uses. Clara headed for the bridge, crossed over it and made her way to Hester Pinner's house.

"Tell you what master Jesse, if you stop cryin' we'll go down to the river to look at the moorhens." Ruby said, stooping down to carry him. Millie, through her tears, looked aghast. "We can't do that! Madam said we 'ad to get home and do our chores."

"Go on back then." Ruby heaved Jesse to a more comfortable position in her arms. "He's upset, dear of 'im. He needs cheerin' up – I don't care what *she* says."

Millie trailed behind Ruby as she headed towards the river. "But what about 'is shoes? They'll be covered in mud," she wailed between sniffs. When they reached the river Ruby set Jesse down and watched him run along the bank trampling across the frosted grass and ferns. Millie caught up with her and suddenly began to cry pear drop size tears. Ruby turned round at the sound of her noisy sobs. "For 'eavens sakes, Millie, stop blubbin'. He's only getting a bit of grass on 'is shoes. What's a few grass stains when 'es just seen his dad go off to war?"

"That's what I'm upset about." Millie wailed, wiping her cheeks and nose on her sleeve. "What if all they soldiers don't come back? What if they all get killed?" Ruby turned to keep Jesse in her sight. "Some of 'em won't come back Millie, but most of 'em will so stop frettin'. Just think what a hero your Jake will be when he comes 'ome."

"He's not my Jake," Milled said with a final sniff. Ruby turned and grinned at her. "Yes 'e is, you ol' dark horse. I've seen those ol' moony looks 'e gives you."

Millie smiled. "No you 'aven't. You're making it up." Fancy Ruby thinking she was a dark horse.

Millie patted her eyes dry with the back of her red, chapped hand, then walking with a slight swagger, followed Ruby along the bank to Jesse.

Christmas 1914 was a cheerful affair at Marbal House. In the front parlour on Christmas Eve, Clara decorated the fir tree. As a special treat Jesse was allowed to stay up and watch his mother cover the branches with delicate glass baubles, strings of beads, tinsel and little red candles shaped like barley sugar. The fire crackled with logs, and above it the mantelpiece was made festive with garlands of holly, ivy and spruce decorated with bows of scarlet ribbon. Jesse sat silently on the sofa, his eyes sparkling at the magic transformation of the parlour.

On Christmas morning his stocking held nuts, an orange, an apple, and a gingerbread man. In front of the tree was a wooden Noah's Ark with ten pairs of brightly painted animals from his parents; and a picture book from his Grandmother, who was spending Christmas at Marbal House, much to the servant's dismay. However, they had each received a box of Bromley soaps from their mistress, and permission to hold their own little party downstairs on Christmas evening, as soon as they had finished catering for Clara's guests upstairs. Clara was in fine spirit, not least because she knew that her last encounter with Albert had not rendered her pregnant, and the prospect of getting pregnant in the foreseeable future seemed wonderfully remote. She played the piano for her guests, which included the Pinners, and happily drank more wine than she was used to.

Jesse, who earlier had been taken up to bed by Ruby, found the unaccustomed sound of jollity from downstairs, difficult to sleep through. He meandered from his bed to the stairs, sitting as he sometimes did under the blue and red stained glass window, now illuminated by a large candle on the sill. With his thumb in his mouth, he silently watched his mother in the hall below as she came from the dining room followed by Hester Pinner. They were giggling like young girls, and then Hester put her arm around Clara's waist twirling her towards a bunch of mistletoe dangling from the ceiling. Jesse watched as they kissed, wondering what it felt like to be kissed by his mother who looked so fine and beautiful in her frock of deep green shot silk that changed with the light to all the colours of a peacock's feather.
He suddenly remembered the last time his father had kissed him, before he went off on the train; a bristly kiss that tickled his face. Without knowing why, Jesse felt sad. In the hallway below, his mother and Hester Pinner were laughing, and then linking arms they disappeared into the noisy parlour. Jesse began to cry.

Later, when Ruby was on her way upstairs to place Mrs Marbal's stone hot water bottle in her bed, she came across Jesse curled in a ball fast asleep, his thumb still in his mouth. She lifted him up off the stairs smiling, bemused. "Whatever are you doin' out of bed master Jesse?" she whispered over his sleepy head. "It's all been a bit too much excitement for you my bird, hasn't it?" Weaving a little from the effects of Mrs Grundy's punch, she carried him back to his bed, tucking his covers tightly around him.

38

Clara climbed into her warm bed feeling a little wine dizzy. She smiled contentedly in the darkness. It had been a most enjoyable Christmas Day, although admittedly strange with Albert not being there to accompany her to church, or to carve the turkey. Rain and wind were beating against the window, making Clara feel cosy, although a little anxious for Albert. Where exactly, was he right now? she wondered. What did soldiers in trenches do to celebrate Christmas? The day had probably not been too unpleasant for them, - all men together, drinking, joking, able to play out their Jesse James fantasies, shooting the enemy, and becoming heroes. At least, she hoped Albert had enjoyed the day. Perhaps she would receive a letter from him soon. Absence and wine were beginning to make her think fondly of him. She would write to him tomorrow, tell him how well Jesse had played with the Noah's Ark they had given him, and how the vicar had said a special prayer for all the brave soldiers from the diocese. Clara stretched, and with her arms resting above her head, fell in to a deep, untroubled sleep.

From the 1st Battalion trench on the Messines Ridge, Albert was carried to the field hospital. He lay on a hard narrow mattress, his head and body full of lice, his boots full of mud and his trousers full of his own shit. He trembled as he had done for much of that cold and bloody winter, but now he trembled and perspired at the same time. He felt thirsty and very sick. The sound of the artillery like a giant's wrath, reverberated in his ears and behind his closed eyes was a brightness that hurt. He searched in that white light for Clara, to see her face. Gradually, like a turning kaleidoscope fragments came and settled; her hair, her eyes, her mouth. The fragments formed together. Her green earrings glistened in the light; her eyes sparkled as she looked back at him. Then slowly iridescent feathers began to flutter down over her. The light began to fade. Large wings of black net covered her, and then there was darkness.
"Dysentery", the M.O. said to his attending nurse. "The poor sod came all this way to die of dysentery."

Chapter 3

It was an unusually warm day in March when the letter came. Millie, who had just finished scrubbing the front porch, was wiping her hands on her hessian apron and absently looking at the profusion of daffodils lining the path, when the telegraph boy propped his bicycle by the hedge and opened the garden gate. Millie, who knew by now what it meant to be visited by the telegraph boy, took the letters with trembling fingers. She placed it on a silver tray on the hall table and went downstairs to change her apron. "The telegraph boy 'as brought us a letter for the mistress," she said in a hushed voice to Mrs Grundy. Mrs Grundy turned pale. "You don't think the master 'as – no surely not. P'rhaps it's not too bad. Maybe he's gone missin' or maybe 'es a bit poorly an' their sending 'im home." Her voice was unsteady in spite of her attempt to sound positive. Millie said nothing. She tied the ribbons of her white apron and took the letter upstairs to Mrs Marbal.

Clara had recently begun to dabble in watercolours. On the table in front of her was a clear glass vase holding the four irises that she was deftly painting. This was to be her still life contribution for the local exhibition to be held in the Town Hall. She was pondering over what to call it, and had just decided that Irises in a Glass Vase was as good a title as any, when Millie knocked on the door. "Come." Clara dipped her brush into the palette. A very pleasing indigo, mixed with a touch of ochre stained the bristle tips. She held the brush poised over her work. "What is it Millie?" Millie bobbed a little curtsey and held out the silver tray. Clara put down her brush and picked up the envelope. "Thank you Millie. You may go."

"It is my painful duty," Clara read, "to inform you that a report has been received from the War Office notifying the death of," and there handwritten next to Name was "Albert Clive Marbal." Clara read it twice, and then went on to read his rank and number, the name of his regiment, the place, and the date, "by his Majesty's Command I am to forward the enclosed message of sympathy from their Gracious Majesties the King and Queen. I am at the same time to express the regret of the Army Council at the soldier's death in his Country's service." Albert was dead then, he had died serving his country. Albert was a hero. It was far too much to take in. Clara stared ahead of her. She had never for one moment seriously considered that Albert might not come back. He was only twenty-seven and somehow didn't seem the type to die. Of course plenty of men had already died during the war, but foolishly she hadn't thought Albert would be one of them. She had assumed that at the end of it he would come back, boring her with tales of hardship and bravery. She smiled wryly and sighed. Poor Albert. She wished she could feel terribly sad and cry, but she couldn't. She felt nothing more than a numb sort of confusion. What did she do now? For some moments she sat staring ahead trying to assemble her thoughts. Jesse would have to be told of course, but beyond that she could think of nothing. Eventually she decided she would send for her mother, but first she would visit Hester and Dr Pinner. They would direct her; they would know what to do.

A couple of weeks following the news of Albert's death, Clara summoned Ruby and told her that her services were no longer required. Hester had often said that Clara having three servants was an excess, particularly since Albert had gone off to war, and there was only herself and Jesse to be cared for. One maid, Hester said, was quite sufficient. With her mother to take care of Jesse until she organised a more permanent arrangement, Clara decided this was the ideal time to get rid of Ruby.

"I'm sure you will find work on a farm, with so many labourers away at war. In fact I have heard farms are desperate for workers, so you see Ruby, it would be quite selfish of me to keep you here when your services are - well needed elsewhere." Clara sighed. "And of course, my own circumstances have changed since the death of my dear husband." She added that for sympathy in the knowledge that Ruby wouldn't dare ask in what way her circumstances had changed, because they hadn't, apart from financially. Now she was much better off. She had been well provided for by Albert. Everything was now hers. Apart from the capital he had left and the money from the insurances, there was the rent from the cottages Albert's father had left him. Marbal House however was Jesse's. That part of the will had come as a surprise to Clara, not that it bothered her unduly. She couldn't sell the house, but she was entitled to live in it for the rest of her days so the fact that it legally belonged to Jesse, seemed irrelevant.

Ruby, standing in front of Clara, felt a gripping heaviness inside her as the words of her mistress registered. After five years of faithful service she was being dismissed, cast aside without a thought for the feelings she had for little Jesse. That was the bit that hurt. She couldn't bear the thought of leaving him and handing him into the charges of goodness knows who – someone who didn't know the first thing about him and could never love him the way she did. "What about Jesse, Madam?" she blurted. "Who will take care of 'im?"

"Why Ruby," Clara replied tersely, "I hardly think my son's welfare need concern you."

"But your son's welfare has been my concern since the day 'e was born," Ruby wailed. "It would break my 'eart to leave 'im now."

"Nonsense. You're only a young girl and no doubt you'll have children of your own before long."

"But madam, please-"

"There is no more to be said Ruby. My mind is quite made up. You will leave at the end of the month." Clara turned her back on Ruby to signify the meeting was at an end. Unable to hold back her tears, Ruby ran from the room and dashed downstairs to the kitchen.

"Whatever's up now?" Mrs Grundy cried as Ruby rushed in flinging herself down at the kitchen table. Mrs Grundy's eyes were puffy from continual sobbing since learning the fate of her master. She had been employed at Marbal House since Albert was a young boy and since his death had stated daily that it was

42

like losing one of her own; that she'd never actually had one of her own was a fact nobody wanted to point out.

"I've been told to go." Ruby wailed. "How am I gonna tell Jesse, when he has only just lost his father? He'll feel abandoned. He'll think it's my fault and whose gonna look after him proper? Not 'er, not his mother tha's for sure. Poor little mite, I shall miss him so much."

"She hasn't gone and dismissed you ,has she?" Mrs Grundy said, with her knack for asking the obvious. She went over to Ruby and put her arm around Ruby's heaving shoulders. "There, there now. Millie stop gawpin' and make us a pot of tea. I don't know how all this is gonna end, I don't really. First the dear master goin' and now Ruby. 'Tis all too much at my age. I can't cope with much more, I can't honest."

Mrs Grundy's voice began to crack, and tears began to flow almost as fast as Ruby's. Millie, whose day had started off exceedingly well with a postcard from Jake, looked on in dismay. "Where will you go Ruby?" she asked. She felt guilty now that her mail had made her happy, even though it had been a strange sort of postcard, pre-printed with bits crossed out by Jake so that it ended up reading, "I am going on well I have received your letter letter follows at first opportunity Jake." Ruby sat upright and dried her eyes. "I dunno where I'm gonna live", she sniffed. "I'll go an' see my sister Demelza tomorrow." She blew her nose loudly. "I 'aven't seen her for a while, so I'll take a walk over to the farm in the mornin' when Mrs Treverton is out with Jesse. She's taken him out every mornin' since she's bin 'ere. And if she gets back before I do, well flippin' 'ard luck." She sniffed again. "I can't get sacked for it can I?"

"I reckon this is all that Mrs Treverton's doing," Mrs Grundy said in a low voice in case Mrs Treverton might somehow overhear. "She's nothin' but an interferin' ol' busy body and has been ever since master Jesse was born."

"You don't need to whisper," Millie said as she poured out the tea. "Mrs Treverton is out with Jesse. Ruby jus' told you she takes him out every morning." Mrs Grundy glared at her. "There's no need to take that tone with me, my girl. I don't know when it was that you got so sharp, but I'll tell you this, I liked you much more when you was a mousy little thing."

The following morning after Ruby had dressed Jesse for his outing and handed him over to his grandmother, she put on her coat and left the house. It was a fine April morning and she would have enjoyed the walk across the fields to her sister's cottage if only she wasn't shortly to be bereft of her job, her home and her beloved Jesse. She had spent the night crying between patches of light sleep. She would have to tell Jesse that she was leaving, but later, once she had got used to it herself. It took Ruby nearly an hour walking across country to her sister's tied cottage. Demelza was outside hanging up washing as Ruby walked up the cinder path. "Well you'm a sight for sore eyes." Demelza pegged a sheet to the line and then gave her sister a hug. "So what brings you out to this neck of the woods?" Ruby shook her head sadly.

"You won't believe it when I tell you." Demelza gave her a quizzical look. "You aren't up the spout, are 'e?"

"Chance would be a fine thing," Ruby said giving her sister a friendly shove.

"Well you'd best tell me all about it then." Demelza ushered Ruby into the kitchen, shooed a chicken out and cleared a chair of clothes for Ruby to sit down. "Peaceful, innit?" She said. "My lot are all at school now. Mind, I do find it a bit quiet day times without 'em to be honest and if my Matthew was 'ere I'd probably go and have another one. No hope of that while he's soldierin', though is there? Like you said, chance'd be a fine thing. Come on, sit down." Demelza poured Ruby a glass of barley water, then folded her arms and looked critically at her young sister. You've lost a bit o' weight since I last saw you I reckon- and you're looking as miserable as sin, so what's up?"

Ruby told her. "I feel like little Jesse's mine," she concluded. "I've done everything for 'm since he was born, dear of 'im."

"Oh the boy'll be alright," Demelza said patting her sister's hand. "It'll be harder fer you than it will fer 'im. Kids get over things pretty quick. You've got to start thinkin' about yerself. If you've got to be out by the end of the month, you've only got a couple of weeks to get sorted. Course, you can always stay 'ere at a push – if you don't mind sharing with the three boys. And I daresay they'd be more than grateful to take you on at the farm. You'd find it 'ard though, after what you've bin used to."

"Thanks" Ruby said. "Sounds some inviting, that does."

"I'm only bein' honest." Demelza rubbed her arms thoughtfully. "Bit of a sod though, innit? After all you've done for that ol' bitch and she turfs you out just like that and there's nothin' you can do by it. You'll just have to try and look on the bright side though," she added with a smile of hope. "You never know, somethin' might turn up. Life's full of suprises an' they're not always bad." When Ruby started walking back across the fields, she had no idea how prophetic her sister's words would be.

Ruby had spent longer with Demelza than she intended and so on the way back decided to take a shortcut back through Voleworth Woods. From there she could take a pathway leading to the church, cross over the road and walk along the canal bank back to the town. Mrs Treverton would be home long before, and Jesse would be anxious to see Ruby, but she thought sadly, the dear mite would have to get used to her not being there, but as for Mrs Treverton – well she could lump it.

The woodland was at first refreshingly cool after the heat of walking across open fields and Ruby picked up speed, hurrying her way through the jutting tree roots and low branches. By the time she had reached a small clearing however, she was beginning to feel flustered and tired from the trek and stopped for a while to get her breath back. She saw, but at first couldn't quite discern, the two entwined figures lying beside a hawthorn tree a short distance in front of her, and her heart began to beat faster from the shock of seeing a couple obviously up to no good. She stood still while deciding what to do. The thought of retracing her steps all the way back down the field, and across the next one, was too daunting she decided. She had no alternative but to keep going forward. Ruby took a few tentative steps, trying to be quiet,

45

although she knew the pair was bound to hear her sooner or later. She glanced furtively across at them and then froze. It couldn't be – yet it definitely was. Mrs Pinner and Mrs Marbal. They were doing things that courting couples did. Mrs Marbal's blouse was undone, and one of Mrs Pinner's hands appeared to be under Mrs Marbal's skirt. Ruby felt sick.

"Oh my God," she exclaimed, in a voice loud enough for Mrs Marbal to come out of the euphoria of sexual arousal and give a piercing scream. Hester Pinner turned around quickly, saw Ruby and scrambled to her feet. "You stupid girl, what do you mean by spying on us like that?" she squawked, her hands flying first to straighten her skirt, then her dishevelled plait of hair. "Stop staring and go away. Go on, go about your business."

"I weren't spying on you," Ruby said. Her initial guilt and shock at having witnessed the two women making love was steadily replaced by anger and indignation. Mrs Pinner had a nerve to talk down to her after what she'd just witnessed, and as Ruby had already lost her job, she could tell Mrs Pinner what she thought of her without reprisal. "What sort of person do you take me for that would want to spy on a disgustin' scene like that? You're not fit," she went on, getting braver at the sight of Mrs Pinner's astonished but silent open mouth, "to look after decent sick people. And as for you Madam," she said with mock politeness, glaring boldly at Mrs Marbal, "you're not a fit person to bring up a child." Mrs Marbal's fingers trembled as contrived to button up her blouse.

"I really can't imagine what you're talking about Ruby or why you're here when you should be … but whatever you think you saw … Mrs Pinner and I were – were merely resting."

"What?" Ruby scoffed, "with 'er hand up your skirt? Funny sort o' resting that is. Oh no, I know what I saw all right and I'm only glad that the poor master can never know about it. Though what Mrs Treverton and Dr Pinner will say, 'eaven knows." Clara was on her feet now, clutching at Hester for support. "Don't you dare, Ruby. Don't you dare breathe a word to anyone."

"She wouldn't dare," Hester said with more hope than conviction. "Who would believe her word against ours?"

46

"Well, we'll 'ave to see won't we?" Ruby scowled at the two women. "I'll have to tell for the sake of my conscience. I reckon Master Jesse has already seen more than he should. He told me 'es seen you two kissin' for a start." Hester out of fear and anger took a step towards Ruby, her hand upraised as if to strike her. "I'm warning you, you stupid little bitch, you say a word to anyone and you'll regret it."

"Hester stop," wailed Clara. "You're making things worse."

"Yes she is," Ruby agreed. "If she threatens me again I'll tell the police." Clara began to cry. "Please Ruby don't tell anyone."

This was the second time Ruby had power over her mistress and realising it, knew also that her problems could soon be over; provided Mrs Pinner didn't kill her before she had chance to get out of the woods. "Well it's only Jesse I'm bothered about – bein' left with you that is, without me there to make sure he's alright," she began craftily, "course, if you was to let me stay on madam, well," Ruby shrugged, "what you did would be yer own affair."

"Blackmail," Hester hissed. "Don't let her blackmail you Clara."

"Oh shut up Hester." Clara snapped. "This is all your fault. You're too – too forceful. Very well Ruby, you may stay. But you must promise me on my son's life that you will never breathe a word of this to anyone." Ruby nodded, almost moved to tears with relief. "I promise," she said, "I won't never say a word about it – for Jesse's sake." She was true to her word. She never mentioned it to anyone, although Clara herself did, many years later.

Ruby happily told anyone who was interested that Mrs Marbal had simply had a change of heart, and had reinstated her. Mrs Treverton was as pleased as anyone. Acting the role of doting grandmother in the face of her grandson's sad loss was wearing her out. She was more than relieved at not being obliged to take Jesse out and entertain him every morning, and so was Jesse. At the first opportunity, Mrs Treverton returned home to Truro. Clara broke off her affair with Hester. The fright and shame of being caught in the act by Ruby, of all people, soured the relationship beyond repair. Viewing it from the distance of time, Clara

47

gradually realised that Hester, forceful and competent in a way she admired, had entranced and then manipulated her. She wasn't sure how the physical side of their relationship had come about. Hester had been so subtle. And she had to admit that she enjoyed sex with Hester far more than she ever had with Albert, but the truth was, she realised, that she didn't particularly need sex with anyone. Hester had taught her to become more assertive, had boosted her self-confidence and after the initial whack to her pride at being caught in the woods by her maid, Clara revelled in being her own person, doing what she wanted without interference from anyone. In the main this meant painting, first in watercolours and then in oils. It also meant cutting off her long hair into a fashionable bob, buying a motorcar and learning how to drive. Clara never forgot Hester. The moment Hester had said, "I can give you something for the pain", was the moment Clara felt a great surge of love for her, and in her detached way she continued to love Hester for the rest of her life, which was more than could be said for her affection towards Albert.

Mrs Grundy didn't see the end of the war. In 1916 she had a stroke and died in hospital a few weeks later. Millie and Ruby who had gone to visit her on a couple of occasions, said her death was a great relief. Following the stroke Mrs Grundy could only dribble and utter incoherently from the side of her mouth, one eye staring straight ahead, while the other was forever shut. Millie said it gave her the creeps to look at her, even though she'd often wished Mrs Grundy's sharp eyes and tongue to be less so. Now they were, she was unable to enjoy the poetic justice of it. Ruby was saddened by Mrs Grundy's terminal illness. Seeing her lying in the hospital bed trying in vain to communicate was most upsetting. Ruby never quite knew whether her responding yes and no's were said in the right place or what it was exactly that Mrs Grundy was trying to ask her to do. She often wondered whether in the end Mrs Grundy gave up and died from the sheer frustration of it all.

After the war, Ruby married and moved to Bristol with her new husband who had found work at the Bristol Aircraft factory. Jesse now seven years old was sent to boarding school at Truro, which would have been his fate regardless of Ruby's marriage. Even after she had children of her own, Ruby often thought of Jesse with great affection, and for several years they corresponded with each other. Ruby managed to visit him on occasions at Marbal House when Clara was away on her sojourns. Clara had taken to travelling, which was fortunate for Millie, because she was required to look after Marbal House in the absence of Mrs Marbal, and also to be conveniently on hand when Jesse was home from school. This meant Millie retained her live-in job, even after her marriage to Jake.

Jake had come home on leave only once during the war. Late one balmy July evening just before he returned to the front, he gave Millie one of the brass buttons from his uniform, looped through a piece of string. As he hung it around Millie's neck he told her it meant they were now engaged and then he ravished her behind a cowshed. Millie was ecstatic until he left and then she lived in a constant state of nervous dread that he might not return. When he did return at the end of the war, it was minus a leg, shell shocked and exhausted. He was haunted by the horror of the Somme and told Millie how he often woke up at night crying like a baby and that now he wasn't fit for anything let alone to be her husband. Millie told him he had to marry her because they were engaged and now that she was no longer a virgin, no one else would want her. As she said it, it occurred to her that no one else would want her anyway whether she was a virgin or not. If Jake thought the same, he at least had the grace not to tell her, besides he had no illusions about his own eligibility on the marriage stakes.

Where they would live and what Jake, handicapped as he was, would do for a living, was solved by Clara. Her motives were not entirely selfish. Like most people, it was not until the war had ended that she became aware of the horrific suffering soldiers had endured. She would have shown Albert more affection when she saw him off at the station had she known what he was letting himself in for, although she imagined if he himself had known what was in store, he probably wouldn't have gone. To help her assuage her guilt at sending Albert off to his fate without a thought for his safety, she suggested that when Jake and Millie married they could share the attic room at Marbal House. There was nothing she could do about poor Albert, but Jake had survived and needed help. Jake could do maintenance work around the house and in the garden. Millie could do as she had always done, only less of it, because most of the time, with the exception of school holidays there would only be Millie and Jake living at Marbal House. However when Clara was in residence, she sometimes regretted her decision in allowing Jake and Millie to sleep upstairs in the attic. There was no servants' staircase at Marbal House so the only route to the attic was passed Clara's bedroom door. The sound of Jake's wooden leg as he thumped across the landing and up another, uncarpeted flight of steps often roused Clara to lip biting irritation and she constantly had to remind herself that Jake had lost his leg in serving his country; yet it never occurred to her that it might be more convenient all round if they slept in one of the unoccupied bedrooms away from her own. As far as Clara was concerned, live-in servants occupied the attic. And so it was in the attic of Marbal House one night in late September, that Agnes' grandmother was conceived.

Chapter 4

Clara stood by the window of what had once been her drawing room but was now her art studio. She was anxious to get her first glimpse of Jesse's wife. At first Clara had been aggrieved to learn of Jesse's marriage by way of a telegram after the event, and took it as a personal slight; however Jesse's subsequent letter, short though it was, appeased her. Jesse wrote that Joan, his wife had lost both her parents when a doodlebug made a direct hit on their home in Islington. Joan's only sister Muriel was a G.I. bride, living in America, and as Joan had no other family, she wanted a quick registry office marriage with just a couple of friends to act as witnesses. Once Clara realised that that her absence of invitation was not a personal snub, and not being sentimental enough to have wished to have been at her son's wedding, no matter how small an affair, she was almost grateful to him for being saved the bother of attending. Jesse had written little more in his letter other than he had met and courted Joan during the war when they were both stationed at R.A.F. Lynham, and that it hadn't taken him long to realise she was the woman for him. And now at last here they were, de-mobbed and married and bound for Cornwall.

What Jesse hadn't mentioned in his letter to Clara was that Joan had never felt close to her parents, and had been only too pleased to get away from them by joining the W.R.A.F. Her father, a tailor who ran his business from home and was therefore ever present, had been a mean spirited, tyrannical Edwardian, her mother too cowed to stand up to him when he bullied her or either of her two daughters. Joan had revelled in her freedom when she joined the R.A.F. and even when she went back to Portland Road, Islington and stared at the rubble where the family house had once stood she found it difficult to grieve for her parents who had been buried beneath it. What Jesse also and understandably omitted to tell his mother was that Joan was the hottest bit of stuff he'd ever had the good fortune to encounter. She was crazy for sex, whipping off her knickers at every opportunity. They'd had sex on a train, in cars, in her office, in fields, up an alleyway, behind a sand dune,

51

and once, although he sometimes had a pang of conscience about it, in a church, half-way up the belfry tower.

Considering her strict upbringing, or perhaps because of it, Joan was extremely uninhibited. She was also very forthright and down to earth. What you saw was what you got, as Ruby used to say, and apart from sex, that's what Jesse liked about Joan the most.

Clara hoped she wouldn't feel jealous towards Jesse's wife. Clara had grown very fond of Jesse from about his fourteenth year onward. He had turned into a well-mannered young man of whom she was justifiably proud to take with her on some of her excursions abroad. She appreciated the way he stood up when she entered the room, drew back her chair at table, opened and closed doors for her, and never forgot her birthday. He did all of these things with an air of detachment, which she particularly liked. He wasn't close or cloying; he didn't fret about her, or try to dissuade her from sudden urges of recklessness. He was in fact rather good company and furthermore he admired her paintings and encouraged her artwork. She had constantly prayed for his safety during the war years and had a photograph on the piano of him in his R.A.F. Officer's uniform looking handsome and smiling broadly. And now the war was over, and he was coming home with her – this Joan whom Clara knew practically nothing about.

At the sound of a car pulling up at the kerbside Clara open the curtains a chink wider. It was Jesse. He climbed out of the car and walked around to the passenger side to open the door for Joan. Clara peered closer. Her daughter-in-law wore a red hat perched at what the fashion magazines would term a jaunty angle, a tight fitting grey suit, and had a fur of some sort slung around her neck. She was quite stocky and her ankles looked rather thick, Clara thought. She was too far away to see Joan's face clearly, but she heard Joan laugh at something Jesse had said and then suddenly she looked right up at the window where Clara stood, and waved. Clara, feeling ridiculous at having been caught spying at her, dropped the curtain back into place as Joan linked arms with Jesse and swaying provocatively walked up the garden path.

Clara opened the front door to her son and his wife with a pre-fixed smile. This was their house now, but as she had no intention of living out her life elsewhere, she would have to make every effort to get on well with Joan or life would be very unpleasant for them all. Joan was smiling back at Clara, and then being as tactile as Clara was reserved, leaned forward and kissed her cheek. "Nice to meet you at last," Joan said, happily unaware that Clara had flinched from her touch. "So what am I to call you then, Clara or mother?"

"Clara - most definitely." Heaven forfend, she thought, that I should become mother to anyone else. "I'd like to say I've heard so much about you Joan," Clara said with a false, tinkling laugh, "but I'm afraid Jesse has told me very little." She looked up at Jesse who smiled back at her and gave her cheek the briefest peck. "Joan is my wife. What more is there to tell? You're looking well, mother." To Clara's dismay, Jesse picked up his wife, who gave a little squeal of surprised delight as he carried her across the threshold. "Welcome to Marbal House, Mrs Marbal." Joan flung her arms around his neck and kissed him fully on the mouth with such blatant disregard for Clara presence that she found it hard to conceal her disdain. "Mrs. Marbal of Marbal House," Joan said, laughing. "How grand does that sound? I'm not sure it suits me at all." Jesse grinned at her and gently eased her arms from his neck so that she was standing upright again. "Bit pretentious really isn't it? Don't you get embarrassed Clara, when you have to give your name and address?"

"Not at all," Clara replied stiffly. "However I rarely have to give my name and address. The family is well known around here as you will find out."

"My grandfather had the house built," Jesse added, "so we Marbals have been here for three generations." He hoped his mother hadn't already formed a bad impression of Joan. If she had, Joan was oblivious to the fact, and happily looking around her, touching the flock wallpaper, removing her hat and adjusting

53

her hair at the mirrored hall table. Clara was trying to overcome Joan's apparent shortcomings. It was far too early to get their relationship off on the wrong footing. "Jesse will show you around the house later, after you've warmed yourself by the fire and had tea," she said, making an effort to sound pleasant. "Did you have a good journey down from London?"Jesse, well aware of how his mother abhorred public displays of affection and realising that Joan had already embarrassed her, gave Clara a grateful smile.

"Very enjoyable. We started out yesterday and stayed overnight at Bath. Joan hadn't been there before. We found a really delightful hotel, didn't we darling?" Joan smiled in agreement.

"Is the fire lit in the parlour?" Jesse opened the parlour door and Joan peered around him for a quick look inside.

"Yes it is, so go along in," Clara said. "Violet has set out cakes and bread and butter. Sit yourselves by the fire while I make a pot of tea."

"This certainly is a big house," Joan said. "All these doors everywhere – I shall get lost. And what's down those steps, the kitchen?" Without waiting for an answer she began to descend the steps to investigate. Clara gave Jesse a bemused look. He shrugged back at her and grinned. "Well I'm going to thaw out by the fire even if Joan isn't, so I'll leave the pair of you to get acquainted." Clara followed Joan into the kitchen.

"Blimey, you've still got servant's bells." Joan said. "Do they work?"

"Oh yes," Clara said. "They still come in very handy – when I'm in my studio and need Violet for something."

"Really? I can't imagine ringing down for someone," Joan said, and before Clara could reply wheeled round to face the oven. "Oh thank God you've got a proper gas cooker. Jess told me you had an old kitchen range. My cooking is bad enough I can tell you without having to wrestle with a bit of antiquity like an old range."

"But you won't have to cook," Clara said. "Violet sees to that."

"Oh I don't know," Joan frowned. "It doesn't seem right not to cook for your husband- although I'm not very good at it, so he might prefer it if I didn't. But to be honest Clara, I'm not really comfortable with this servant lark, particularly as Violet is like a kid sister to Jess."

Clara raised an eyebrow. "A sister? I hardly think so. Violet is the daughter of –."

"Millie and Jake, I know. Jess told me .He was quite upset when Jake died last year." Joan decided against telling Clara that Jesse had also said Jake had been like a father to him. She sensed that was something Clara wouldn't want to know. She rifled through her handbag and brought out a packet of cigarettes and a lighter. She offered the packet towards Clara who declined with a small shake of the head. "So, where is she then, your Violet?"

"Violet has gone to see Millie. She lives in one of those dreadful little houses the council have put up on the other side of the town." Clara lit a gas ring on the oven and placed the kettle on it to boil.

"I don't suppose Millie thinks it's so dreadful," Joan said puffing smoke up at the ceiling. "I should imagine she's only too happy to have a place of her own at last."

"I'm sure Millie is delighted with her home but it doesn't alter the fact that the council estate has been built on what was a most pretty piece of countryside. Now it's destroyed by dreadful, ugly buildings. Of course people must have houses – it's where they are built and how they are built that I take issue with." Clara wondered if she'd sounded too indignant, but her daughter-in-law unperturbed, was looking around her and not finding an ash-tray, using a pot of geraniums on the window-sill to flick her ash into. Clara turned her attention to the bubbling kettle. She wasn't too impressed with Joan. She couldn't help thinking that Jesse could have done much better for himself. Joan was a little coarse she felt, and Jesse had been out with much prettier girls. Joan wasn't pretty at all, really. She had the sort of lips that reminded Clara of a goldfish. However, Jesse had taken long enough to find himself a wife and, as he had chosen Joan, Clara would have to make the most of it. "Why don't you go back up to the parlour with Jesse?" she said. "It's rather cold in here. I'm sure you'd rather be sitting by the fire."

"Don't you want a hand? I could carry the tray up, or something."

"I can manage, thank you."

"Alright, if you're sure. Actually I could do with a wee first though. Where's the toilet?"

"There's one out in the yard." Clara said, intending to add that it was the servant's privy but that she would find the lavatory on the first floor landing next to the bathroom; however, as Joan was already making her way out of the back door, Clara decided not to waste her breath.

"So how are you and mother getting along?" Jesse held his hand out to Joan as she came to join him in the parlour. "She told me to come in here and warm myself with you." Joan said, pressing herself against Jesse as he stood in front of the fire. She moved her hand slowly and deliberately across his crotch.

"Stop it, you tease," Jesse said. "She might walk in on us."

"It's our home, isn't it?"

"Yes but we have to show her some respect darling. After all it's going to be difficult enough for mother to adjust to you running the house, without subjecting her to lewd displays of behaviour – nice though it is."

"I suppose you're right." Joan took a final drag on her cigarette and threw it into the fire. "She's a bit of a snob your mother, isn't she?"

Jesse laughed. "Whatever gave you that idea? Actually no, I don't think she's a snob. You have to remember she's been used to a different way of life; servants to do everything for her, standards to be kept. I think she's adjusted pretty well to the world she now has to live in."

"She's taking a bloody long time to make the tea. I'm starving." Joan muttered, looking at the inviting cake stand of saffron buns and jam-covered scones topped with thick, yellow cream.

"She's probably not used to doing it." Jesse said. "I'll go and carry up the tray from the kitchen for her – and then I'll fetch our cases in from the car."

As soon as Jesse had left, Joan took a scone and ate it while giving the room a closer inspection. There was a pair of Staffordshire dogs on the mantelpiece separated like book ends

56

by a deep ruby Bristol glass vase, stuffed to capacity with dried flowers and next to that a glass domed carriage clock. A bevelled mirror spanned the width of the mantelshelf reflecting the whole of what Joan considered to be a dreary room. She moved across to the piano, picked up the photograph of Jesse, and smiled lovingly at him before replacing it. She looked towards the fireplace. The Staffordshire dogs would have to go, she decided, along with the bulky corner display cabinet filled with an assortment of glass and china ornaments. She sat down on the edge of the sofa. It felt hard and unyielding, stuffed no doubt with horsehair. That too could go, along with the term parlour. Who on earth had a parlour in this day and age? Then there were those dreadful, drab velvet curtains. Joan searched in her handbag for a handkerchief to wipe the tell-tale smears of jam from her fingers. She'd have to start making lists. It would take months to get Marbal House modernised. Of course she'd discuss her plans with Clara first, but changes there would be whether Clara approved, or not.

After tea, Clara decided to drive over to Rock Beach. She needed fresh air and time on her own. Joan, she'd discovered was inclined to talk rather a lot and although she constantly asked questions, seemed reticent to talk about her own past, particularly her childhood. Joan had also sat throughout tea as close to Jesse on the sofa as was possible. Clara thought it shameful the way Joan's thighs were pressed tightly against Jesse's, and the way her hand was forever resting on his leg, his arm his hand. Married they might be, but in Clara's day shows of affection were kept strictly to the bedroom, or in her case not shown at all. "Violet will be back in an hour to start dinner," she said, standing in the doorway already dressed in her hat and coat, "I'll see you both at seven."
"But it's so dark outside," Joan said, following Clara out into the hall. "You won't be able to see anything. Why do you want to go out now?"
"I happen to like walking in the dark," Clara replied tersely.
"You should get a dog then," Joan suggested. "Then you'd have a reason for walking in the dark."

"I most certainly should not get a dog," Clara replied. "And the only reason I need to do anything, is because I want to do it."

Joan winced as the front door was shut with more force than was needed. "Oh dear. I didn't mean to upset her." She turned to Jesse. "Your mother and I don't seem to be getting on too well, do we?"

"Don't worry, you'll get used to her, besides she's always taking herself off somewhere – for weeks sometimes."

He put his arms around Joan's shoulders. "Now, why don't I give you a tour of the house? Where shall we start?"

"Oh how exciting!" Joan rubbed her hands together. "I've been longing to have a proper look around. Let's start with the bedrooms." She followed Jesse up the wide mahogany staircase, stopping briefly at the stairs turn to admire the stained glass window.

"It's really attractive in the day time with the sunlight shining through." Jesse said. "When I was a kid I used to sit on that step where you're standing, and look at the carpet and wall all magically bathed in blue and red. It used to make me feel warm and safe."

"How sweet. I bet you were a sweet little boy."

"I was."

Joan, reaching the landing wrinkled her nose. "What's that strange turpsy pong?"

"It is turps," Jesse said, "mixed with the smell of oil paints and mother's Du Maurier's."

"So she does smoke then?"

"Oh yes – chain smokes when she's painting, but always with a very elegant cigarette holder. Her studio is here, at the front of the house and her bedroom is the room opposite."

"Clara has both the rooms facing the front garden then," Joan said, opening the door to Clara's studio and peering in.

"Well yes. That's always been her bedroom and her studio needs to be facing north for the light. You don't mind, do you?" Jesse wanted to tell Joan that she really shouldn't be going into Clara's studio. It was her retreat, entered by invitation only. Joan however wasn't particularly interested in the racks of canvases, the squashed, rolled tubes of oil paints, the brimming ashtrays and the all-pervading odour. She shut the door. "Of course I don't mind. Any bed with you is fine by me. So which room is ours?"

"This one, on the other side of the bathroom. This has always been my room and it looks as if Violet has made it ready for us – but you can choose one of the other two if you prefer."

"No, this will do beautifully." Joan stood in the doorway looking at the high, brass double bed. "Doesn't it look inviting?" she said. "Crisp white sheets, and such a pretty, soft eiderdown. And this is where you slept as a boy, when you were virginal and innocent?"

Jesse stood behind her and put his arms around her waist. "It certainly is Mrs. Marbal, and I bet you can't wait to corrupt my chaste bed, can you?" Joan grinned, pressing her buttocks hard against his groin. "You're absolutely right, but I'm trying to control myself until I've seen the rest of the house." Jesse smiled. "You – control yourself? That doesn't happen often. Come on then' I'll show you the other two bedrooms."

"One day," Joan said, as they continued their tour, "we'll fill all these bedrooms with children. Wouldn't that be wonderful?"

"I don't know about filling them," Jesse said. "But one in each room would be nice."

"Alright. I'll settle for that." At the end of the hallway Joan saw the steps leading to the attic, and began to climb them.

"There's nothing up there apart from Violet's room", Jesse told her, "and we can't very well go in without asking her permission."

"But she's not here to ask, is she?" Joan said. "I only want to take a peep so that I've seen every room upstairs before we start on the rooms downstairs. Don't look so worried darling, I'm not interested in whether Violet hasn't made her bed or whether she's left her knickers on the floor. I'm just curious to see the room."

The thought of Violet's knickers lying on the floor persuaded Jesse that maybe it wouldn't hurt to have a look. Joan flicked on the light switch beside the door and a single bulb dangling from the middle of the ceiling cast a shadowy and dim light over the room. There was a double bed once used by Millie and Jake, a curtained clothes rail and under the sloping roof, a chest of drawers that doubled as a washstand with a porcelain bowl and jug on top. Jesse was rather disappointed to see how neat the room was, with nothing lying on the floor apart from a pair of black leather shoes carefully placed beneath the cane chair. And then he noticed a white towel over the back of the chair and on top of the towel an even whiter brassiere. Violet's plain but very large brassiere with crease lines across the cups where her very large confined breasts had pressed against them. At the sight of such a personal item of clothing, Jesse found himself thinking about Violet in a way he's never allowed himself to do before; her soft brown hair, and her doe brown eyes, her quiet ways, and her breasts that looked pillow soft. "It's a bit Spartan in here, isn't it? And chilly – I need warming up." Joan slipped her arms around Jesse's waist, pushing herself as close to him as she could. Jesse's thoughts, which had already taken an erotic turn, and were now exacerbated by Joan's limpet proximity, aroused him in a way, she didn't fail to notice. "You can't wait for it, can you poor darling? So why don't we do it here and now. In fact," she continued, unbuttoning the front of Jesse's trousers, let's bonk our way through every room in the house, starting here, right at the top, and ending in the cellar, if you've got one."

"We can't do it in Violet's room," Jesse said without much conviction. "She could come back at any minute."

"I know – exciting, isn't it?" Joan's hands were inside the waistband of his shorts, tugging at them to ease them over his hips. Jesse felt a pleasurable sensation of cool air over his warm, newly exposed parts. His eyelids felt heavy and closed momentarily. When he opened them again his vision briefly focused on Violet's brassiere with its enticing creases. In a rush of passion he pushed up Joan's skirt and whipped down her knickers before she had time to do it herself.

It wasn't until hours later when Jesse lay in bed with Joan asleep beside him making soft put-put noises through her half opened mouth, that Jesse felt uncomfortable about his behaviour in Violet's bedroom. It was a form of violation not to have respected her privacy and to have leered at her underwear. And if it wasn't bad enough that he'd behaved like a smutty school- boy, he'd also fantasised while having sex on the attic floor with his wife, that she was Violet. What madness, he wondered, had gotten into him? And it hadn't ended there, if he was honest with himself. Later, when Violet had called them down to dinner, he'd been brazen enough to give her a warm brotherly kiss and tease her jut to see her fluster and blush. In future he would make sure he behaved in a more responsible way, though he could never treat Violet like the servant she indubitably was. She felt like family – after all, he'd known her since she was a baby, and they'd practically been brought up together. God, he'd be thirty-six next birthday and had behaved like someone half his age. Jesse turned on his side and tried unsuccessfully to blank out his feelings of guilt. He'd slyly ogled Violet all evening. What had made him do that when he loved Joan so much? He placed his arm over her waist and she sighed in her sleep. Joan was bright and fun to be with. Violet was sweet, but, well not very bright, not even pretty really. Sweet though. A sweet shrinking Violet.

Joan was surprised and dismayed when as the months passed, she failed to become pregnant. She and Jesse had carried out their intent by bonking their way through every room in the house – with the exception of Clara's two rooms because neither of them fancied doing it there - Jesse out of respect and Joan because she couldn't stomach the smell of the studio, or of Clara's bedroom which had an aroma a of rose-water and camphor and reminded Joan too much of her parent's bedroom. Jesse and Joan enjoyed so much unprotected sex that most mornings Jesse found it difficult to summons the energy to get out of bed and go to work. It seemed impossible that under such a barrage of sperm, Joan would fail to conceive; yet the months passed without successful fertilisation and although Jesse said that it was good fun trying, Joan began to feel their sexual exploits were turning into a mockery. All those nights of passion only seemed to highlight the fact that she couldn't become pregnant. Her appetite for lovemaking began to wane and her energy diverted into transforming Marbal House.

The celebration of their first wedding anniversary had not long passed when Jesse began to work on late in his photography studio – the studio that in his childhood had belonged to Oats. Jesse worked late because it was more peaceful at the studio than it was at home. Joan's refurbishing and renovation lists seemed endless, with an assortment of builders, plumbers and decorators taking turns to create havoc until their particular tasks were completed. Clara was agreeably acquiescent over the changes to Marbal House, although as Joan pointed out to Jesse, apart from having gas and electricity installed, Clara obviously had never given decorating much thought. Every room in Marbal House retained Edwardian wallpaper and furnishings, chosen Joan reckoned, by Clara's mother-in-law. However, Joan was grateful for Clara's indifference, Clara's only request being that her bedroom and studio remain exactly as they were. And so while paper was being scraped off walls and all the bedroom fireplaces except her own were ripped out, Clara stayed in her room, smoking, painting, listening to the wireless and planning her next holidays. She appeared downstairs only for meals, which due to the chaos around the rest of the house, were eaten in the kitchen. But it was not only the presence of the workmen that persuaded Jesse to work until early evening. His preoccupation with Violet's soft, rounded body, and doe-eyed simplicity hadn't waned since the first night he had brought Joan back to Marbal House and it troubled him. The only way out of the situation he decided would be to ask Violet to leave and so rid himself of her tempting presence. It would be best for Violet too. She was young enough to do more with her life than endless chores for his family. What had been acceptable for her mother and dear old Ruby was not appropriate for Violet. The world had moved on and in everyone's best interest, so should Violet.

As soon as Joan had taken off for good the woollen scarf that she wore wound over her head and knotted in the front, and had discarded her paint splattered slacks and his old white shirt, as soon as the last workman had left the house never to return, and

Joan had laid down her paintbrush and was free to return to the household chores allocated to Violet, he would find a way of asking her to leave. However, this resolution, although seriously intended, never came to fruition. The spiralling effects following the events of one evening late in the summer of 1948 changed everything.

Jesse, deciding he'd had enough of being cooped up all day working on his latest commission, Colourful Cornish Calendars, locked up his studio at six p.m. and began a leisurely saunter home. There was still plenty of heat in the day, and by the time he had reached the top of the hill, he had removed his linen jacket, slung it over his shoulder and loosened his tie. He decided that after dinner he would take Joan to the pub by the river front where they could sit shaded by trees and down long, cool drinks. He opened the garden gate, noticing at first the earth strewn across the path and then two well staked cherry tree saplings planted by the garden wall. Jesse groaned. Surely now that Joan had finished revamping the inside of the house, she wasn't about to start on the outside? He unlocked the front door to the familiar smell of fresh paint, mixed this evening with the aroma of what he hoped wasn't stew but smelt suspiciously like it, and hung his jacket on the hall stand. The hallway, he had to admit, appeared a good deal brighter since Joan had the old wallpaper replaced with ribbed stripes of white and gold, yet he missed the cosy familiarity of the old red flock, even though it had become bald in places.

"Is that you, Jess? I'm in the kitchen." Joan called out. As soon as he entered the kitchen doorway Joan rushed across to him, and threw her arms around his waist. "I'm glad you're home Jess," she murmured, snuggling against his chest. "I've had a bugger of a day."

"Have you darling?" Jesse stroked her hair from the top of her head down to the nape of her neck, where it was pinned up over some sort of padding. Jesse liked the soft glossy feel of the underside of Joan's hair, although the sausage padding it was pinned to had given him a bit of a shock when he first encountered it lying on Joan's dressing table and hadn't a clue what she used it for. "So," he said, "tell me about your bad day."

Joan sighed. "I will, after you've eaten." As she broke free of him Jesse wondered if she had been crying. Her eyelids looked slightly puffy and there were fine traces of earth smeared across her cheeks as if she'd brushed away tears with muddy fingers.

He'd never seen Joan cry, and he decided not to mention it. She didn't like fuss, and would tell him what was upsetting her when she was ready. "I saw the saplings you planted," he said. "You should have left that for me."

"Why?" Joan said, suddenly defensive. "There may be some things I can't do but I can dig a couple of bloody holes." She began to ladle something from a saucepan onto a plate.

"Is that stew?" Jesse asked tentatively.

"Yes. And if you're thinking of complaining about it, don't. I've already had your mother moaning that my dumplings aren't as soft as Violet's. I told her she could make her own blinkin' dumplings next time."

"I wasn't going to complain," Jesse said, trying not to dwell on anything of Violet's that was soft. "It's just that the weather's a bit warm for stew, isn't it?"

"Maybe, but we had salad yesterday," Joan said as if stew was the only alternative. "Do you want a glass of wine with this?" Jesse glanced at the bits of vegetables and meat and one lumpy dumpling covered in thin, pale gravy, and shook his head. "You have one if you want. I'll get myself a glass of water. Why are you doing the cooking anyway? Where's Violet?" he asked, filling a tumbler from the kitchen tap.

"Violet's at the hospital."

"The hospital – has she had an accident?" Jesse tried to stay calm. So Joan *had* been crying and Violet was in hospital. Something was dreadfully wrong. He tipped back his head and drank the water too quickly; it dribbled from the sides of his mouth and down his chin.

"It's not Violet, it's Millie." Joan was saying. ""She was taken into hospital this morning with pneumonia. I'm afraid she's dying Jess."

64

Jesse thumped his glass down on the wooden draining board and wiped his mouth with the back of his hand. He felt suddenly angry. "Well thanks Joan," he said. "Thanks for getting around to telling me."

"But you've only just walked in," Joan wailed. "I told you as soon as I could."

"Where's mother? Is she at the hospital with Violet?"

"No. She had to go down to her friends with the gallery in St. Ives – Stanford I think they're called. She drove Violet to the hospital before she went, though."

"Well that was good of her wasn't it?" Jesse said with sarcasm. He sat at the table and stabbed his fork into a chunk of carrot. "Violet should have someone with her at a time like this. Couldn't you have gone?"

"No, Jess I couldn't. I know you're very fond of Millie but –"

Jesse grunted. "Not that fond as a matter of fact. She always worried and fussed too much – got on my bloody nerves most of the time. Still, it's a shock to find out she's dying. She dedicated her life to this family. The least we can do is give Violet some support." Jesse put down his fork. He still felt angry that neither his mother nor his wife had put themselves out to be with Violet. Joan obviously felt it was more important to plant her damn trees. He glanced over at her and frowned. "Why couldn't you have gone to the hospital with Violet?" he asked impatiently. Surely the trees could have waited."

"The trees?" Joan gave a sad, half smile and then picked up the bottle of wine and topped up her glass. "Actually, I've been trying to come to terms with some bad news of my own. Bad news for both of us." She sat down opposite Jesse and lit a cigarette.

"Bad news?" Jesse's anger immediately disappeared, replaced by concern, not now for Violet, but for Joan. She *had* been crying then and obviously not because of Millie. "Go on," he said. "Tell me."

Joan sighed and drew hard on her cigarette. "I drove over to Truro today to get the results from some tests that were done last week. I had an appointment with Mr Norman, he's a gynaecologist."

65

"Why didn't you tell me you were going to see a specialist?"

"I wanted to find out why I hadn't got pregnant yet. I thought I could get the problem sorted out, whatever it was, and then one day I could surprise you by saying, hey Jess, guess what? I'm pregnant." Joan chewed on her bottom lip and then drew furiously on her cigarette. "Only, that's never going to happen I'm afraid, because I can't have children."

Jesse stared at her, for a moment speechless. It was hard to comprehend, to take in the full impact of never having his own kids. He looked at Joan, her face pale, her lip trembling as she fought back her tears and realised that no matter how bad the news was for him, it was even worse for her. "Oh God, Joan – you poor darling." He scraped back his chair, intent on going to her, holding her, giving her some comfort but she put out her hand to fend him off. "No – please don't make a fuss of me Jess, or I'll start crying again, and I've done enough of that for one day."

"Alright, fair enough." He puffed out his cheeks and sighed. "I think I need that glass of wine after all." No sons to carry on the name of Marbal, no cute little daughters to spoil. It was a sod of a thing to come to terms with. He'd always assumed he would have kids one day – just went to show you shouldn't assume anything in life. Even his plans for a pleasant evening by the river with Joan had turned sour.

He poured himself a drink and refilled Joan's glass. "Maybe we should get a second opinion."

Joan shook her head. "No point. I had peritonitis when I was a kid and it buggered up my fallopian tubes." She made a brave attempt to smile. "That's not the correct medical term but it's what it all boils down to. I'm really sorry Jess. I know how much you wanted us to have babies."

"It's tough for both of us – but it's not your fault."

"No – it's my dad's fault. I can remember telling him and mum that I was in terrible pain, but they didn't believe me. The daft sod told mum to give me cod liver oil and she was stupid enough to do it. Between them they nearly killed me." Joan rolled the stem of her glass between her thumb and forefinger. "Mr. Norman said," she began tentatively, "that we should consider adopting." She looked at Jesse to gauge his reaction, but his expression told her nothing. "What do you think, Jess? I know it's not the same as having our own baby, but I'm sure we'd love it just as much." Jesse raked his fingers through his hair. "Steady on Joan. I've hardly had chance to come to terms with never having my own children – let alone take on someone else's."

"No, of course not. I'm sorry. It's still a shock for you isn't it? I've had all day to let it sink in."

"Why didn't you come to the studio as soon as you were back from Truro? You shouldn't have dwelt on it by yourself, Joan. You should have shared it with me. "

"That's not my way though is it? I cope best when I'm left alone." Jesse smiled fondly at her. "Too bloody independent by half, that's your trouble. Look, I was going to suggest we went to the Volesworth for a few drinks, but to be honest I don't really feel like it now unless, of course, you'd like to go". Joan shook her head. "Nor me," she said. "Besides, you'd better go over to the hospital and find out how Millie is."

"Will you come with me?"

"I'd rather not, if you don't mind. I feel depressed enough without hanging around with Violet waiting for her mother to die." Jesse noticed Joan's words were beginning to slur and as she reached out to the bottle to refill her glass, he put his hand over hers to halt her. "What are you doing?" Joan glowered at him. "Blimey, if you were prepared to take me out for a few drinks you surely can't object to me drinking in my own home."

"But have you eaten Joan? I don't want you getting ill over this and you've had about four glasses of wine already. If you want to drink any more, at least eat first."

"I have eaten. I had a plate of stew with Clara before she dashed off, so stop fussing. Oh – by the way, I haven't mentioned to Clara that I can't have kids. I haven't told anyone, and I'd rather you didn't either, Jess. I don't want people looking at me as if I'm a freak, or feeling sorry for me. You won't say anything, will you?" Joan looked at him, with a vulnerable, hurt look in her eyes. Jesse cupped her face in his hands and kissed her mouth tenderly. "Of course I won't say anything. The important thing is that we have each other and – well, I expect we'll sort out something in time."

"You mean adopt?"

"Maybe. We'll see."

Jesse drove his car into St. Luke's car park. The convent run hospital was newly built of Cornish granite and looked inviting enough with hedges of rhododendrons and camellias and a profusion of Damask roses that filled the air with their heavy scent. Even so, Jesse was mistrustful and uneasy about hospitals. As far as he was concerned they were debasing places where you either died or recovered, and if the latter, were obliged to show humbling gratitude to the staff who had nursed you through. He wished Joan had come with him and yet could understand her reluctance to do so. As he walked towards the hospital entrance he hoped Joan was all right at home on her own, and that she wouldn't drink too much. Now he thought about it, she had been hitting the bottle quite a bit lately. Oh well, this evening she'd probably drink herself into a lethargy, have an early night and bounce straight back by the morning. Joan was like that. She was tough. He suspected Violet on the other hand, was not.

He pushed open the double swing doors and entered the hospital. There was no heavy smell of Damask roses here; there was a clean and somehow intimidating smell of strong antiseptic. The walls gleamed with white tiles, the highly polished floor reflected starkness. Jesse heard the distant sound of a trolley being pushed; a trolley wheeling something as innocuous as teacups probably, but that was the thing with hospitals, you could never be quite sure what was being wheeled on a trolley. Then he heard the tip-tap of shoes over the glossy floor, and down the corridor walked a young nun dressed as white as the walls, apart from a dark crucifix that dangled against the starched crispness of her virginal breast. She eyed Jesse with surprise. "May I help you?"

"Yes, I'm looking for Mrs. Parker. She was admitted today with pneumonia but I've no idea which ward she's in I'm afraid."

"Mrs. Millicent Parker would that be?"

"Millie – yes."

"Are you a relative, sir?"

"Yes." Jesse lied. "I'm here to visit her if that's alright."

The nun laid her hand briefly on Jesse's arm. "You're too late I'm afraid. I've just come from her room. She passed away about fifteen minutes ago. Her daughter was with her and it was a peaceful end." The nun gave Jesse a gentle smile. "Would you like me to take you to her?"

"Violet – Miss Parker?"

"No, I meant her mother, Millicent." Jesse paled at the thought. "Oh no – thank you. I'd umm rather –"

"Remember her as she was," the nun finished for him. Jesse had the impression it was a cliché she'd heard many times. "I understand. I'll take you to the Day Room and let Miss Parker know you're here."

Jesse followed the nun rustling in her starched uniform, as she led the way down the corridor. She stopped at an open doorway and ushered him into a room with an unfinished jigsaw puzzle on the table and tidy piles of battered books on a shelf beneath the window. "If you'd like to wait in here. Miss Parker is in Sister's office. She shouldn't be long now."

"Thank you." Jesse looked out of the window. His car was solitary in the car park. Visiting time must have been long over. As he looked out onto the shiny green leaves of the bushes and the blood red Damask roses he thought of Millie and tried to comprehend that she was dead. Life over, final curtain, so that was it then. He sighed. Not much of a life really, poor old Millie.

"Jesse." Violet stood in the doorway holding a carrier bag of what Jesse supposed was Millie's personal belongings. Jesse gave Violet a sad, sympathetic smile. "Violet, I'm so sorry to hear about your mother." He went over to her and held her close. She nestled against his chest and gave a small sob. Jesse drew her even closer to him. This wasn't the time to be thinking about her plump body pressed up against him; it wasn't the time to enjoy the feel of her arms anchored tightly around his waist, yet he couldn't stop himself. She felt as wonderful as he had known she would. After a while Violet loosened her hold on him and Jesse said, "If you're finished here, shall we go?" Violet nodded. "I'd like to go back to mum's if that's alright."

In the car Violet said, "It was nice of you to come, Jesse. I didn't really feel up to walkin' anywhere."
"I'm not surprised," Jesse said. "You've had a traumatic day. I'm only sorry I didn't arrive earlier."
"Mum wouldn't have known whether you were there or not," Violet said in a flat voice. "I don't think she realised I was there. Still, at least she didn't drag on for days like poor ol' dad." She was silent for a while and then added, "Mum was never the same after dad went. I like to think they're together again now."
"I'm sure they are," Jesse murmured, although he doubted it very much. Violet smiled. "I'm glad you think so too." She said. When Jesse pulled up outside Millie's council house, he turned to Violet and said, "Would you like me to come in with you for a while? I don't think you should be on your own – unless of course you want to."
"No – I'd like you to stay for a bit. As a matter of fact I feel a bit trembly," Violet forced a smile. "Shock, I expect." She unlocked the front door and they walked into the dim, narrow hallway. Violet dropped the carrier bag she had been holding at the foot of the stairs and squeezed passed Jesse. "We'll go in the front room," she said.

After the lofty rooms of Marbal House, Jesse felt oppressed by the smallness of the room he'd followed Violet into. The three-piece suite was far too bulky for the limited space and everything seemed to have a protective covering, adding to the claustrophobic ambiance of the room. When had Millie planned on removing the obscuring layers to enjoy what was underneath? Jesse wondered as he looked around. There were antimacassars draped over the backs and arms of the chairs, a piece of oilcloth over the occasional table, a strip of felt across the top of a glass cabinet and off- cuts of swirly carpet placed like stepping stones over the patterned carpet beneath.

"It seems really strange, you being here." Violet said, rubbing at her arms. "Just give me a minute to stop shakin' and I'll make a pot of tea."

"I think you need something stronger than tea, "Jesse said. "A drop of brandy wouldn't do you any harm."

"There's a bottle of brandy in the cabinet. Mum never drank as you know, but she always got a few bottles of spirits in at Christmas just in case anyone called in who –" Violet suddenly began to cry. "I'm sorry Jesse, I'll be alright in a bit," she mumbled, dabbing at her eyes with a wet, crumpled handkerchief. Jesse was uncertain whether or not he should cuddle her again, but decided it was probably best if he didn't. "You cry as much as you need to. I'll pour you that brandy." He squashed himself sideways between the two armchairs in order to get to the cabinet behind them, and managed to open the doors just wide enough to look for the right bottle.

Violet pushed her handkerchief back up the sleeve of her blouse. "D'you mind if we just have a few candles instead of puttin' the light on?" She sniffed. ""It just seems the right thing to do, somehow."

"Light candles for Millie, you mean?" What a quaint idea, Jesse thought. On the other hand candlelight would be better than nothing, particularly as the room was getting dimmer by the minute and he was having difficulty in seeing the brandy as he poured it out. "Why not?" That's a sweet thought, Violet." Violet left the room and returned minutes later with a cardboard box of used candles and a few odd saucers. She knelt in front of the fireplace and arranged the saucers across the tiled hearth. When she had put the candles in place she fumbled with a box of matches as she tried to light them. "Here, let me do that." Jesse handed Violet her glass of brandy and crouched down beside her. The space was so confined that their thighs rubbed against each other as Jesse leaned forward and put a lit match to each of the candle stumps. Violet took a large gulp of brandy and gasped as

71

it seared down her throat. "Sip it," Jesse said, turning his head towards her. Her doe eyes were moist with tears and her wet eyelashes had formed shiny black spikes. Her skin looked almost translucent in the candle glow and so soft that Jesse couldn't resist stroking her cheek with the back of his hand. "Are you feeling any better?" Violet smiled at him and nodded slowly. "That's good." With effort Jesse forced himself to move away from her and sat down on the settee. "I shall have to get this place sorted out," Violet said. "The council will want it back."

"There's plenty of time before you need to worry about that." Jesse said. "You don't need to worry about anything yet. Perhaps this isn't the right time to mention it, but I'd like to take care of the funeral expenses. I'll do whatever I can to help. You know you only need to ask."

"It's good of you to offer Jesse." Violet stood up and came to sit next to him on the settee. "The funeral isn't a problem though 'cos for years mum's been payin' into the Co-op for it."

"Really?" Jesse frowned. "Is that what people do? Seems a bit morbid to me."

"We all have to die some time, Jesse." Violet looked at him wide - eyed with surprise that he shouldn't find the idea of spending your life planning for your funeral the most natural thing in the world. She sipped at the brandy. "I'm an orphan now. A homeless, twenty five year old orphan." Jesse twisted round towards her and patted her firm, plump arm. "You know you'll always have a home at Marbal House, Violet. Good gracious, we grew up together. You're like a sister to me – in some ways."

"It's nice of you to say that Jesse, but I've been thinking, it's probably time for me to move on. I don't have mum to consider now, so there's no reason for me to stay around here really."

Jesse looked at her, surprised. "You're thinking of going away?" Although before Millie had died it had been his intention that Violet should move out of Marbal House, he hadn't considered that she might want to leave the district altogether. "What will you do?"

"I've been thinkin' about trainin' as a nurse," she replied. "I reckon I'd be quite good at that."

"So you've thought of leaving for a while then?"

72

Violet nodded. She downed the last of her brandy. "I think I could do with another one. Have you got time to stay and have a drink with me, Jesse?"

"I can stay for as long as you need me here." Jesse rammed himself between the chairs again, and refilled Violet's glass before pouring out a drink for himself.

"Joan won't mind then?"

"No, of course not. She wanted me to look after you this evening." He handed Violet her glass and settled back onto the settee. "Seems strange me callin' your wife by her first name, but she's always insisted on it. I mean I wouldn't dream of callin' Mrs Marbal Clara", Violet said. "But then, Joan's not a bit stuck up, is she? Not that I meant Mrs. Marbal -"

Jesse smiled. "It's alright, I know what you mean. No, Joan isn't stuck up." She swears like a trouper, smokes like a train and shags like a ram when the mood takes her, he thought. Violet stared ahead at the candle flames and said softly, "You haven't been alone in the same room with me since you came back home, Jesse. I thought I must have done somethin' wrong."

"Don't be silly," Jesse was taken aback. He'd no idea that Violet had noticed he'd been avoiding her. As far as he was concerned she just went about her work in that quiet way of hers without thinking very much about anything. He suddenly felt very benevolent towards her and took her hand and placed her fingers to his lips and lightly kissed them. "How could you possibly do anything wrong?" Violet smiled then pulled her hand away. "I expect I stink of the hospital," she said, unwittingly breaking a tender moment. "Would you mind if I had a quick bath and got changed, Jesse? I don't feel very fresh, not with bein' at the hospital all day."

"Would you like me to leave now?" Jesse said, " because If you want to go to bed –"

"I want you to stay Jesse. I know you're married an' all. . . . but we probably won't ever get another chance. That's if you want to stay, of course." Jesse smiled, wondering what she had meant. Won't get another chance for what, he thought. Had it been said by anyone other than Violet, he would have suspected her of trying to seduce him - albeit clumsily. Surely Violet wasn't flirting with him? He would have to stick around to find out. "Go and take your bath," he said. "I'll wait here for you."

 When she had gone he took off his jacket and tie and slung them over the back of an armchair. He stretched out his legs and stared at the row of candles lined up like soldiers across the hearth. Maybe the candles weren't really for Millie. Maybe it was Violet's idea of a romantic touch. The thought was so absurd that Jesse nearly laughed aloud. He could hear Violet running water into the bath upstairs and decided he could do with a drop more brandy.

Bored from sitting in the semi-darkness with nothing to do other than contemplate and sip at his drink, Jesse switched on the electric light and studied the photographs set out on the mantelshelf. In the middle, in a silver plated frame, was a picture of Millie and Jake on their wedding day. Millie wore a plain white, calf length dress and satin shoes with almond shaped toes and buttoned straps across the ankles. Her lace veil pinned flat against her hair, looked like a large, limp tray cloth. Millie and Jakes faces were in profile, with Millie's bad eye away from the camera. She peered up at Jake with a squintless but surprised look, while Jake gazed down at her looking equally astonished. They both seemed, Jesse thought, surprised to be at their own wedding. Next to it was a sepia photograph of Violet as a chubby toddler with dark curls and a dreamy smile, and next to that was a photograph of him-self. Jesse picked it up. It was taken in the back garden of Marbal House. He was kneeling up on a chair at a table helping Ruby shell peas. Dear Ruby. He missed her still. Jesse picked up the photograph and looked at Ruby's alert rather handsome face with deep affection. He had no recollection of the photo being taken. He guessed he was about four years old at the time. Jesse studied the child in the photograph with detachment. He looked like a boy from a picture book with his cliché fair curls long lashes and comically intent expression. Maybe if he'd had a son, he would have looked cute like that. He'd never know. The sound of gushing water brought Jesse out of his reverie. Violet had finished her bath. Jesse replaced a couple of gutted candles with fresh stumps from the cardboard box, lit them, and switched off the light. He settled back on the settee and waited for Violet. When she walked into the room she was wearing a dressing gown tightly tied at the waist accentuating her unfettered breasts. Jesse tried not to notice how they swayed as she stood in front of the fireplace rubbing at her hair with a towel. "I haven't been too long, have I?" she asked.

"No time at all." Jesse could see that she was wearing some sort of cotton nightdress under the dressing gown and that was probably all she was wearing. Jesse's throat felt dry. She sat in front of the empty grate, still drying her hair and looked at him. "You never knew, but I went out with a chap durin' the war. Tom his name was. He was stationed at St. Eval and I met him one night when I'd gone over to Newquay with a friend. Poor Tom never made it, though. He went off on a bombin' raid one night and never came back." Jesse leaned forward, his hands clasped between his knees. "Were you fond of him?"

"In a way, I was. I'm fond of *you* Jesse, I always have been. I only stayed on at Marbal House 'cos I hoped you'd come back."

"Violet you're very sweet. I'm fond of you too." So she definitely was making a play for him. Jesse knew that the sensible thing to do would be to leave, go home to his wife, and although he didn't want to be sensible, he might have left if Violet hadn't said, "I expect you think I'm a virgin, but actually I'm not." Jesse was taken aback, not so much by the revelation as the revealing of it. "You're surprised about that, aren't you?" Violet said, laying the towel at her feet. "Yes, I am a bit," Jesse said. "Who was it – the R.A.F. chap?" Violet nodded. "I'm glad I did it. I would've regretted not doin' it, especially as Tom got killed. My dad always used to say regret was the saddest word in the English language."

I bet the poor bugger would have regretted saying that if he'd known his daughter was going to get laid on the strength of it, Jesse thought wryly. He cleared his throat. "Violet," he said gently, "why are you telling me all this?"

"Well," she looked away from him, toying with the belt of her dressing gown, "Don't think bad of me Jesse, but I want you to –

you know – do it with me. We'll probably never have another chance like this, and I only want to do it the once with you Jesse, just so I'll have somethin' special to remember. Then I can go away with no regrets and start off a new life without wonderin' what it would have been like if we had....done it." Jesse felt his heart pound faster. *Christ* his sweet shrinking Violet was offering it to him on a bloody plate. "Violet, I'm not sure this is such a good idea," he heard himself say.

"You don't fancy me?"

"Yes, - yes I do."

"Is it Joan then – you don't want to be unfaithful to Joan?"

"No – well yes, but it's you too Violet. You're not thinking straight. You're distraught and you've had a bit to drink. I couldn't take advantage of the situation, it wouldn't be fair."

"You wouldn't be takin' advantage of me Jesse. Nobody need ever know, but if you don't want to.. ." she sighed. "Well I feel really awful now. Really cheap."

"Hey, come on," Jesse said. "I never said I didn't want to make love to you." He leaned towards her and suddenly found that he had no trouble in ignoring his alter ago. He pulled open Violet's dressing gown and knew there would be no going back. The nightdress underneath was sprigged with tiny flowers, the neckline was low and lace trimmed. Jesse saw the fine trail of talcum powder she had poured between her breasts. He smelt the sweetness of it, felt its silky dryness on his fingertips as he slowly followed its tantalising path. He wouldn't be like Millie. He would remove the protective layers and enjoy what lay beneath.

In the early hours of the morning Jesse parked his car behind Clara's black Austin and walked up the darkened path into Marbal House. He quietly unlocked the front door and took his shoes off in the hall. Moonlight shone through the blue and red window giving sufficient light for him to make his way to the bedroom. He pushed the door open a fraction and heard Joan's light, snuffling snore. Best not to wake her. Best that he slept in one of the guest rooms.

When he was in bed he lay with his arms behind his head. Women – he was no judge of women that was for sure. Shrinking Violet – Christ. It was just as well she was leaving or he might be tempted again. Voluptuous was the word for Violet. She hadn't done a lot, just lay back and revelled and wriggled in pleasure. That had been fine by him. To think he'd felt guilty just thinking about having sex with Violet. Now he'd done it and he didn't feel in the least bit guilty. He felt bloody good, as a matter of fact. They had been disrespectful though, he couldn't get away from that. Jesse looked up towards the ceiling. I'm sorry Millie. I had no intention of making love to your daughter, particularly tonight of all nights, but I think it took her mind off grieving for you for a while, so I hope you'll forgive me. He drifted off to sleep savouring the taste of Violet's talcum powder on his tongue. Violet too slept well.

Neither of them could have known that as they slept, Jesse's sperm was swimming to imbed itself in Violet's newly ovulated egg and that in forty weeks Violet would give birth to Agnes' mother.

Chapter 5

Joan came down the stairs with a bundle of washing in her arms. She propped it under her chin in order to free a hand to scoop up the mail from the hall mat, then continued on her way to the kitchen. "More Christmas cards," she said to Violet and after dumping the washing in the sink, sat down at the kitchen table to open the post. "Mrs. Marbal," she said, looking at the first envelope. "For me or Clara, I wonder? I may as well open it seeing as Clara's jaunting around London - again." She ripped open the envelope and drew out a tondo shaped card of the Virgin Mary who looked no more than twelve years old. Her new-born baby sat upright on her lap with remarkable balance. He looked endearing enough, in spite of the anomaly of his back muscles. Christmas is for children, Joan thought sadly – for some maybe but not, apparently for me. She turned the card over to find out the name of the painter. "Well, obviously Fra Angelico," she said to Violet, "was under the illusion that Mary had only just entered puberty when she gave birth to Jesus." Joan opened the card. "Oh, I might've guessed. It's from the Stanfords. Jesse took me to their art studio in St. Ives last summer."

"Mrs. Marbal is plannin' a trip to Italy with them," Violet said without looking up from the Christmas cake she was icing. Joan took another glance at the baby with his yellow lamb's wool curls and chubby limbs and sighed because she didn't have a baby to sit on her lap and cuddle. She put the card to one side and opened the next envelope. "Very festive," she said. "Snow, a nice fat robin and a bit of holly, I like traditional cards." She held up the card for Violet to see but Violet kept her head bent and silently carried on smoothing white icing over the marzipan. She was never very talkative, but today she was definitely more reserved than usual and Joan wondered whether it was because this would be Violet's first Christmas without Millie. Christmas could be a poignant time and even though Millie had been a dry, humourless old stick, she was Violet's mother after all and they had seemed quite close. It had only been three months since Millie had gone. Out of consideration for Violet, Joan decided to open the rest of the cards later and pushed them aside. "Fancy a cup of tea?"

"Tea?" Violet blanched at the thought of it. "No thank you, not for me."

"How about a coffee then, with a drop of whisky to keep out the cold?" Joan offered cheerfully, rubbing her hands together. Whisky at this hour of the morning. Violet didn't dare open her mouth to answer in case she threw up. She shook her head once, slowly, and went over to the sink to pour a glass of water. After a few sips the nausea began to subside.

"I told Jess we should have taken up the flagstones before we had the lino laid," Joan was saying as she poured herself a cup of coffee. "The cold comes right up through this floor. I'm trying to persuade him to have an Aga put in; that would make it really warm in here, not that I'd know how to cook on an Aga. I'd have to learn though, wouldn't I? Because when you go off to start your nurse training in January –"

"It's a pity Mrs. Marbal had the old range taken out," Violet said quickly. She wouldn't be going off nursing in January. Not now. She didn't know what she was going to do. Just thinking about it made her prickle with panic. "That old range cooked a treat and it was good for dryin' off the clothes."

Joan groaned. "The sodding washing. That's something else I'll have to do when you go. To be honest, I'm not as domesticated as I thought I was." She unscrewed the cap from a bottle of Teacher's and poured a liberal amount of whisky into her cup. "What was the date again?"

"What date?"

"The date you start training."

Violet's heart sank. She bit her top lip. Oh God, if only she could turn the clock back. She'd felt so proud of herself when she'd been accepted at Exeter General. Now she wouldn't be going. Now she didn't know what she was going to do. She was in such a mess. She went back to the table and dipped the palette knife she'd been using into a jug of water.

"Isn't that water supposed to be hot?" Joan said. "It looks bleedin' stone cold to me. Here, hand it over, I'll fill it up from the kettle. Is it the first or second week of January? For some reason the tenth rings a bell. I must say I envy you in a way – going off and doing something worthwhile with your life. Not that I could be a nurse, I couldn't cope with that, but to be honest I had a really great time when I was in the WRAF. Working and living together with other girls forges a special camaraderie. You make friends you never forget. Course some of them were a pain in the arse but…"

I wish she'd shut up, Violet thought. Shut up Joan, shut up. Violet sat down and stared at the Christmas cake in front of her while a voice inside her head kept repeating I can't go away and I don't know what I'm going to do.

"I was in admin which might sound boring, but believe me we had such laughs. I shouldn't say it really, but even though there was a war on, I had the time of my life. I bet you will too, when you get to Exeter and start making new friends to go out with." Joan placed the refilled jug on the table and sat down opposite Violet. She lit a cigarette and then took a sip of her laced coffee. "Ah, that's better. I feel warmer already." She squinted at Violet through a haze of cigarette smoke. Violet was rubbing at her arms, her eyes still focused on the cold, white blandness of the iced cake.

"Well come on then. Don't tell me you've forgotten when it is you're going."

"I'm not going and I don't know what to do," Violet said in a small voice.

"Sorry?" Joan cocked her head to one side. "Did you say you *weren't* going?"

Yes she had said it, she actually had. The burden was too great to keep to herself any longer. Violet looked at Joan and nodded. "I'm not going."

"Don't be daft Violet, you must go. You probably feel a bit nervous about it now but once-"

"I can't go."

"Can't?" Joan drank her coffee and drew on her cigarette. The combined smell made Violet feel queasy again. " Why- ever not?"

80

"Because I'm – I'm pregnant." There, now she'd done it, she'd said it, although she immediately wished she hadn't because Joan was looking at her in a strange and terrible way. And she didn't know the half of it – not yet, she didn't. Joan suddenly gave a crooked smile. "Do you know Violet, I thought for a minute you said you were pregnant."

Violet swallowed hard. "I did." Malevolence was in Joan's eyes again. There was a heart stopping silence before she said, "But how the hell can you be pregnant?" The words were said in a tone so harsh, so cold that Violet felt weak.

"How the hell can you be pregnant when the only night in the week you leave the house is a Friday to go to the cinema and even then you come straight back. Same old routine. You come in, make yourself a bloody cocoa and then go straight up to bed with such regularity that frankly there's been times when I've wished you *had* stayed out You haven't even got a bloody boyfriend – unless of course you've been lying to me and you haven't been going to the cinema. Is that it? Have you been sneaking off every Friday with some bloke and not telling me?" Joan knew she was being unreasonable; she knew she shouldn't be shouting at Violet who was after all, old enough to lead her own life. Nevertheless, she had to shout because she was angry. She was angry that Violet was pregnant and she wasn't.

Violet shook her head. "I haven't. I haven't been lying".

Joan ground her cigarette hard against the bottom of the ashtray. Shards of tobacco splayed against grey ash. "So, you don't have a boyfriend?"

"No," Violet said in almost a whisper.

"Who do you think you are then, the Virgin Mary?" Joan picked up the Angelico Christmas card and threw it across the table at her. "You're either a liar Violet or you're bleedin' mad."

"I'm not, honest I'm not."

Joan glared at Violet sitting there rubbing at her arms, trembling. And then another thought occurred to her. "It wasn't rape, was it?" Her tone was milder. God, what if Violet had been raped on the way back from the cinema and had

81

been too scared to tell anyone? But Violet was shaking her head again. Joan sighed, exasperated. "What the hell are you playing at Violet? How can you be pregnant if you haven't been with a man? I suppose you do *know* that you need a man to get pregnant?" Joan's sarcasm made Violet flinch. She knew she'd set herself on a course that would take her straight into the flames of hell, but it was too late to stop. She was going headlong into fire with quickening speed. "It was a man," she answered quietly.

"Really? Who the hell was it then?"

Violet cleared her throat noisily and looked down at the table. Beads of hard white icing dotted the bleached wood. She wanted to pick them off one by one but couldn't move her hands down to the table; it seemed too far, too big a task. She began to rub her arms again. The fires of hell were licking so close she felt almost suffocated but it was too late to go back. She took a deep breath. "Jesse," she said. "It was Jesse."

For what was probably only seconds but to Violet seemed an age, Joan said nothing. Her mouth had dropped open and her eyes stared ahead glazed and unblinking. Violet had seen fish look like that. Dead fish, mackerel that her dad had sometimes brought home for her to cook. Only she knew Joan wouldn't stay like a dead fish for long. In fact she was already reviving. "Are you telling me that you've been to bed with my husband, in my house?" Joan's voice was dangerously steady and ice cold.

Violet's mouth felt dry and tasted of metal. Fear, she decided, tasted like sucking on a fork. "I'm really sorry Joan. We only did it the once and Jesse doesn't know I'm pregnant. It didn't happen here though", she added quickly. "It was at mum's house."

"When? When did you do it?" The words were spat out now, and the pitch higher.

"The – the night mum died."

"Oh God, how could you?" Joan put her hand to her mouth, horrified at the blatant lack of respect signified by the timing. She remembered that night only too well. She'd told Jess she couldn't have children, sent him off to comfort the bereaved Violet. Well he'd done that all right. How *could* Jess have done that to her – thrown himself into the arms and legs of fat, stupid Violet? He knew how upset she'd been that night, the hard-hearted, selfish bastard. "You're both bloody animals," Joan yelled at Violet. "Having sex with poor Millie hardly cold and me grieving because I can't have children. I bet you had a good laugh about that, didn't you? You slut!"

Violet summons the strength to stand. "No of course not. I didn't know nothin' about that. I – I never wanted this to happen, honest. But I had to tell you, didn't I? Because I don't know what to do about it. I just wanted to go away an' start a new life. I was really lookin' forward to it but now –"

"Don't stand there snivelling, telling me you don't know what to do!" Joan yelled. "You knew what to do with my husband didn't you? You ungrateful, conniving bitch!" The ashtray was the first thing she hurled. It hit the opposite wall with a crackling thud. Violet gasped and flinched as glass shattered. "Stop it Joan, you're frightening me," she wailed. The cup of coffee followed the path of the ashtray then the jug of hot water. Violet backed towards the steps that led out of the kitchen. "I'll leave," she said shakily. "I'll leave and get rid of the baby – and well you'll never hear from me again. I'm sorry, I'm really sorry for what I've done."

"Damn right you'll leave!" Joan got up from her chair and kicked it out of the way. She picked up the Christmas cake and using both hands hurled it at Violet as she fled from the kitchen. The cake hit Violet in the small of her back, sending her sprawling onto the steps; gasping and sobbing she stumbled into the hall, white icing dripping from her skirt.

Jesse was photographing a wedding. It was beyond him why anyone would want to get married two weeks before Christmas, when apart from any other considerations the weather was certainly going to be cold, if not wet. Today it was both. The bride and groom stood in the church porch smiling stoically through chattering teeth. "Just one more,"

83

Jesse said, "then we can get off to the reception." Some of the guests had already set out for the Volesworth Arms; only a handful who had thought to bring umbrellas remained. The bride's mother was one. "That would be the thing to do," she said to Jesse, "seeing as most of his lot have scarpered anyway. She nodded towards the groom with a disdainful look on her face. "Hurry up and take it then love. Even me fox is shakin' with the cold." Jesse glanced at the dead animal wrapped around her neck. Glass eyes looked balefully out of glistening wet fur.

Once he'd taken photographs of the cake being cut, Jesse was free to leave. He was anxious to get home because he had at last come to a decision and couldn't wait to tell Joan. One of the wedding guests, who had been loquacious even before she'd started on the sherry, had commandeered Jesse to arrange a studio sitting for her little boy.

"I 'spect 'twill cost me an arm and a leg and me ol' man will probably go up the wall, but I don't care. Once they're grown up you forget what they looked like dun 'e? So I'd like a real nice photo of my William while 'es still young an' gorgeous looking". As she had ushered the child into the foreground of most of the wedding photographs, she would have plenty of reminders of William in years to come, but Jesse wasn't going to bring that to the woman's attention and lose out on a commission. "You're obviously very proud of William," he said as the mother hauled him out from under a table where he'd chased a squealing little bridesmaid. "Proud?" She planted a kiss on the child's cheek before setting him down to run off again. "Best day of my life when we 'ad 'im. He can be a little Turk sometimes, but then he's a boy in' 'e?"

Jesse smiled. "He's certainly that alright."

"Have you got any kiddies then?"

"No, no yet."

"Well you don't want to leave it too long. We kept puttin' it off, then it turned out we couldn't have none."

"Oh – so William isn't yours then?"

84

"Oh yes 'e is." The mother said defiantly. "Mine by adoption. We got 'im from that there new orphanage run by they Catholic nuns. There's loads of little kiddies up there all wantin' good homes. I'm thinkin' of getting another one in a year or two, when William's properly settled in." She made it all sound, Jesse thought, like choosing a puppy from a pet shop window. He grinned at the child's antics as it laughed and rolled around on the floor. Annoying little sod really, still there was something pleasing about seeing a child so obviously loved and happy. Living with an adoring family had to be preferable to being in an orphanage no matter how well the nuns had looked after him.. There was nothing to compensate for the love and security of doting parents Jesse thought – not that he'd had much in the way of parental love himself. Maybe William's new mother was over doing the doting, and a bit of discipline wouldn't be amiss, but even so she'd brought happiness into a kid's life, which was more than he'd been prepared to do. Selfish really – he had a nice home, a big house with room for children. He liked kids and the woman was right. He shouldn't leave it too late. There'd be no harm in going to the orphanage and having a look around. Joan would be thrilled to know he was warming to the idea of adoption. She would no doubt think it was a better Christmas present than the red leather shoulder bag he'd bought her and secreted at his studio.

For a while after hearing Violet leave by the front door, Joan sat motionless at the kitchen table. Her anger was beginning to subside and be replaced by hurt and confusion. Why had Jess betrayed her? What had she done, or not done to deserve this? It was hard to believe Jess could be unfaithful to her. Men had affairs, of course they did, but other men. Not her Jess. Yet he had, he'd destroyed everything. And Violet – God, mousy Violet. How the hell had she managed to tempt him? Joan didn't want to think about it. They'd done it now and were welcome to each other. She stood up and slowly, mechanically, began to clear away the broken pieces of china and glass. She wiped down the walls and moped up coffee and sodden clumps of cigarettes and ash from the floor, then she looked at the Christmas cake lying in unpalatable lumps on the kitchen steps. Her dad had a destructive temper, and it dismayed her to think she'd inherited it. Provoked though she was, she shouldn't have thrown the cake at Violet. Joan derived some consolation from the fact that it wasn't as heavy as it might have been because they couldn't get the fruit, even so, she shouldn't have done it. Joan swept up the cake and threw it in the dustbin. She wondered where Jess had put the suitcases. Not that she intended leaving without seeing him. Oh no, he wouldn't get off that lightly, but she wanted to be packed and ready to leave just as soon as she'd finished with him -in more ways than one. Feeling empty and exhausted, Joan made her way upstairs.

There was a chill in the bedroom causing Joan to regret not for the first time, at having had the fireplace taken out. Not that it mattered now, because she would be leaving and Jess could have his cold and empty bedroom to himself. She looked for the suitcases. They weren't on top of the wardrobe where she'd hoped to find them – but of course they wouldn't be. Jess liked order. Perhaps he'd put them in one of the spare bedrooms, somewhere out of sight. Joan took a cursory look but the bedrooms were too cold to hang around in for long. She clicked her tongue in annoyance and went back to her own room.   How the hell could she pack without a suitcase? She sat on the double bed, and then slid under the eiderdown to keep warm. Only hours earlier she had been snuggled up in here with Jess, happily oblivious of his affair.

Her comfortable life was suddenly shattered, and all because Jess had been weak and stupid enough to have sex with Violet. And if Violet hadn't become pregnant, Joan would never have known. Perhaps ignorance would have been better than knowing and having to go through this anguish. Joan curled up into a ball and tried to plan a course of action, but couldn't. The more she thought about it, leaving aside the satisfaction of a dramatic exit, the more she realised that she didn't want to leave Marbal House.

86

Why should she go? She'd done nothing wrong and besides she had no family apart from her sister in America, and very little money of her own. There was nowhere *to* go. She'd never again get what she already had, a big house and a certain amount of status that went with the name of Marbal. She closed her eyes and wondered how it was possible that she could hate Jess as much as she did, and yet still feel that life without him would be meaningless.

Joan was roused by the sound of Jesse calling her from the hall. "I'm up here!" she yelled back. Her legs felt stiff from the cramped foetal position she'd fallen asleep in. She eased herself off the bed and had just stood up when Jesse entered the room. He looked so handsome standing there, face glowing from being out in the cold weather, eyes sparkling as he smiled at her. Joan imagined him giving Violet that smile. She took a step forward, brought back her hand and slapped it hard across his cheek. "That," she said, "is for shagging Violet, and this," she brought her hand back and hit him again, "is for getting her pregnant!" Jesse stood unflinching, speechless.

Joan shouted and raged at him but he wasn't listening to a word of it. She had said Violet was pregnant. The news shocked him more than the realisation that he'd been caught out and Joan knew about his infidelity, although that was shocking enough but God, who would have thought it possible; he'd had sex only once with Violet and now he was going be a father after all. In spite of the circumstances, he had a feeling of wonder, and yes, he admitted to himself, pride. He allowed Joan to strike him again, and then as she raised her hand a fourth time, he grabbed her wrist. "Alright, that's enough now. Calm down."
"*Calm down*? Violet tells me you've slept with her, made *her* pregnant when I can't have a baby, and all you can say is calm down? Ironic really – I can't have one and she's got one and doesn't want it. That's two women's lives you've fucked up – so you could at least tell me you're sorry, you bastard!"
" Yes - yes I could tell you I was sorry but then I would be lying."

Joan recoiled from him. If Jess had rolled his hand into a fist and hit her, she wouldn't have felt as stunned as she did now. "Well that's it then. Now I know." Her voice was suddenly empty of fight. "Well I'm not leaving Jess and I won't make it easy and divorce you either."

"Divorce? I don't *want* a divorce Joan." Jesse said. "I'm sorry I've hurt you and you're quite justified in being angry with me. I know I deserve it. But it was a moment's weakness with Violet, that's all. It happened once and neither of us had any intention of it happening again. I know that doesn't make it right, I know I shouldn't have done it, but – she's pregnant Joan. She's expecting *my* baby."

Joan paled. "I'm only too well aware of that. So what are you expecting me to say – congratulations? Congratulations Jess, you can be a parent but I can't. Why don't you rub it in a bit more, you cold hearted ..." Joan's voice began to crack but she wasn't going to give him the satisfaction of making her cry. Her dad had never seen her cry, neither would Jess.

"*We* can be the child's parents." Jesse said. He hated seeing Joan so upset, knowing that he was the cause of her distress and deeply regretted that she'd found out about him and Violet in such a hurtful way. All the same, her stubbornness to accept that the outcome could mean happiness for them both was beginning to irritate him. It wasn't as if Joan was a particularly moral person, in fact she wasn't at all moral really. He'd watched her flirt with men at parties and he knew she'd had an affair with a married chap before they were wed. True, she had always been a faithful wife, but his one night of lust with Violet could hardly be termed an affair. "Joan, I understand how you must feel," he began, but she cut him short with a derisive, brittle laugh. "Bollocks. You haven't got a clue how I feel. How could you betray me like that? I trusted you Jess. I thought you were different from other men. But you're not"

He tried again. "Look, naturally you're angry with me and hurt, I know that – but you haven't allowed yourself to think this through."

"Think it through? I've thought about nothing else." Her eyes narrowed and her mouth hardened, tight lipped with anger. He was getting nowhere. He raked his fingers through his hair despondently and walked towards the door. "Is Violet in her room? Perhaps the three of us ought to go downstairs and talk this over together."

"No she's not in." Joan said tersely. And what had he meant when he'd said *they* could be the parents? If he thought for one minute she was going to mother Violet's child, he wasn't only insensitive, he was mad. She gave an involuntary shudder and wrapped her arms tightly around herself. "I'm going down stairs anyway," she said, "not because of anything you have to say, but because I'm too bloody cold to stay up here."

Maybe it's just as well Violet isn't in, Jesse thought. Best sort out a few things with Joan first. He waited for Joan to swish passed him and then he sneaked a quick look in the dressing table mirror at the bruised cheek she had given him. He touched it tentatively and winced, then followed her down stairs.

Jesse lit a fire in the living room. The fire was usually roaring away by the time he came home from work, but there was nothing normal about this day. As he placed sticks on top of rolled up pieces of newspaper, he wondered why Violet hadn't had the sense to tell him she was pregnant instead of going to Joan. It was true they'd done their best to keep out of each other's way since the night at Millie's house, but she could have come to the studio. Violet should have allowed him to tell Joan. Somehow he would have found a way to break it to her gently. He regretted that his night of passion locked in Violet's thighs was causing misery to both her and Joan, but he didn't regret it enough to wish he hadn't done it. He touched the newspaper with a lighted match. Flames devoured the printed-paper and headed towards the sticks. The three of them were in a mess, but it didn't need to stay that way. He shovelled coal on top of the flames, squashing them for the moment, but soon they would rise stronger than ever.

"If you want a sandwich, make your own." Joan pulled a fireside chair as close to the grate as she could, and sat hunched forward, trying to feel the heat.

"I'm alright. I had something at the reception." Jesse perched on the chair opposite her. "We ought to discuss this together before Violet gets back." Joan said nothing. As far as she was concerned Violet wasn't coming back. She reached out for her packet of cigarettes on the mantelpiece, drew one out and lit it. "Discuss what, exactly?"

Jesse looked at her through a curl of exhaled smoke, aware that she was deliberately looking away from him. "Bringing up the baby as our own. You said Violet didn't want it, well it's my child too, and I certainly want it. Come on Joan, what do you say?" He tried to keep the excitement from his voice but couldn't manage it. He knew she wouldn't want him to be happy, she would expect him to be penitent, probably for some time to come.

"What makes you think that I'd want to look at a child who was a constant reminder of your unfaithfulness to me?" Joan still couldn't bring herself to face him. She gazed absently at the fire, at the flames licking and spitting around lumps of coal. Jesse's frustration at her attitude heightened. All right, he was being selfish and unreasonable to expect her to feel the excitement he felt about the baby, but she was the one who had been so keen to adopt.

"There is nothing either good or bad but thinking makes it so," he said aloud. Joan wasn't impressed. "Whoever said that was talking bloody tripe." she snapped.

"How about this then," Jesse said, "Heav'n has no rage like love to hatred turn'd, nor hell a fury like a woman scorn'd." He hoped she would at least show a glimmer of a smile, but no, she just bit pensively on her bottom lip and then said, "I'm glad you realise that."

Jesse's frustration bubbled into annoyance. "Now look here Joan - I fully appreciate why you're mad at me, but the fact is, you've pestered me to adopt a baby ever since you found out you couldn't have one, and now we can have a child who is at least partly ours you're putting up barriers. If you were prepared to take on a baby not knowing a thing about its background, you could at least consider bringing up mine."

"Yours and Violet's. You haven't given a thought to the gossip and scandal there'd be, have you?" Joan gave a forced and bitter laugh. "Respectable Jesse Marbal, having it off with his servant, getting her in the family way. You never know what goes on behind closed doors do you?" she mimicked. "It's the wife I feel sorry for, although some say they indulged in a bit of ménage a trios." She shook her head. "Oh no, I don't think so, Jess. And I'm sure Clara wouldn't either. The shame of it would kill her."

Jesse had already thought of the scandal Violet's pregnancy would bring to them all. "No-one needs to know it's Violet's baby. We could pretend it was yours," he said.

Now Joan did face him. "Mine? Don't talk such drivel. God, do you really think I'd spend the next six months pretending I was pregnant – with a cushion stuffed up my skirt? Just to save you from humiliation? Think again."

"Not for me, for us and the baby – and Violet. She could get on with her nursing career and we'd be a proper family at last."

"We're not even a proper couple anymore." Joan turned her face away from him again. "You've destroyed my trust in you. You've ruined our marriage."

"Oh for God's sake Joan!" Jesse's temper was beginning to get the better of him. The best form of defence, he decided, was attack. "Will you stop feeling so bloody sorry for yourself? I love you, always have and always will – you know that. I'll tell you again, I'm sorry. I'm sorry I've hurt you but I'm human and on one occasion gave way to temptation. Alright, I was weak and stupid, but you could come out of this situation with the one thing you want, if only you'd bury your pride. So if you must feel sorry for someone, feel sorry for Violet. She's the one who's going to suffer most, not you. And I'll tell you something else. I'll never agree to adopting a stranger's child, so make your mind up." Thank God, he thought, that he hadn't had chance to tell her about his proposed visit to the orphanage. "It's either this baby, or no baby – ever." Joan flinched. It wasn't often Jesse shouted at her and she didn't think it was fair that she should be shouted at now when after all, she was the injured party. She was afraid that he meant what he said though; he would never adopt if she didn't agree to

91

take on his child. She also knew deep down, that part of her would rather bring up Jesse' baby than a stranger's. She sighed at the mess of it all. "Violet would never agree to it, anyway."

"She hasn't got a choice." Jesse had definitely detected a softening in Joan's tone and said a silent prayer of gratitude. He was getting through to her. "I'd never agree to Violet having an abortion, and she couldn't have one without my consent. But we need to talk to her, get all of this sorted out. When are you expecting her back?"

"I'm not."

"What do you mean, you're not?"

Joan shrugged. "When she left, she said she was going to have an abortion and that I'd never see her again. So frankly I don't know where she is."

Jesse began to feel anxious. "My God, you don't think she's already done it do you? Do you suppose she's booked into a clinic, or found a dodgy back street abortionist?"

"For goodness sake stop being so dramatic. There are no dodgy abortionists around here and no professional would do it either, not unless there were medical grounds - and even then it's doubtful. Besides where would she have got the money? Stop worrying." Joan however, was beginning to feel a little worried herself. She really shouldn't have hit Violet with the cake. "How long has she been gone?" Jesse was asking.

"Several hours." Joan said. "I suppose it was around ten o'clock when she left."

"And you don't know where she went? She's pregnant, and upset no doubt, and you just let her go off in this weather to walk the streets – or chuck herself in the river. Even given the circumstances I'm amazed you could be so hard."

"It's not my fault she's pregnant," Joan didn't protest too much; snippets of the morning's violent events floated back to her, making her uneasy.

"We'll just have to take the car and find her, although where the hell we start looking when she's been gone for at least four hours, I don't know." Jesse was already on his feet, pushing his fingers through his hair, the way he did when he was anxious.

"Go on your own. If she sees me she might get nervous, and run off again." Joan hoped Violet hadn't started to miscarry. She had fallen quite heavily on the kitchen steps and could well be at the hospital this very minute. Jess would never forgive her if Violet lost the baby.

"Why should she get nervous?" Jesse eyed Joan with suspicion. "What actually happened here this morning?"

His voice was very cold. Joan fleetingly wondered how it had come about that he now had the upper hand, and she was the one feeling guilty. "I was angry with her." Joan said defensibly. "Given the circumstances, what woman wouldn't have been?

And I wasn't sorry when she said she was going; I was glad to see the back of her. But I suppose when you find her, you'd better tell her I said it's all right. She can come back – for a while."

"*If* I find her." Jesse gave Joan a worried look then went out into the hall picked up his car keys from the hall table and unhitched his coat from the stand.

Violet had managed to grab her coat and handbag from the cupboard under the stairs before leaving Marbal House by the front door that morning. Ordinarily, she used the kitchen door, but to go back into the kitchen now would have been nothing short of suicide. She buttoned up her coat as she hurried down the path and out onto the pavement. There was a slight ache in her back where the cake had hit her, and her knees were sore from falling on the stairs, but her injuries didn't concern her half as much as the hole she saw in the knee of one of her black stockings. She gazed in horror at the florin sized white flesh on show, knowing that as she walked the hole would get bigger. She tried to walk stiffly on that leg, with minimum bend to the knee; even so, she could feel the nylon fibres insidiously splitting apart. She pulled her coat over her knee, but it was impossible she found, to hang onto the hem of her coat and walk stiff legged. The wind however was in her face, and did a pretty good job on its own in flattening her coat across her legs. The fact that cold drizzle was also blowing into her face didn't bother her. It felt refreshing; it cooled her cheeks and cleared her head. She had known Joan would take her affair with Jesse badly, but she hadn't expected her to get violent. She didn't quite know what she had expected really, and now she was out of the house, she didn't know where she was going either. She gave a huge sniff and patted a few tears and raindrops from her face, then mechanically started off down the hill towards the town.

Outside the Plaza Cinema Violet stopped to look at the stills displayed behind glass. Brighton Rock would be on next week. It looked quite scary. In one of the stills Richard Attenborough had a desperate look on his face, a trilby perched on the back of his head and a gun in his hand. The woman in the picture was chewing her fingers in terror, her eyes wide and her brow furrowed. How did she do that? Violet, forgetting her troubles for a moment, gave a furtive look around her, and then opened her eyes as wide as she could and tried to frown. She could see her reflection in the glass. Her eyes were crossing. Violet gave up. She wished the cinema was open, even though Camille, the film she'd seen the night before, was still running. She wished she looked like Greta Garbo, she wished she could meet someone like Robert Taylor and most of all she wished she could pay over her 10d, sit down on one of those faded red plush seats and lose herself in the dark, musty, dusty cinema. She loved that moment when the house lights went down, and the spotlight shone a huge circle of red on the curtains as they swished and swayed to the sides of the screen. You could forget everything for a couple of hours, and even when you came out of the cinema, for a while you somehow believed you were part of the film and walked like a film star and pretended you looked like one. It only ever lasted until halfway up the hill though, by which time the illusion had faded and everything became boringly familiar again and Greta Garbo had turned back into Violet Parker. She walked away from the Plaza and decided she would have to talk to Jesse about her plight. He would probably hate her as much as Joan did, when he found out that Joan knew about their night together, and the rest of it. Still it was Jesse's fault as much as her own that she was pregnant. She'd promised Joan she would have an abortion, but

94

how would she go about it? Violet had heard that drinking gin in a hot bath sometimes did the trick but as she no longer had access to either gin or a bath, Jesse would have to sort something out.

The door to Jesse's shop was locked. As Violet's hand fell away from the handle she remembered he was photographing a wedding that morning so goodness knows when he would be back. Tears of frustration and self-pity pricked her eyes. By now the wind and drizzle were making her feel cold and damp. Her mother's house had quickly been taken back by the council, so she had nowhere to go, and no one to turn to. Joan had been the only woman she could talk to, not as a friend exactly, but she'd always treated her fairly and they'd had a few pally moments together as they went about the household chores. She couldn't blame Joan for throwing her out and although she'd told Joan in the heat of the moment that she'd never see her again, Violet realised that just wasn't practical. She needed to go back to Marbal House to collect her possessions – but where to take them? Violet ambled aimlessly on down the street. She couldn't go back to Marbal House until Jesse was there; hopefully wouldn't throw her out until she had somewhere to go.

The shop windows were decorated gaily for Christmas, making Violet even gloomier. There was bustle and excitement in the air and one or two people that she'd known since childhood hurried pass with a quick "Alright then, Violet?" No she was far from all right. She wanted to go somewhere warm and have a hot drink. Then she thought of the railway station. There'd be a fire lit in the waiting room, and as it was Saturday the cafe might be open and she could get a mug of hot chocolate and a biscuit.

There were several people milling around at the station, mainly women with children waiting for the train to Bodmin. Violet sat in the cream and brown café, sipping her luke warm supposedly hot chocolate. She kept her eyes downcast, hoping to remain unnoticed. However a woman who lived a few doors down from

95

where Millie had lived, soon spotted Violet and got up from her own table to eagerly came across and offer commiserations.

"I was so sorry to hear about your mother. Millie Parker was a lovely woman," the neighbour said. Violet looked up at her. Her mother had been many things, but lovely wasn't one of them. "She'd turn in her grave if she could see the state of 'er house now, with this new lot what's moved in. I'll say that for Millie, she always kept her nets white and you could eat off her floor 'twas that clean." The woman sat down opposite Violet to further extol Millie's housekeeping and to ask a few questions about her death that hadn't been filled in by local gossip. She savoured the tit-bits Violet gave her, and then moved on to enquire after the Marbals. "You're still up there workin' then? Only I heard you was thinkin' of movin' up country." Violet licked away a smear of hot chocolate she could feel on her top lip. The woman's questions were beginning to make her feel panicky "I might move away. I haven't decided yet." The neighbour swept her gaze over her with intensity and then gasped, "My word, Violet Parker!" in such a shocked way that Violet blushed with guilt wondering for a second whether the woman had super natural powers and could tell she was pregnant. "Have you seen your stockin' dear? I never saw such a great 'ole. 'Tis half-way down yer leg."

Violet, still feeling guilty but less so, quickly pulled her coat across her tattered stocking. She knew the woman was thinking that Millie would do another turn in her grave if she could see her daughter in such an untidy state and she would be right. The woman's mercurial mind however, had already found another place to settle. "Look at the time. The train will in before we know it – we'd best get out on the platform. I hope it's not too packed up Bodmin. I don't know about you, but crowds do make me claustrophobic." Violet found herself following the woman out of the café. She may as well go to Bodmin for a few hours – she had no-where else to go and even the prattle of an old busy-body was better than dwelling on her own muddled thoughts, or listening to that reverberating inner silence called loneliness.

96

Jesse parked his car outside his shop and then walked slowly back through the town. He peered in shop windows hoping for a glimpse of Violet. He realised that he knew nothing about her social life; whether or not she had a close friend that she might have called on, or some special place that she liked to visit. He knew about her weekly visit to the cinema, but as there was no matinee performance it was useless looking there; besides which, he had no idea what state of mind she was in. Had she felt desperate enough to want to kill herself? It was a thought he didn't like to dwell on, but even so he hurried down to the riverbank. He peered in at the grey water, at the surface broken by slanting rain -drops. What was he expecting to see? Violet floating downstream with her hair spread out around her and a bunch of wild flowers in her hand, looking like Ophelia? If Violet was in the river she would be at the bottom of it, but that was unlikely because had she had jumped off the bridge, or waded in from the bank, she would have been hauled out again by the locals and the news would have reached his ears long before now. She could have gone into Volesworth Woods. He walked back to his car, and drove to the church where he had earlier photographed the wedding. Pieces of confetti, brightly coloured paper horse -shoes and bells were glued to the wet path as if in mockery of his anxiety. The little gate behind the church was cold to his touch, and beyond it Volesworth Woods stretched out shrouded in rain and darkening skies. Jesse walked down towards the tangled branches, his best leather working shoes slipping on the slimy wads of leaves. And then he stopped. This is bloody stupid, he said to himself. How the hell can I scour the whole woods?

He cupped his hands to his mouth and yelled "Violet!" more as a release to his frustration than in hope that she would call back to him. Then in silence added, for *Christ's sake*, come home.

As Jesse was driving back along the road, wondering whether he might as well return to Marbal house, he heard and saw the steam train across the river heading towards the station. For the first time it occurred to him that Violet might have bought a train ticket to somewhere – anywhere. She could be miles away by now.

97

The only way he would find out would be to ask the station master if he'd seen Violet boarding a train that day. It would be tricky trying to sound casual about it; he'd have to think up a feasible reason for asking, but ask he must, if only and hopefully to eliminate the possibility that Violet had left the town.

Jesse parked outside the station and hurried towards the platform. Then he saw her. Violet was casually walking along with some woman with bulging shopping bags dangling from both arms. The woman with the bags saw Jesse first. "Look who's here Violet. Mr. Marbal's come to give you a lift home. He's some good boss, I must say!" Violet's doe eyes looked at Jesse with surprise; her mouth fell open a little. Jesse felt like shaking her for the worry she'd caused him yet he also had an urge to hug her because she was safe after all. The emotions of a parent finding an errant offspring, he realized and wondered whether his main concern had been for Violet or the random assortment of replicated chromosomes within her that would grow to be his child. "This isn't as gallant as it appears," Jesse said to the woman with the bags, "I didn't come to collect Violet, but now that we're both here," he turned to Violet, "of course I'll give you a lift home." He had to allay suspicion; no one must ever know that anything untoward had happened between himself and Violet, or even guess at a relationship between them other than employer and employee. Out of politeness he asked the woman if she would like a lift, but thankfully she declined saying that her husband would be meeting her off the bus.

"Don't ever go off like that again." Jesse said as soon as both he and Violet were in the car. "I've been frantic trying to find you."

"I didn't have no choice," Violet said. "I came to the studio but you weren't there."

"You didn't tell that woman you were pregnant, did you?"

"So you know then?"

"Of course I know." Jesse started up the engine and eased the car out onto the road. "It's not something Joan would forget to tell me, exactly is it? So – did you tell that woman you were with?"

"Course I didn't. I'm not stupid."

Jesse grunted. "You weren't exactly clever telling Joan everything." Violet chewed on her lip. "I knew you'd be mad at me," she said. "I didn't mean to tell Joan, but she kept goin' on about how much I'd enjoy goin' away to be a nurse and I just couldn't take any more." Violet began to cry. "You can't imagine what it's been like. I was really looking forward to makin' somethin' of meself – and then this. I had nobody to turn to."
"You should have come to me – unless of course…"
"What?"
"Unless of course you planned all of this," Jesse said. He hadn't, until then, considered that she might have tried to trap him. "Did you, Violet? Did you hope Joan would leave me when she found out you were pregnant? Because if you did, you'd made a seriously wrong assumption." Violet's tears stopped. She was now too angry and shocked by his accusation to cry. "Stop the car," she said in a tight- lipped voice. "If that's what you think I don't never want to see you again." She pulled at the handle, opening the car door. From the corner of his eye, Jesse saw Violet lurch forward towards the gap between her and the road. He grabbed the handbrake and then Violet's arm, forcing her back into her seat with a strength he hadn't known he possessed.
For a second they both sat in silence. Violet began to cry again. Jesse reached across her and slammed the door shut. He took a deep breath to steady himself before starting up the car again. "I'm sorry Violet. I shouldn't have said that. Stop crying. Everything will be all right. I'm not really mad at you. It's just that – I've had a bugger of a day," he added, knowing he was echoing Joan's words on the day all of this had started.

"So you found her then." Joan said as Jesse and Violet walked into the hall. Jesse said nothing, and Violet, with eyes downcast, began to unbutton her coat. Jesse took it and put it on the hallstand with his own, then noticed Violet's skirt. "What on earth's all that white stuff on you?"
"Icing sugar," Violet said. Jesse laughed, hoping to break the tension between the three of them. "Icing sugar? What did you do – sit on a wedding cake?

"Why don't you go upstairs and change," Joan said, before Violet had chance to reply. She looked tired, drained even, Joan thought, but at least she didn't look like a woman having a miscarriage. "I'll make tea and we can have it in front of the fire – so don't take too long." Violet looked at her with uncertainty. This was a different Joan to the one she had left that morning. Whatever had Jesse said to placate her? Violet walked slowly and heavily upstairs to change her skirt and stockings.

Without a word to Jesse, Joan went down to the kitchen and busied herself cutting stale cheese to make Welsh rarebit. Jesse brought down the coalscuttle from the living room and went out into the yard to refill it. On the way back he stopped and watched Joan as she put bread under the grill, and rattled tea -cups onto a tray. There was an unforgiving air about her and he desperately wanted them to be close again. "I don't know what to say to you," he began. "All I can think of is I'm sorry and I love you. That's not enough though, is it?" Joan carried on putting scoops of tea into the teapot. "Trouble with you Jess," she said, "is that you're selfish. You put your own needs first and to hell with everyone else. I suppose you get that from your mother. I daresay you are sorry now – but it will take a long time, if ever, before I'll forgive you. Right now, I think you're a bloody rat."
"I see." Jesse picked up the coalscuttle. Oh well, it was no more than he deserved or expected and Joan hadn't warmed the teapot – again. Shame; he could do with a good cup of tea. Jesse wondered at himself for thinking such trivia at a time like this. Perhaps Joan was right. Perhaps he was a selfish bastard and all the other names she'd called him. He loved her though, and he hadn't meant to hurt her - or Violet. Even so, that was exactly what he had done.

When they were finally all seated in the living room and had munched on Joan's black edged toast thinly covered with piping hot cheese, and eaten the remains of a Victoria sponge cake that Violet had made several days before, Jesse decided it was time they came to some decisions.

"I think we should get down to business," he said, aware that he sounded like a chairman addressing a board meeting. He cleared his throat. Both women looked at him, stared at him, with emotions that were a blend of love, disappointment and downright contempt. "Violet, I'm sorry I've got you into this mess. I know you're devastated to find yourself pregnant and I know how much you were looking forward to becoming a nurse."
Joan snorted. "She should have thought about that before she –"
Jesse held his hand up to silence her. "Please Joan, I know this is hard for you, but we won't get anywhere unless we're adult about this."
"You mean like you and Violet were?" Joan said. "You two certainly behaved like adults, bloody irresponsible, self- indulgent lecherous adults." Violet lowered her head and looked as if she was about to cry. Jesse chewed the inside of his cheek and looked exasperated. "Yes, you're right we did behave that way and we apologise, but nothing is going to change the fact that Violet is pregnant, so can we please get on without any more recriminations – for now, at least?" Joan glared at him moodily but silently. "Right. Now Violet, what I suggest is that you let Joan and I bring up the baby as our own. As far as anyone else is concerned, Joan will be the baby's natural mother, and you'll be free to get on with your own life." He was surprised to see that Violet looked dismayed and not relieved as he had expected "What's the matter, don't you like the idea?" he asked tersely. "Joan told me that you planned to have an abortion but that's completely out of the question, so to be honest Violet, I don't see any alternative. My suggestion will be the best way out for all of us, not least the baby."
"When did you both decide all this, then?" Violet said, in a small, perplexed voice.
"*We* haven't decided anything." Joan said tartly. "This is all Jess's idea. Of course, being a man it's easy for him. But I'm expected to get over the shock of finding out I've been betrayed by the pair of you and then be prepared to welcome your offspring as if it were my own – all of this in the space of a few hours."

"I know it's asking a lot from you but we have to act quickly," Jesse said. "We need to plan everything before mother comes back from London. It's also imperative that no-one else finds out Violet is pregnant. No one knows you can't have children Joan, apart from the three of us, and of course that specialist you saw, so for you to have a baby would seem natural enough." A thought occurred to him. "Have you been to a doctor, Violet?" Violet shook her head. "No. I couldn't bring myself to do it."

"Well that's all right then, no-one else knows about you either." Jesse considered this for a second and then said, "So how do you know you're pregnant?"

"For goodness sake, she doesn't have to answer that," Joan said. "Do you suppose she'd have told me unless she was completely sure?"

"It wouldn't be easy," Violet muttered, "to give birth and then hand the baby over- especially as I know you don't really want it Joan."

Joan lit a cigarette. "Well, you could always keep it – but you'd have to sacrifice nursing of course and be prepared to be ostracized by everyone who knew you. There's such a stigma attached to being an unmarried mother, but if you think you're tough enough to cope, get on with it." Part of her was beginning to feel sorry for Violet. Of course the stupid girl only had herself to blame, even so, she wouldn't want to be in her predicament. Jess, she was glad to see, was looking decidedly displeased with her. "Anyway, whether I want the child or not," she continued between puffs, "I don't see how this scheme can possibly work. For a start I refuse to go around like a poor deluded woman pretending to be pregnant," she looked icily at Jesse, "while Violet on the other hand would have a bloody hard job disguising the fact that she *is* pregnant."

"Violet can go away after Christmas just as she'd planned to do, only not to Exeter, obviously. We'll find a little flat for her in – Plymouth, say. Everyone here will assume she's started her training so no-one's likely to ask awkward questions. You'll have to write to the hospital in Exeter Violet, with some excuse to start later on in the year."

"There's another intake in September, they might let me start then" Violet said, although still unsure that Jesse's plan was her best option; however the thought of having her own little flat and her career back was beginning to appeal to her far more than being an unmarried mother.

"Excellent. I'll get a telephone installed here – it's something I've been meaning to do it for a while now. So, we'll only be a phone call away should you need anything. When the time comes for you to give birth, Joan and I will travel up to Plymouth. We can say we're going on holiday and -"

"And reappear with a baby?" Joan scoffed. "Bit unlikely anyone is going to believe it's my baby, I should think."

"They will if you've said beforehand that you're expecting a baby," Jesse said. "And that will be the truth – you will be expecting a baby, only not your own. You needn't go in for padding or anything like that", he added. "That red winter coat of yours is pretty full anyway, isn't? You could indulge yourself so that you put on a bit of weight and then wear one of those loose top things." Joan gave him an arched look. "There's more to looking pregnant than eating a few extra chocolates and wearing a maternity smock. Your mother lives with us for goodness sake. She's bound to get suspicious."

I don't see why," Jesse said staunchly. "You know mother. She probably won't be the slightest bit interested."

"Mrs. Marbal won't be here in May," Violet said quietly. "She's goin' to Lake Como with the Stanfords." She looked shyly across at Joan, "You know, them people she had the card from. Anyway, that's when I reckon the baby will be born, around the beginning of May."

"Really? Well then, when mother gets back we'll present her with her grand-child." Jesse said, with a smile. "I think all of this will work out perfectly."

"Except," Joan said, "that I haven't agreed to it yet."

"Neither have I," Violet said. Jesse stood up and stretched. "No – but you will," he said confidently. And they did; slowly and with questions that he always had an answer for, they began to accept the inevitable. Violet would give birth to Jesse's child, and Joan would accept her as her own. On the 6th May 1949 Agnes' mother was born.

Chapter 6

Finding a place for Violet to live in Plymouth hadn't been as easy as Jesse had anticipated. Although redevelopment had begun replacing commercial buildings and homes destroyed in the blitz, there seemed to be far more people wanting accommodation than was available. Eventually, Jesse had to pay out rather more than he could comfortably afford renting the ground floor flat of a three-storey house near the Hoe. Violet and Joan had spent most of the winter and spring indoors, Joan because she didn't look pregnant, and Violet because she did.

It was with a sense of great relief that Violet awoke on 6th May, to the tug of contractions banding her large girth. Once the baby was born she could come out of hiding, and resume her life. At ten o'clock with her contractions progressing fiercely she phoned Jesse, who sounded extremely excited and within three hours was standing with Joan, on her doorstep. Violet led them into her living room and offered them a cup of tea.
"For heaven's sake, you sound so calm!" Joan said. "Shouldn't you be sitting down, or something? I'll make the tea, you put your feet up."
"Shouldn't we set off for the nursing home?" Jesse said. "I don't think we should be hanging around drinking tea."
"There's no need to fuss," Violet said. "I'll make the tea, only it might take a while if I get another con-"she stopped, gripped hold of the mantelpiece for a while and gritted her teeth, "traction."
"Bloody hell," Joan murmured.
"That one was a bit longer and a bit stronger," Violet conceded. "P'raps we should get goin' soon."

Violet had been booked into The Elms Nursing Home under the name of Marbal. She had given her name as Mrs Marbal ever since arriving at Plymouth and wore a Woolworth's wedding ring that Jesse had given her. He had insisted that she pretended to be Joan and that she told people her husband was working abroad as a freelance photographer. Not that Violet had entered into conversation with anyone very much, apart from May, an old lady who lived in the flat above. May wasn't particularly interested in whether Violet was married or not and certainly didn't believe a word of her jumbled story. May was just as lonely as Violet, and for mutual company they would sometimes sit out the evenings together.

May would tell Violet horror stories of the Plymouth blitz; how store windows melted with the heat and became rivers of molten glass, how meat frizzled on butchers' shelves and how fur coated shop dummies blazed like well-dressed Guy Fawkes effigies.
She also told her about the fourteen new-born babies and three nurses who died when the General Hospital took a direct hit. Violet listened to it all, wide-eyed and speechless. May grew fond of Violet. She liked a good listener.
"I'll have to say good-bye to the old lady upstairs," Violet said, as Jesse picked up her suitcase to take out to the car. "I'd rather you didn't," Jesse said. "Best not to draw attention to ourselves."
Violet sat in the back of the car with Joan beside her and fiddled with her pretend wedding ring. Once she'd handed the baby over she'd have to take off the ring for good. She looked down at her finger. The best part about all of this had been pretending she was married to Jesse.

A nurse at The Elms took Violet onto a side ward, and told Joan and Jesse to wait in the visitor's room until she'd found out how far dilated Violet was.
"What did she mean?" Jesse asked Joan when the nurse had left.
"She meant, how far – oh, never mind Jess. Don't bother yourself with the biology of it all. Basically she should be able to tell us how advanced Violet's labour is." Jesse nodded and raked his hair. God, how he hated hospitals. He couldn't understand why anyone would want to work in them. He felt tense and wanted the whole business to be over with as soon as possible. The sooner Violet's ordeal was over the better. Seeing her in pain had made him feel, well a cad really. He held out his hand to Joan for reassurance. She gripped his hand and smiled. "Don't worry. She'll be all right. She's as tough as old boots." Jesse put his arm around Joan's shoulders.

"I don't know what I'd do without you," he said. Joan nestled against him. They were close again now, but only after painful months when she had cried out her misery in private and kept Jesse out of her bedroom. Cutting off your nose to spite your face, that's what her mother used to say, and so eventually accepting that nothing could undo the past, besides which sexual frustration was driving her mad, she took Jesse back.

"Well now," an entering nurse said, casting a suspicious eye over Joan and Jesse as they stood cuddled together, "Mr. Marbal is it, and -?" She nodded towards Joan.
"My sister," Jesse said, disengaging himself from Joan's clasp "This is Miss Marbal, my sister." He wondered if the nurse believed him and if she did, she must have thought they had a very close relationship.
"I see." She sounded unconvinced. "Well I suggest you both go away for a few hours, have some lunch and then call back. Your wife certainly took her time coming here, but fortunately all is well. I wouldn't be at all surprised if baby doesn't arrive before tea-time."
"Could we see her?" Joan asked, "Just to make sure she's alright?"
"I'm afraid that's out of the question," the nurse said indignantly. "We don't allow visitors to patients in labour. Good heavens, this isn't the place for a family outing." Joan opened her mouth to retaliate, but Jesse led her towards the door. "That's fine," he said to the nurse. "We understand. Perhaps you would let her know that we're thinking of her?" He had wanted to say, give her my love but Joan would probably have read more into it than he intended and the last thing he needed to do at this critical stage was to alienate Joan.

They walked out into a spring sunshine that gave little heat. It was the sort of weather Joan hated. Glassy was how she described it, clear and cold with a feeble sun giving anticipation of hotter days to come; the sort of weather when a coat was too much to wear and a cardigan too little. She was glad to sit in the car next to Jesse and feel the warmth magnified through the windscreen, even so she shivered. "Are you alright?" Jesse

107

asked. She nodded. "Not sorry to leave this place though." They drove down the private lane lined with elms and out onto the main road. "Where now?" Jesse pondered. "Shall we do as we were told and have lunch?" Joan smiled. "Yes. Let's find a pub somewhere."

They drove into Plymouth, passed Charles Church that stood without windows or roof, destined to remain in its ravished state as a testament to the destruction of war. Jesse's child would in later years pass by the church in its dereliction, and half- heartedly wonder why no one had rebuilt or demolished the eyesore. For now, Joan looked at it and the gaps where houses had stood and the piles of rubble and thought of the disruption war brought to ordinary people; plans made that could no longer be realised, ambitions that were quelled, futures that were lost. "War is a bloody inconvenience, isn't it?" she said to Jesse. "One day everyone is going about their business, kids at school, men at work, women cleaning, shopping and gossiping and the next day, wham, a bomb drops on their street and blows their life away." Jesse looked across at her. "Inconvenience? That's an understatement, if ever I heard one." Evidence of the blitz, he decided, had led Joan into thinking about the death of her parents. Perhaps losing them had affected her more than she let on. Today however was not the time to be retrospective. "Plymouth will be a wonderful new city when they've finished building it," he said. "We have to look to the future – just like the town planners." Joan laughed. "God Jess, you do sound old sometimes."

They chose the first pub they saw. Joan sat at a rickety wooden table while Jesse went over to the bar to get their drinks and enquire about the possibility of having something to eat. "There's crisps or cheese sandwiches," he said when he came back. "And the sandwiches were offered as a favour. What do you think – do you want to move on to a restaurant?" Joan shook her head then sipped at her gin and tonic. "No, I'm not really hungry. A sandwich will do." She took out a cigarette case and a lighter from her handbag. She felt uneasy. This day that she been looking

forward to was beginning to churn up emotions she hadn't counted on. Jealousy, for a start. It should be her lying at The Elms, labouring to give birth to Jesse's child, not Violet. She gulped at her gin and inhaled deeply. That's what wives did, they gave birth to their husband's children. Not her though, she would never know what it felt like to be in labour with her hair stuck in strands to her forehand from the sheer exhaustion of it all, or know the feeling of having her own baby placed warm and dependent in her arms. On the other hand she would never have to experience dictatorial nurses telling her when to push and not to scream and whatever else it was they said to women at their most vulnerable. Jesse came back and placed a plate of chunky sandwiches on the table. "You look deep in thought Joan. What were you thinking?" He sat beside her and took a deep draught of beer, licked the froth from his top lip and made an umm sound of appreciation. Joan thought about her reply. She wouldn't mention her feeling of jealousy. There was no point. It was something she would have to live with. "I was thinking how exciting it is now that the baby's finally on its way. A few more days and it'll be all snug in the nursery."
Jesse nodded. "I know. Doesn't seem possible does it?" He picked up a sandwich. "I wonder how Violet's getting on," he said.

When they returned to the nursing home, a nurse informed them that Mrs. Marbal had given birth to a girl and took them to the glass fronted nursery to peer through at the infant. Only two of the four cots were occupied. Both babies were tightly bound in woolly shawls; one slept peacefully, the other wailed lustily. "Yours is the noisy one," the nurse said to Jesse. He grabbed Joan's hand and gazed with instant love at what he could see of his daughter, a delicate white neck, an angry red face, and a shock of fluffy black hair. His eyes misted with tears. "Can I hold her?" The nurse shook her head. "We don't want her to get into bad habits. She has to learn from the start that the only time she gets picked up is for feeds." Joan looked at the howling little scrap of humanity. It seemed so unnecessary not to be allowed to cuddle her, particularly as Jess, she knew, was aching to do so.

And he after all, was paying the nursing home. She turned to the nurse. "Mr. Marbal would like to hold his daughter," she said calmly. "So would you fetch her for him please?" The nurse looked at Joan with disdain. She could smell trouble on her breath. "I really don't advise it," she snapped.

"Now if you would - please."

The nurse turned to Jesse. He smiled at her. "Just for a moment, then I'll hand her back." With a loud click of tongue and heel the nurse entered the nursery and bent over the baby's cot. Jesse squeezed Joan's hand and grinned at her. "Well done darling. I don't know why, but people in starchy white scare the hell out of me." Joan smiled back and watched as the baby was placed in Jesse's arms. She felt a tightening in her chest. Jess may not have loved Violet more than he loved her, but already he loved his daughter more. Joan moved to get a closer look at the child who had filched her place from Jesse's heart and who she would have to love as her own. The baby stared back and cried.

They gave Violet the flowers they had bought for her, and then stood either side of her bed. Jesse lightly kissed her forehead, Joan briefly held her hand. "So, how was it? You look well."

"I'm tired," Violet said, "but it wasn't as bad as I'd thought." She struggled to sit up in the bed. Already colostrum was oozing out from her and staining the front of her nightdress. She pulled the sheet up higher so that Jesse wouldn't see. "What do you think of her, then?" she asked him.

"She's lovely". He gave her a tender smile. "I suppose we ought to decide on her name." Violet shrugged. "It's up to you two, isn't it? It's nothin' to do with me." Suddenly her mouth curved downwards and she began to sob. Joan quickly handed her a handkerchief. "Shush, Violet, we don't want the old dragon in here wondering what all the fuss is about."

"I'm sorry," Violet said gulping to hold back her tears, "but I can't do it. I can't give her up!" Jesse visibly blanched. He felt panicked and suddenly angry. No, she couldn't change her mind, not now. They had an agreement. "What do you mean, you can't give her up?" he demanded. "It's too late – "

110

Joan shook her head at him. "Violet's exhausted, Jess," she said quietly. "Go for a walk and leave us alone for a while."

When he had left the room Joan pulled up a chair next to Violet's bed. "Look Violet," she said, "if you want to keep the baby, you can." Violet looked at her with suspicion. "But it will mean giving up any thought of having a career and probably a husband, too come to that. In fact your life would be very hard as a single mother. You know how people are; you'd be an outcast. The baby wouldn't have much of a life either, would she? I mean not compared to what Jess and I could give her."

Violet blew her nose. "Jesse would have to pay for her keep." She said. "It's his baby as much as mine." Joan sighed. "Well, that's it y' see. He wants her so much that he'd probably take you to court to get custody. You might win though, who knows? It's up to you Violet. You must do what you think is best." She stood up to leave. "Now isn't a good time to worry about it. I've read women's hormones do funny things when they've had a baby, so decide after a few days when you're feeling stronger."

"I don't understand," Violet said. "I thought you'd be angry with me for wanting to keep her."

"I knew you'd want to keep the baby when it was born," Joan said truthfully.What woman would want to part with a baby she'd just given birth to? "Only wanting to keep her, and doing what's best might not be the same thing. That's for you to decide."

Violet twisted at her handkerchief. "Not really," she said.

"I haven't got a choice, have I?" No, Joan thought. And neither have I. She opened the door and then turned back to Violet, "What name would you like to give the baby?" she asked.

"Elizabeth," Violet said.

Joan smiled. "After the princess?"

"No Elizabeth Taylor. She was lovely in National Velvet, wasn't she?"

Jesse was outside waiting by the car. "Well?" he said to Joan as she scrunched over the gravel towards him. "Did you manage to talk Violet into seeing sense?"

111

"She'll hand over the baby if that's what you mean." Joan lit a cigarette and leaned against the car. She watched the smoke drift upwards and then looked towards a fathomless sky glittering with myriad stars. Only it wasn't the stars you saw but their reflected light. Nothing was as it seemed.

"Thank God for that," Jesse said. "I thought we were going to have problems."

Joan glanced across at him. You haven't got a bloody clue when it comes down to it, have you Jess?"

"I'm sorry?" Jesse opened the car door. "A bloody clue about what?"

Joan shook her head and climbed into the passenger seat. "It doesn't matter," she said.

Jesse and Joan stayed at Violet's flat while she was at The Elms. They packed her few possessions because it wouldn't be safe for Violet to come back. Somebody might wonder where the baby was, might start asking difficult questions. Jesse had found a bed-sit above a tea -room in Exeter where Violet could stay for the summer, before she started her training at the hospital. He hoped she'd find herself a job as soon as possible so that he could stop supporting her. Not that he would mention it for a while. As the days went by, Violet became more and more attached to the daughter she had to feed and care for and became more depressed and tearful because she knew her time with the baby was limited. After ten days, Joan and Jesse collected them both from the nursing home. Violet sat in the front seat of the car. Baby Elizabeth fretted in her carrycot in the back with Joan beside her making solicitous clicking noises.

Violet's bed-sit overlooked the Cathedral Green. As she opened the leaded paned window and looked out, she smiled for the first time in days. "It's lovely here," she said. Jesse and Joan exchanged gratified glances. The view was inspiring, but Joan could detect dampness in the room and Jesse had spotted mouse droppings on the windowsill. "Hopefully it will do until you live in at the hospital," he said. "The rent is paid for six weeks. You should be able to find work after that. In fact, the sooner you get a job the better. It will take your mind off - things."

Violet turned back towards the room. "I 'spect I'll be able to get a job easy enough." She looked at the carrycot, where Elizabeth cried lustily. "She's hungry," she said. "I'd best show you how to make up her bottle Joan, and how to change her nappy." Joan picked up the baby and wondered how long it would be before the feelings of guilt and sadness left her. Hopefully she'd be all right once they were at home, and she didn't have to face Violet anymore. Jesse whistling cheerfully, went out to the car to fetch Violet's suitcase and the holdall of newly purchased immediate requisites for Elizabeth. Violet tried to focus on her future and to hold back her tears on this last day with her baby. It would be easier once she was gone. She'd have a good life with Jesse and Joan, better than her own life had been. And that was why she was doing this, wasn't it? All this pain was for Elizabeth's benefit. If she didn't look at her and didn't pick her up, she'd get through it. She wanted them to leave, get it over with. She wanted them to stay and never leave.

Eventually, after the baby had been fed and changed, Joan stood up and put on her coat. "Oh I nearly forgot," she said, "that old lady in the flat above yours in Plymouth, gave me this for you." She brought out a brown paper bag from the holdall and passed it over. Violet took out a matinee jacket knitted in thick, yellow wool and fastened with over large white plastic buttons. Violet looked at it with tenderness, touched by the old lady's kindness. "Dear old May," she murmured, laying the jacket aside before tears got the better of her. "What must she think of me goin' off without sayin' good-bye?"

"I told her we were moving to Dorset," Jesse said. "And I made your excuses for not coming to see her before you left, she was alright about it. We'd better start back." This was the moment Joan had been looking forward too yet adversely dreading; the moment she would take Elizabeth away and become her mother. "We'll just go," she said, picking up the holdall. "We won't say anything, we'll just go."

Violet nodded numbly. "We bought you these," Jesse said, laying a package on the table, "something for you to look at when we've gone." He smiled at her and holding the carrycot began to follow Joan out of the room. He turned in the doorway. "Good luck, he said. "And – well thank you, Violet."

Violet stood without moving for some time. When she had estimated that enough minutes had passed for Jesse's car to be well on its way out of town, she braced herself to move. The first steps without Elizabeth, unwrapping the parcel they had left her, her first action without Elizabeth. She hadn't crumbled, disintegrated into a pile of dust as she feared she might. She was the same Violet Parker, on the outside at least. The opened parcel revealed a small box and a book. She removed the lid of the box and took out a watch with a silver fastening and numbers on it that were upside down, until of course you pinned it on your uniform, then you could see the time. A proper nurse's watch. She glanced at the book and flicked through the anatomical drawings. They had taken her baby and left her a watch and a copy of Gray's Anatomy. Violet picked up the matinee jacket May had knitted. She could tell by the look on Joan's face when she unwrapped it, that Joan would never have dressed the baby in it. Violet was glad Joan hadn't taken it, because she wanted to keep it forever. She took off her Woolworth's wedding ring and looped it over one of the over-sized buttons and then folded up the jacket and put it back into the paper bag. Later on she would unpack and change her clothes, but for now she would sit in the window seat and hug herself and smell the milk and talc smell which was all she had left of Elizabeth.

Chapter 7

When Elizabeth, or Lizzie as she was known, was ten, a letter arrived from Joan's sister saying that she was coming to visit. Joan gave a whoop of excitement as she scanned the sheet of blue airmail paper. It was breakfast time and she sat in her dressing gown at the kitchen table, a cigarette bobbing between her lips and the ashtray, a cup of tea in front of her. "Oh my God," she exclaimed to Lizzie, "Your Aunt Muriel and Uncle Chuck are coming over for Christmas. Isn't that exciting?"

Lizzie was watching a piece of toast under the grill. "Is that my Aunt Muriel who lives in New York?" she asked.

"Of course it is – how many Aunt Muriels do you think you have, you dope?" Joan began to re-read her letter, slowly this time, smiling with pleasure.

"D'you think she'll bring me a Christmas present from America?" Lizzie said.

"Umm, I expect so."

"Oh my God," Lizzie said, now as excited as her mother. The toast she was holding slipped between her fingers and fell to the floor. She picked it up and brushed it off against her skirt. "I expect she's seen loads of film stars. Wait until I tell Clover. She'll be so jealous."

"She'll also be waiting for you *again* if you don't hurry up and get ready for school. Oh I'm so thrilled Lizzie. I haven't seen my sister in years." Joan rushed over to Lizzie and hugged her with childlike joy. She smelled of cigarettes and a sickly sweet smell that Lizzie didn't like very much. She pulled away, and began to butter her toast. She wondered what Aunt Muriel looked like. She expected she was beautiful, not because she thought Joan was, but because Muriel lived in New York and everyone in America was beautiful and rich. Halfway through her contemplative munching and crunching, the doorbell rang. "That'll be Clover," Joan said. "Go and let her in. Oh God Lizzie, you've left the grill on again. It stinks of fat in here now."

"That's because you didn't wash out the grill pan - again," Lizzie said, rushing toast in hand out of the kitchen. "If you must know, my toast *tastes* like fat."

"Guess what?" Lizzie said to Clover as soon as she'd opened the door. "My Aunt's coming over from America and she's bringing me a Christmas present from *America*!"

"Gosh, you're so lucky, Lizzie." Clover knew that was the right thing to say. Lizzie beamed smugly and following Joan's yelled instructions from the kitchen went upstairs to fetch her school raincoat and satchel. "And don't forget your home-work," Joan said, coming into in the hall. "Hello Clover." Joan smiled at Lizzie's friend.. She was such a dainty little thing. "You always look so neat and tidy. I wish Lizzie was as neat as you."

Clover said "Hello Mrs. Marbal," and smiled back. She had no choice but to be tidy. Her mother fussed about everything and laid out her polished shoes and clean clothes for her to wear each morning. Clover's mother washed her hair and bound it in rags every Saturday so that it would be shiny and curly for church on Sunday morning, and for Sunday school in the afternoon. Clover's life was a set routine, right down to the meals her mother cooked each day of the week. Today being Thursday was quite good because it was pork pasty day. Lizzie came bouncing down the stairs, her wonky plaits flying up and down with every thud. "Here's your tuck, darling," Joan said. "Do your coat up; it's really frosty today. And where's your scarf? Clover's wearing her scarf, Lizzie. Go back upstairs and get yours."

"Oh I don't know where it is. I'm alright." Lizzie took from Joan a packet of crisps and an apple for break-time, and stuffed them into her satchel. "By the way, Grandma says can she have her breakfast now 'cos she's been awake for ages and she's starving." Joan groaned, but didn't say the rude things she normally said when Clara was demanding, because today Joan was in a good mood. In a couple of weeks she'd see her sister again.

Lizzie's unbuttoned raincoat flapped around her skinny legs as she hop-scotched along the pavement Her brown Clarke's brogues were scuffed and her knee- high socks spiralled towards

116

her ankles. Clover trotted along beside her. Her white socks were anchored in place by bands of knotted elastic that bit painfully into her legs and would be the prime cause of varicose veins that she would develop later on in life. Lizzie secretly envied Clover's shoes. They were shiny black patent, with a strap and buckle and leather bottoms that made a satisfying tap, tap noise as she hurried along the pavement to keep up. Lizzie's shoes were regulation school shoes, sensible, expensive, with durable thick crepe soles and no end of petulance would induce Joan to buy her anything else.

"I've got sixpence from Grandma," Lizzie said. "Shall I buy some Spangles or fruit gums?"

"I'm not allowed boiled sweets," Clover said. "They're bad for your teeth." That settled it then. Lizzie pushed open the half glass door of Todd's Tobacconists, and picked up a packet of Spangles from the display shelf. She still had threepence left, and deliberated over aniseed balls, sherbet dips, liquorice sticks and sweet cigarettes. "Lizzie," Clover groaned, "hurry up or we'll be late."

"Alright, keep your hair on," Lizzie said. Sweet cigarettes would be good fun, because on a day like today you could puff on them and the cold air would look like smoke coming out of your mouth. She handed over her sixpence to Mr. Todd and waited for her penny change. She wanted to dawdle in the warmth of Todd's shop, and look at the Christmas decorations and rows of glittery snow scene cards set out on a trestle table covered with red crinkly paper. But she and Clover had already been given one after-school detention for lateness that week and Clover's mother had sent Clover to bed early and threatened that if she was late for school again, she would be in serious trouble and banned from calling for Lizzie in the mornings. Outside the shop, Lizzie opened the packet of Spangles. The top one was red, and she popped it into her mouth. A green Spangle was underneath. "You can have that one if you like," Lizzie said. "I don't like the green ones." Clover took it, and hoped she didn't develop toothache. She probably would. She always got caught out when she disobeyed her mother. Lizzie, with a Spangle lodged between her teeth and the inside of her cheek, placed a Barrett's cigarette between her

117

lips and pretended to smoke. "Look," she said with delight. "Look at the smoke coming out of my mouth!" Clover managed to smile. Sometimes Lizzie was a bit thick, but she was still her best friend. They crossed over the road, and increased their pace to narrow the gap between themselves and some other late stragglers. Lizzie suddenly thought about her Aunt Muriel's visit and a tingle of excitement leading to a rare moment of bonhomie washed over her.

"You can have last week's Girl comic if you like," she told Clover as they neared the school gates. "It's got a really cute picture of two white kittens, and guess what they're called?" Clover couldn't. "Candy and Floss. Get it? Candy Floss! I'm gonna keep that picture, but you can have the rest of the comic."

"Oh thanks Lizzie," Clover said. She wondered what was on the back of the kitten page. She hoped it wasn't Belle of the Ballet. Belle of the Ballet was her favourite.

Duty teacher Miss Prinn blew her whistle as the girls ran across the playground to get into line. Miss Prinn glared at them as they fell in behind the rest of their class. "Just made it," Lizzie whispered.

"Marbal!" Miss Prinn yelled. "Get that disgusting thing out of your mouth and be quiet!" Lizzie quickly nibbled down the length of her sweet, powder-coated cigarette. It tasted even better mixed with a red Spangle.

At break time, when the rest of the class filed out to the enforced ten minutes of fresh, freezing air, Lizzie dawdled by the oilcloth map pinned on the back wall of the class-room. She'd never taken much notice of the map before, but now she had an urge to find out exactly where New York was. America was a big continent. Lizzie's ink stained finger roamed across it. Miss Prinn looked up from the crossword puzzle she was trying to complete. "Why aren't you outside with the others, Lizzie Marbal?" Miss Prinn's eyebrows were arched with surprise, not primarily because Lizzie hadn't gone out to the playground, but because she was looking at a map. Lizzie had never shown interest in anything

118

geographical before, or indeed any of the other subjects Miss Prinn tried to teach. "I was just lookin' for New York, Miss Prinn." Lizzie said, her finger still pressed against the map. "But I can't find it." Miss Prinn stood up and edged her way between the desks. "You can't find it Lizzie Marbal," she said tartly, "because you're looking at Africa. New York is in America." Lizzie nodded. "I know it is, Miss Prinn."

"So why are you looking at the continent of Africa?"

"I thought it was America Miss Prinn".

Miss Prinn sighed. "No Lizzie, it's here look – over to the west. And New York is right here, right on the coast." Lizzie's eyes swept around the tip of Miss Prinn's pointing pen nib.

There was a bit of land sticking out of New York shaped like an arm with a hand and a thumb and a beckoning finger. "Why the interest in New York?" Miss Prinn asked.

"Because I'm going there, Miss Prinn," Lizzie said, focusing on the beckoning finger.

"Indeed?" There's obviously money in the photography business, Miss Prinn thought. "And when is this visit to take place?"

Lizzie shrugged. "I don't know. As soon as I've saved up enough money." Miss Prinn briefly closed her eyes as a wave of despair swept over her. "Daydreaming again, Lizzie Marbal? Out you go. Clear your head with some fresh air, child." Lizzie ambled over to the door. She wasn't daydreaming.

She would go to New York one day and those other places encircled by the tip of Miss Prinn's pen – Baltimore, Philadelphia, Boston and somewhere else beginning with N. She'd go to them all.

Lizzie went out into the playground. Clover was watching a couple of girls slithering over a wide strip of ice, wanting to have a go herself, but too mindful of her shoes to try. Lizzie gambolled across, her arms out-stretched ready for her slide as she ran at the frozen patch. The friction caused by her rubber-soled shoes made her stop so suddenly that she nearly fell over. She just managed to keep her balance by stumbling forward, her arms flapping like a demented bird. The girls laughed, Clover bit her lip so that she wouldn't giggle. If she did, she could forget all about having Lizzie's Girl comic, with or without Candy and Floss. Lizzie regained her equilibrium and punched at the ice with the heel of her shoe. "Bloody Clarke's brogues," she said.

Once she had broken up from school for the Christmas holidays, Lizzie was able to join Joan in a cleaning blitz on Marbal House. Lizzie wasn't by nature a tidy child yet she did, when in the mood, find a great deal of satisfaction in polishing and cleaning. Turning the little catch on the side of a new tin of Ronuk and smearing a piece of old rag across the smooth, orange polish before applying it, perhaps a little too liberally, onto a piece of furniture was almost blissful. Now the dull patina on the dining room table became vibrant and glossy, perfect for Clara's old silver candelabra that Joan had buffed up with Silvo, and fitted with red candles. The chair backs came in for a waxy treat too, the legs less so, as Lizzie wasn't keen on doing the legs of things. Large items she attacked with a zest, and once the downstairs rooms were sweet smelling and shiny, she started on the bedrooms. The guest room delegated to Muriel and Chuck caused a big dip in the Ronuk and a dull ache in Lizzie's wrist. The dressing table mirror was one minute smeary pink with Windolene, the next, sparkling clear. Even Clara's bedroom, her sanctuary until Lizzie was tall enough to open doors, came under attack.

"Lizzie, how many times have I told you to knock, before you enter my room?" Clara said, as Lizzie burst in with her basket of cleaning materials.

"But you're not doin' anythin', are you Grandma? You're only listenin' to the radio, so you probably wouldn't have heard me if I had knocked." Lizzie set down her basket and looked around her, wondering where to begin.

"Well now that you're in here, what do you want?" Clara eyed the polish and dusters with suspicion. "I hope you don't intend disrupting my peace with your incessant cleaning."

"It has to be done, Grandma," Lizzie said. "Every-where's got to look nice. Auntie Muriel and Uncle Chuck are comin' on Christmas Eve."

"Not into my room, they're not," Clara said stoutly. She was only too well aware of the impending visit of Joan's sister and brother-in-law. It was hard to tell who was most excited by it, Lizzie or her mother. And the more ebullient they became, the more despondent Clara felt. At her age, she really couldn't be doing with guests at Christmas.

"They might open the wrong door by mistake," Lizzie said, beginning to dab at her polish, "an' come in. Anyway it stinks horrible in your room, like mouldy ol' apples so it could do with a bit of freshnin' up."

Clara scowled."Really, Lizzie, you're the most incorrigible child I've ever known." Lizzie smiled. She had no idea what Clara meant by *incorrigible*, but she suspected it wasn't good and wasn't particularly bothered whether it was or not. What anyone thought of Lizzie had little impact on her- which was both a puzzle and a fascination to Clara.

Ten years previously, on Clara's arrival home from Italy, Jesse had been impatient and proud to present his four weeks old daughter. As Clara scrutinised Lizzie sleeping in her cot, her first feeling was one of gratitude to her for not having inherited Joan's goldfish lips. As Lizzie grew it was apparent that she hadn't inherited Joan's stout ankles either – in fact as far as Clara could see there was nothing of Joan she had inherited, and little of Jesse either, come to that. Lizzie had her father's blue eyes yet smaller. Her hair was much darker than Jesse's and candlestick straight and with none of the auburn tones that Joan's had. Although not particularly tall for her age, Lizzie's legs were long and gangling so that when she ran, with her stick legs bent up behind her she invariably kicked herself. Lizzie had never been through a chubby stage; she had always been coltish. She was far from pretty, yet she wasn't plain either. She was, Clara thought, rather a strange child – a cuckoo in the nest. Not that she seriously doubted Lizzie to be the product of Jesse and Joan. Joan had looked pregnant during the months prior to Lizzie's arrival. Clara had no reason to suspect that layers of warm clothes caused the bulk under Joan's button through smock;

121

clothes that Joan was pleased to wear during the cold winter months. Clara had expected her grandchild to arrive by the time she returned from Italy, and sure enough the child had. The fact that Joan had been foolish enough at the end of her pregnancy to go off on a shopping spree in Plymouth causing her to give birth there, was as far as Clara was concerned, just another testament to Joan's headstrong nature. Clara was never inclined towards babies, and her own grandchild was no exception. However, when Lizzie was about four and had stopped crying for no good reason and could get around without falling over or bumping into things and had stopped breaking any object within her reach, Clara began to pay her more attention. By the time Lizzie was six, it was obvious to Clara that the child possessed a very independent and indifferent nature. Jesse worshipped his daughter, but for all his indulging, Lizzie showed little affection in return. Joan might scold her, yet Lizzie never outwardly showed remorse. She was, thought Clara, like a ship on a chartered course ploughing through choppy seas and sailing through calm waters with equal measure of insouciance. People, it seemed, were of small consequence to her. Clara didn't doubt that Lizzie's excitement over the arrival of Muriel had little to do with her, but everything to do with the fact that she lived in America. America was the land of film stars and opulence, home of the rich and the famous, and that in Lizzie's view, was something to get excited about. But for all that, she was an unusually dispassionate child; Clara was, for the most part, glad of her company.

"Don't touch anything on my dressing table," Clara said, watching Lizzie pick up a glass candlestick.

"It's all dusty," Lizzie said. "Your dressing table hasn't been cleaned for ages."

"I'll do it myself, later. You might break something. Besides, you really should have a rest now child. Why don't we look through my jewellery together? You like that." Lizzie did. She replaced the candlestick, put down her duster and went to the bottom of Clara's wardrobe where she knew she would find an old chocolate box with a Renoir painting on the lid. She placed it on Clara's bed and dipped in to the strands of coloured glass and sparkly broaches.

122

Clara, sitting in her armchair, next to the bed and in front of the fire, looked at the necklace Lizzie held in her hand. White glass daisies that Clara's mother had given to her on her seventh birthday. Lizzie's little friend Clover liked to know the personal history behind each piece of jewellery, not so Lizzie, She was content to rummage through the box and loop anything that caught her attention around her neck or pin it to her jumper – often several pieces at once, so that she would look, Clara told her, like the Queen of Sheba. Sometimes Clara allowed the girls to look at her real jewellery, the stuff she kept in a locked, leather jewellery case. In here she kept the emerald ear-rings Albert had given her, a diamond dragonfly broach, a sapphire ring belonging to her grandmother, pearl chokers and droplet earrings of ruby, amethyst, coral and amber. Her special pieces, she called them. Once, when Clover was holding one of the emerald earrings up to the light, Clara had a sudden and vivid memory of Albert. In a voice inadvertently subdued by such a clear and unexpected picture, she told the girls that she had worn the earrings the night before her husband went off to war. Clover sat back on her heels and asked what became of him. "I never saw him again," Clara said. "He was killed fighting for his country." Clover thought that was a really sad story and carefully returned the earrings to their padded satin. Lizzie dangled the sapphire ring on her thumb and said. "Is this worth a lot of money, Grandma?" Clara could remember a time when she had been that indifferent, but now, in old age, she had mellowed. Her failing eye-sight, and arthritic fingers made it impossible to paint. With knees that ached and creaked, she couldn't walk very far. For most of the time she sat in her room listening to the radio or turning her thoughts back to the past, pointlessly wondering what she might have done differently with her life.

Lizzie was aware of a car pulling up outside the house. "Daddy's home," she gave a little gasp of excitement and quickly jumped off the bed. "And it's Wednesday." Clara raised an eyebrow. "Well I'm glad you're pleased to see your father, but you're not leaving this room until you've put away my jewellery." Lizzie, with an

123

impatient sigh scooped up the jewellery in careless handfuls and slammed the lid back on the chocolate box. She ran across to the door and opened it just as Jesse downstairs in the hallway called out, "Where's my princess?"

"I'm coming!" Lizzie called back. "Where's my Girl comic?" Clara slowly nodded. That was why Lizzie was in a hurry to see her father. It was comic day. Something glinted on the bedspread catching Clara's eye. She peered at it from her chair but it remained a frosty blur against the dark eiderdown. Rubbing at her knees, she got up and steadying herself on the bedstead, picked up the small object. A white glass daisy. And now she could see other daisies, broken from their thread and scattered across the green satin eiderdown like wild flowers in a meadow. One by one she picked them, cold and pretty in her hand and then returned to her chair by the fire. She held the daisies tightly and, with misted eyes, stared ahead at nothing.

"Are you ready for dinner?" Jesse stood in the doorway, and then moved slowly across to Clara. "You look pensive. Are you all right? Lizzie hasn't been bothering you, has she?"

Clara looked up at her son. He was still good looking, even though he was nearing fifty and his hair was more grey than fair. She smiled at him "No. Not at all – Lizzie's been polishing my room for me, ready for the guests." With Jesse's help, Clara stood up from her chair. "Just wait until you see downstairs. Lizzie's done a wonderful job. Joan's delighted with her." Jesse said proudly. "I can't remember the last time I came home to such a gleaming house."

"Probably when we had servants." Clara said. Jesse chuckled. "Well my Lizzie is as good as any servant we ever had. She's a most unusual kid."

"She certainly is." As she passed her waste-paper basket, Clara unclenched her fist and threw in her childhood memory. The daisies dropped soundlessly. Clara took Jesse's arm to steady herself. They were only glass beads, she told herself. Only glass beads.

Lizzie was allowed to have Clover to stay over the night before Christmas Eve. Lizzie wanted Clover to stay because she knew she would be able to curl her hair in rags. Joan didn't know how to and neither did Clara. Clover did. She arrived with setting lotion and ribbons of cloth. "You're my hairdresser," Lizzie told her, "and I want my hair very curly because I'm expecting important guests from America, tomorrow."

"We'll have to shampoo it first," Clover said, "so shall we do it after tea, when we've got ready for bed?" Lizzie sighed, "Hairdressers don't say that," she said impatiently, "they say, I can fit you in at eight o'clock, if that's all right madam."

"Well I don't know what they say," Clover, not realising she was supposed to have been in character, looked crestfallen. "I've never been to the hairdressers."

"I have," Lizzie said, "loads of times." Twice anyway, she thought, and both times to wait for hours while her mother had her hair permed. The hairdresser had let Lizzie pass her the little squares of tissue paper that she wrapped around each strand of Joan's hair and then wound up tightly on blue rubber, bone shaped curlers. Lizzie had swept the floor of cut hair, and arranged fat, round curlers soldier straight on a trolley of plastic trays. And after that she'd became bored.

Clover liked Lizzie's bedroom. The wallpaper was bubble-gum pink matching the satin curtains around the glass topped kidney-shape dressing table, and rose-bud pink was the colour of the carpet. To have a carpet of any colour on your bedroom floor was a luxury Clover could only wish for. She had to make do with a rag rug beside her bed that her granny had made and was not only cold to her early morning bare feet, but painfully knobbly as well.

Both girls were now in their pyjamas. The collar of Lizzie's pyjama jacket was wet from the misaimed jug-fuls of water Clover had tipped over Lizzie's soapy head. It was Lizzie's howls that the water was too hot, too cold, that the shampoo had blinded her, that there was water in her ears which would probably kill her if it got to her brain, that unnerved Clover into tipping the water with such swift uncertainty. She had decided to pretend she'd rinsed out all the shampoo rather than put up with Lizzie's yells, and had draped a towel quickly over Lizzie's head to stop her complaints and to hide the bubbles of soap.

Lizzie shivered. The bathroom was big and cold and it had been bad enough having to kneel on the lino with her head over the snow white, snow cold bath without having icy water dripping down her neck. Back in the relative warmth of the bedroom, she glowered at Clover from under her towel. "Fine hair dresser you make. I'm soaking *and* I'm probably deaf and blind as well." Lizzie looked so comical peeping out from under the towel, fronds of black, water-beaded hair over her eyes and matted to her face that Clover started to laugh. It was nearly Christmas and she was feeling happy enough to be reckless. Fortunately, Lizzie too was excited that tomorrow would be Christmas Eve, and began pulling silly faces in the dressing table mirror, so that by the time Joan arrived with mugs of cocoa and bread and butter for them both, the girls were laughing uncontrollably at nothing in particular. Joan set down the tray and smiled indulgently at them, then picked up the towel from the floor and began to rub vigorously at Lizzie's hair. "Don't you do it," Lizzie said, squirming away. "Clover's got to do it." Joan saw the traces of shampoo on Lizzie's scalp, and felt she really ought to rinse it out, but threw the towel for Clover to catch. Joan too, decided that putting up with Lizzie's shrieks was more than she could be bothered with, besides she was eager to get back to the warmth of the fire down stairs and have a cigarette, and a glass or two of claret with Jesse. "Another hour," she said to the girls, "and then it's lights out, alright?"
"Yes Mrs. Marbal," Clover sipped at the frothy bubbles covering her hot chocolate.
"Right, I'll leave you to it then. Good night both of you."
"Good night Mrs. Marbal."
"Night mum." From the dressing table mirror Lizzie watched Joan leave and close the door. "Come on then, Clover," Lizzie said, picking up her mug. "Do my curls."
Lizzie reluctantly set down her milky sweet drink and picked up the bottle of Curly Tops she had brought with her. She liberally

doused Lizzie's hair, and then tugged through it with a comb. "Ow, that bloody hurts," Lizzie said crossly.

"I've nearly done it now." Clover folded the rags in half and began tightly twisting shanks of Lizzie's hair, from top to bottom and then back up again, ending in a knot at the scalp. Lizzie writhed in her seat, with only the thought of seeing her own perfectly formed curls the next morning stopping her from yelling at Clover to end the agony. Instead, she hissed at her, "Why don't you ask me if I want somethin' to read?" and scowled irritably.

"What?" Clover looked at Lizzie in the mirror. Clover was getting into her stride with the twisting and knotting. Doing the ragging was much better than having it done to you. Tomorrow it would be her turn though. Her mother would rag her hair mercilessly in readiness for church on Christmas morning.

"You're supposed to ask me if I want somethin' to read."

"Am I? Sorry. What would you like to read?"

"Madam. You're supposed to say madam."

"Madam."

"I think I'll read a film annual, please."

Clover went over to Lizzie's bookcase and brought back a book with pictures of Clark Gable and Judy Holliday on the cover. Lizzie took it eagerly. Her discomfort subsided as she flicked over the colourful pages to gaze at the glamorous stars. Mitzi Gaynor, Cyd Charise, Piper Laurie, Pier Angeli. Beautiful, stardust names to be stranded together and breathed out softly like a line of favourite poetry.

Lizzie always found it difficult to sleep when Clover stayed overnight. For one thing, there seemed so much more to say once the light was out. Usually Clover drifted into sleep from sheer exhaustion with Lizzie still chattering away, and it wasn't until Lizzie asked Clover a question and didn't receive so much as a sleepy 'umm' that Lizzie realised she'd been talking to herself. This night was no exception. Lizzie could make out the shadowy form of Clover huddled under blankets on the camp bed. "Are you asleep?" she almost shouted at her. "Because you're blinkin' lucky if you are. I can't sleep. Not even sittin' up like you said to try. I won't be able to sleep all night, not with these hard lumps in my hair. Then what will I look like tomorrow? I'll have bags under my eyes, big black, baggy bags." There was no reply from Clover, other than the deep sigh of a child sleeping. Lizzie punched her pillow and tried to find a part of her head that wasn't quite as tightly knotted as the rest. Eventually she decided the only solution was to take out a couple of rags, just enough to give a comfortable space to lie on. After a while she managed to drop off to sleep, but only until she moved her head, and then the bumpy, tight knots would waken her again. Each time it happened, she pulled out another rag, and so in the morning awoke grumpily with curling rags strewn all around her pillow.

Clover opened her eyes and looked across at Lizzie. Then she peered closer. "Oh Lizzie what have you done?" she wailed. Some of Lizzie's hair stuck out straight at odd angles, some of it dangled limply. All of it looked terrible. Lizzie pushed back her bed covers and plodded over to her dressing table. She gave a little shriek at her reflection. "Oh my God Clover, I look a freak! I went through all that agony to end up lookin' like this." She pulled at her hair in dismay. "What am I goin' to do now?"
"We could wash it again," Clover said leaping out of bed. "And p'rhaps put the rags back in."
"No!" Lizzie roared. "You're not ever touchin' my hair ever again."
"It's not my fault. I ragged it properly. It's your fault it's all messed up, you should have left it alone." Clover said. She'd spent ages over Lizzie's hair and all for nothing. Worse really, Lizzie's hair had looked far better before she'd started on it. Lizzie said nothing. It wasn't often that Clover stood up to her, but when she did it came as a mild surprise, like thinking you were drinking a glass of lemonade until your taste buds told you it was water. She picked up her hairbrush and raked it through her hair a couple of times and then threw down the brush and stomped off to the bathroom. Clover decided her best course of action would be to get off home as soon as possible.

128

By the time Lizzie had got back from last minute food shopping with Joan, her hair had become considerably dampened by drizzling rain. Joan was able to plait it and Lizzie added a couple of plastic Scottie dog hair clips and then stopped moaning that her hair was ruined. After lunch she changed into her best grey Gorray skirt and Fair Isle jumper and proceeded to drive Joan, Clara and even Jesse mad by continually asking what time Aunt Muriel and Uncle Chuck would be arriving. "For the last time, I don't know," Joan snapped.

"Go and read a book or something." Her own excitement at seeing her sister again coupled with a niggling worry that she might have forgotten to buy something important and, as the shops were shut, it was too late now if she had, was enough to cope with. Lizzie turned to her father, who had come home from work early as it was Christmas Eve, and was now trying to mend the tree lights that had suddenly and mysteriously stopped working. "They're not coming, are they?" Lizzie said. "They've decided to stay on in London, haven't they?"

"Course they haven't," Jesse said, methodically twisting bulbs tight in their little sockets. "I expect the traffic is heavier than they thought, that's all. They'll be here – just be patient. Oh sod it, I've broken the bloody thing now." Jesse looked at the pieces of broken, transparent red plastic that had hitherto been flower shaped and puffed out his cheeks with annoyance. The telephone rang and Joan rushed into the hall to answer it. From her laughter and joyful tones Jesse knew she was talking to her sister. "I bet that's your Aunt Muriel she's talking to," Jesse told Lizzie.

"I bet they've phoned to say they're not coming," Lizzie said.

"For goodness sake Lizzie stop saying that. Do you think your mother would be sounding so cheerful if your Aunt Muriel wasn't coming? Course she wouldn't. She's as excited as you are – more probably. It's been a long time since she last saw her sister. Now have a look in that box on the table and see if you can find another one of these plastic things."

Lizzie absently fiddled around in the box of spare fairy light bulbs and bits of wire Jesse had brought in from the shed, but her head was turned towards the door waiting for Joan to come back in the room. When she did, Lizzie said, "That was Aunt Muriel wasn't it?"

"Good guess," Joan said. Lizzie thought she looked a bit serious and her heart sank. She wanted to see her Aunt Muriel so much that she just knew it wouldn't happen. "They're not coming, are they?" she said.

"Lizzie I told you to –" Jesse began, but Joan cut across him and said, "You're right Lizzie. They're not coming" For a moment there was a stunned silence in the room. Lizzie was about to cry and Jesse said, "Oh God, what are they playing at?" And then Joan began to laugh. "I fooled you! They are coming really. They'll be here around six o'clock!" Her voice was shrill with excitement. "You should see your faces!"

"That wasn't funny, Joan," Jesse said but he was smiling. "I'm going to get you for that."

"No it certainly wasn't funny." Lizzie said. "It was really stupid." Her parents weren't listening; they were in one of their occasional playful moods. Joan dashed passed Lizzie, out into the hall, squealing with laughter with Jesse following and calling out, "Just you wait until I catch you."

"Really, really stupid," Lizzie grumbled aloud, giving one of the tree lights a vicious twist. To her surprise all the lights immediately sprang back to life, transforming the dull lustre of the baubles into magical orbs of purple, green, silver and red, and strands of tinsel reflecting their colours glittered and shimmered across the branches.

It was close on seven o'clock when Lizzie heard a car pull up outside the house. She dashed across to the window making Jesse cringe in fear of her running into the Christmas tree. Her safety, and the fairy lights going out again crossed his mind simultaneously. Joan had already flung open the front door, and before long Lizzie who could see very little peering through the window out into the gloom, heard car doors opening and shutting and squeals of delight and footsteps hurrying up the path. "I take it the Yanks have arrived," Clara murmured from her fireside chair.

Lizzie followed her father into the hall and edged in front of him to get her first look at Aunt Muriel. She wasn't disappointed. As Muriel and Joan hugged each other and told each other how wonderful it was to see each other again and laughed and cried, Lizzie scrutinised. Muriel had wonderful film-star blond hair, and lips that were full like Joan's only red and shiny, and she was slimmer than Joan, and taller and wore a fur coat and had a heavy gold charm bracelet that jingled every time she moved her wrist.

All the adults took turns to shake hands and kiss and then Uncle Chuck, who was disappointingly round and bald and who also had a heavy gold chain on his wrist, although without the charms, suddenly caught sight of Lizzie hopping excitedly. "Hi there honey! You must be little Lizzie!" he boomed. "Here, come and give your old uncle a kiss." Lizzie froze. She didn't kiss, and certainly wouldn't kiss a fat bald old man, even if he did come from America. Aunt Muriel saved her. "Oh my God, just look at you!" she said, flinging out her arms to Lizzie.
Lizzie allowed herself to be hugged. The fur coat had fallen open and Lizzie nestled briefly against Muriel's honey beige tube dress that felt wonderfully soft and smelled not of cigarettes but of a perfume, Lizzie later found out, was called Chanel No. 5. "Oh Joan you're so lucky to have such a cute little daughter," Muriel crooned making both Joan and Lizzie beam. "But not so little, eh honey? I bet you've got the longest legs in the class." And then the grown-ups took over again, bringing in suitcases and mysterious parcels, going up to the guest room and down again, being introduced to Clara, and eventually sitting down to dinner. Throughout it all Lizzie was never far away from Muriel, hovering quietly, like a bee around the honey beige tube dress and listening to every word that was said.

Lizzie, who wasn't one for reflecting, did however on Christmas morning, look up from the new Girl Annual she was reading, and smile with contentment. This was turning into the best Christmas ever and she felt something akin to being sorry for Clover who was spending Christmas with her mother and boring granny in her boring council house. Lizzie with her legs curled beneath her, sat on the sofa. Beside her were a few of her favourite presents. The tins of Quality Street and Roses had at last been opened, and earlier Lizzie had mixed them with the other sweets Joan had been hoarding, and had put them into Clara's crystal bon-bon dishes. There were tangerines and figs, dates and nuts and bowls of Cox's apples within reach. The fire that Jesse had arisen early to light, crackled with logs bought specially for Christmas. The air had been full of the scent of pine logs and Christmas tree, until Joan had begun cooking the vegetables. The smell of turkey, Brussels sprouts, and parsnips now pervaded with a whiff of cigar smoke coming from Jesse's study. Tree or sprouts, it didn't matter to Lizzie, they were all Christmas smells but none more so than the cigars. Even when she was grown up and didn't want to think about it, the smell of a cigar would remind her of that Christmas and all the other Christmases she'd had at Marbal House.

By the day after Boxing Day, Clara had decided that she'd had as much as she could take of the Yanks. She was tired of them complaining about the cold and hogging the fire with scarves around their necks. She was tired of hearing them brag about their hot water radiators, refrigerator and dishwasher. Muriel always moved in a cloud of scent that made Clara feel quite nauseous. She was brash with her bottled blond hair and painted talons and worst of all, she was turning Lizzie's head with her talk of New York and the wonderful opportunities a girl like Lizzie could have there. A girl like Lizzie indeed. And as for him – Chuck, well that's what Muriel should do, and the further the better. What man worth his salt wore *pink* for goodness sake? Pink shirts and pale lemon jumpers were colours for the nursery, not for the backs of men. And that dreadful after-shave he wore, not to mention the chunky bracelet. Good lord, it was a wonder he didn't top it all off with a pair of earrings and be done with it. Heaven only knew what Muriel's first husband had been like if she'd left him in preference to Chuck. Chuck was a ponce, that was the only word for it: a vulgar ponce, with apparently, plenty of money and a booming voice, but a ponce nevertheless.

132

That evening, after dinner, the four adults indulged Lizzie in a game of Monopoly while Clara sat by the fire, half listening to them and half drifting off into a catnap. In her dreamlike state, yet still hearing the click of the dice, thuds of objects moved around the board and the exclamations brought by good luck and bad, her imagination transported her back in time. It was another Christmas when her hair was fair and piled on top of her head, and her waist was tiny and her shoes satin and buttoned at the side. And Jesse, perched on cushions sat at the very same table that Lizzie sat at now, only then it was covered in a russet chenille cloth and Jesse was very young, no more than two years old. Albert was trying to play snakes and ladders with him. Jesse was good at shaking the dice although more often than not the dice ended on the floor which made Jesse laugh while Albert scrambled down on his hands and knees to retrieve it. Hester was there, sitting on a footstool next to her and every time the dice fell on to the carpet, Hester took the opportunity to covertly stroke Clara's leg or squeeze her hand. Clara opened her eyes. Hester. She hadn't thought of Hester in years. "Well done, princess," Jesse was saying. "You're the winner."

"We haven't finished the game yet," Lizzie said.

"Oh yes we have," said Joan. "We agreed the winner would be whoever had most property after forty minutes, remember? We'd be playing this game all night otherwise."

They moved to the sofa and chairs, except Chuck who stood with has back to the fire, blocking its heat from everyone else. Not that Clara minded that particularly as she was sat next to it and was, if anything, rather too warm, but she did object to not being able to see the fire; instead she had to look at the side view of Chuck in his pale grey trousers and baby blue jumper. Pants and sweater, that's what he called them- another endorsement to the vulgarity of the Yanks. Jesse took orders for drinks and handed Clara her sweet sherry. Lizzie wedged herself between Muriel and Joan and sipped at the ginger beer Jesse had poured into a wine glass for her. Muriel lifted one of Lizzie's plaits and fingered it for a second. "Have you ever thought of having a perm, Lizzie?" she asked.

133

Jesse laughed. "She's only ten – bit young for a perm."

"But I've always wanted a perm." Lizzie said, although she'd never considered it before. "I'd love to have curls."

"Frizz more like." Joan said. "You're too young Lizzie. A perm would ruin the condition of your hair."

"Oh I don't know," Muriel said, "It might improve it." and then added hastily, "There's some pretty good lotions around these days."

"Back home, anyways," Chuck said, bending his knees slightly and clasping his hands behind his back. Clara tilted back her head and glared at him. What did he know? Although she wouldn't have put it past him to have had a perm himself – back in the days when he had hair to perm. Joan was giggling. "Do you remember that time when you came home with a perm Mo? God, did the old man go berserk."

"Sure I do!" Muriel exclaimed, wide eyed. "Jeez, I thought he was gonna strangle me with his tape measure."

"Why did he have a tape measure?" Lizzie asked.

"He was a tailor honey. He always had a tape measure dangling around his neck He worked from home and there was this big room with a concertina door that folded back into another room where he fitted people for suits and things. And that mirror, Joan – remember that huge mirror we had to polish?" Lizzie began to get bored now that the focus of conversation was no longer on her. Joan and Muriel's reminiscences however, intrigued Jesse. Joan rarely talked about her childhood and it pleased him to hear her laugh and talk about the old days. From the corner of his eye he saw Lizzie yawning. "Bed time, princess," he said. Lizzie didn't argue due to an accumulation of late nights that had made her tired anyway and also because in front of Chuck and Muriel, she was being the ideal child. Muriel had, in Joan's words, taken to her and Lizzie wanted to keep it that way. Muriel would be her ticket to America one day. Lizzie had no idea why or how and had never heard of fate, she just knew. When Lizzie had taken herself off to bed, Muriel and Joan continued to remind each other of their past. "Do you remember the time dad threw a plate of rabbit stew across the room and it just missed poor mother?" Muriel said.

134

"That wasn't very funny though was it?" Joan said.

"No." Muriel said, "Poor mother just stood there shaking".

"Just like a bleedin' rabbit." Joan said. They looked at each other and began to laugh again. The passing of time had made the traumas of yesterday safe enough to laugh about. "Silly sod should've stood up to him," Joan said wiping laughter tears from her eyes. Clara frowned at her. Calling your mother a silly sod was going a bit too far, even by Joan's standards.

"Everyone was scared of the old man," Muriel said,"although I guess he must have been pretty much O.K. with his customers otherwise he wouldn't have had any."

"I've just remembered someone who scared the life out of him." Joan said, slapping her thigh like a panto prince, "that woman who came to be measured for a double breasted suit. You know the one Mo... dad thought she was a man until he took his tape measure to her – then wow, did he get a shock."

"Good heavens," Jesse murmured and Chuck gave such an unexpected boom of laughter that Clara nearly spilled her sherry.

"Oh jeez, yes! She called herself Stevie or Billy or something like that." Muriel smiled. "I guess I was about sixteen then and didn't have a clue. I just thought she was some kind of nut but it's obvious now that she was a lesbian."

"Why? Because she wore a suit?" Clara asked frostily.

"That and her tie and her razor hair cut," Joan said. "Who's ready for another drink?" She held out her glass to Jesse.

"I'll get that," Chuck said, draining his own glass so that he could refill it. "Anyone else? No? How about you Clara?"

"Not for me," Clara thought how impolite and pushy it was of Chuck to take over Jesse's role of host, but at least he had moved away from the fire. "Not all lesbians wear suits, you know," she said, the thought of Hester very strong in her mind.

"Oh granted Clara, but I'm not that naive anymore. These days I can tell a dyke a mile off." Muriel said.

"Really?"

"Yep."

"How?

"Good lord, mother," Jesse said, as he cracked open a walnut shell, "Why do you want to know that? I'm surprised you know about lesbians at all to be honest."

Chuck gave another of his hearty laughs. "Wasn't it your Queen Victoria who refused to believe in lesbianism?" He smiled indulgently at Clara, "She just wouldn't believe that women could do – you know, that sort of thing" Chuck handed Joan her glass and sat down next to Muriel, pleased that he'd read that tit-bit of information somewhere.

"That's right," Jesse said, "so there was no law passed against it because apparently Queen Victoria thought it didn't exist."

"I didn't know that." Clara said "But I do know something about lesbians." Joan turned to Muriel to begin another conversation. They're not interested Clara thought dryly. They think I'm just a boring bag of old bones. Little they know. Again she felt Hester's presence and because of it and because she suddenly wanted to shock them all she said, "I know - because I once had an affair with a woman."

The room became instantly quiet. Clara wished her eye- sight was clear enough to see the expressions of the three wise monkeys on the sofa. They were looking directly at her, and she could only imagine their fleshy lips parted, their mouths open with horror. Jesse broke the silence first. He cleared his throat and said, "I think I will have a drink, after all."

"Perhaps you would help me upstairs first Jesse." Clara said, pleased with herself for having managed to shut up the Yanks at last. "I'm feeling rather tired so if you will excuse me, I'll go up to bed now."

"No, don't go," Joan said. After the initial shock of Clara's revelation she was extremely intrigued. "You can't go now Clara, we want to know more."

"Well I'm damned if I do," Jesse said in a flat voice. "I've heard more than enough." He stood up, handed Clara her walking stick and helped her out of her chair. Chuck heaved himself to his feet and wished her goodnight.

Muriel and Joan said night-night in unison and then Clara heard Joan add, "Bloody hell, a skeleton in the Marbal cupboard – who would've thought it?"

Jesse, who had heard it too, thought grimly that his mother's skeleton wasn't the only one in the cupboard. He held Clara's arm firmly as he guided her up the stairs. "You're angry with me, aren't you Jesse?" she said.

"I'm shocked more than angry." Jesse replied. "Whatever possessed you to admit such a thing?"

"I had an urge to be honest."

"You could've chosen a private moment. There was no need to come out with it in front of Joan's family like that."

"I know. It was naughty of me. All right, I admit it, I wanted to shock them."

"But what you said was true?"

"Oh yes." They had reached the landing. "Hester she was called. Poor Hester, I wonder what became of her."

"Hester," Jesse repeated.

"Hester Pinner, the doctor's wife. You wouldn't remember her Jesse, you were far too young."

As Clara opened her bedroom door the stick she was carrying slipped between her fingers. Jesse bent down to retrieve it. As he straightened up, Clara leaned across and kissed his cheek.

"You've been a good son to me Jesse," she patted his arm, "better than I deserve. I'm sorry if I've upset you."

"It's a bit of a shock. I'll get over it."

"Of course you will. I did."

Jesse switched on the bedroom light. "Good night then mother."

"Good night, my dear."

He closed the door behind her and began his way downstairs. Under the stained glass window he stopped and sat on the step, something he hadn't done since he was a boy. There was music coming from the sitting room, Perry Como singing Magic Moments. Jesse could hear Joan and Muriel singing along to the gramophone record. And then he remembered. There had been a different kind of music and laughter. And his mother was kissing someone – the Hester woman, right there in the hall beneath the light. He remembered how jealous he felt and that he'd started to cry. He was missing his father and he desperately wanted his mother to kiss him and not her, not the Hester woman. Jesse stood up. Tonight his mother *had* kissed him and called him my dear. He smiled wryly to himself and continued on down the stairs. He'd waited nearly fifty years for that dry peck on the cheek.

"They had a brilliant party on New Year's Eve. Loads of people came and Aunt Muriel looked gorgeous."
"I know. You've told me." Clover and Lizzie were in Lizzie's bedroom. Lizzie was sprawled on her bed, surrounded by mementos she'd filched from the guest room the day Muriel and Chuck left; a Christmas issue of Harper's Bazaar, a couple of nearly empty bottles of Revlon nail varnish and a pair of Fosta-Grantly sun glasses with diamante frames and a cracked lens. Lizzie unzipped the red leather vanity case Muriel had given her at Christmas and once again sorted its contents of Li'l Angel talc, cologne and bath cubes. "They've got passion pits, in America," she told Clover. "They're called drive-in movies really. They're outside in a big car-park place with a huge screen and you watch the film from your car."
"What happens when it's raining?" Clover said.
Lizzie shrugged. "I dunno, I never asked. P'rhaps it doesn't rain in America."
"Course it rains in America," Clover said, looking out of the window. "It rains everywhere – unless it's a desert."
"I know. I was joking." Lizzie added Muriel's cast offs to her vanity case and sighed. "They've got oodles of money."
"What does he do then, your Uncle Chuck?"
"Grandma says he's in the rag trade."
Clover immediately thought of the hard mat beside her bed and the Saturday night ribbons her hair was twisted in. "Rags? How can there be money in rags?" she asked, incredulous.
"That's just Grandma. Aunt Muriel says they've got three booties and they'll probably open another one soon." Clover wrinkled her nose "Three booties?"

"Yes, Grandma says it's French for small shop, but I expect Aunt Muriel's are really big."

"It's stopped raining now Lizzie. Are we going for that walk or what?"

Lizzie in her Wellington boots trudged dreamily along the canal bank. Clover found an old crisp packet in her raincoat pocket and emptied salty crumb into the water. A moorhen swam across to her and then swam back again. "Aunt Muriel said," Lizzie began. Clover glared at her. *"Lizzie."*

"What?"

"Shut up!"

Lemonade to water. "That she's seen Elvis Presley – twice."

Chapter 8

It came as no surprise to anyone although a secret disappointment to Jesse, when the following year Lizzie failed the eleven-plus and Clover passed. Lizzie was happy enough with her new, green school blazer that had an inside pocket with a silver coloured metal zip, and her new, hard leather satchel, and wooden pencil box containing a rubber, a pencil, and a blue and grey marbled fountain pen. She was content to learn how to make suet puddings and boil hankies while Clover had new subjects to master, like French and geometry. Lizzie was saved the bother of homework; what little she was given she either did hurriedly in the morning before she left for school, or promised her teacher she would hand it in the next day. Nobody seemed to mind very much whether she fulfilled her promise or not. The important issues at Lizzie's secondary modern were to walk on the left hand side of everything and to stand up when an adult entered the classroom. You could do pretty much what you liked when you sat back down again. Clover on the other hand, worked hard at school and did homework most evenings. However, in spite of attending different schools, Clover and Lizzie continued to be friends and met up at weekends. Lizzie soon made it a golden rule that neither of them should talk about their school life when they were together. Lizzie had discovered that Clover became impassioned with certain subjects, subjects that Lizzie found incredibly boring, and so when Clover discovered Shakespeare, Lizzie imposed the ban.

When Lizzie was fourteen, Clara who was now eighty, became so frail she was practically bedridden. Joan, who found Lizzie's teenage mood swings and untidiness wearing enough, constantly moaned about the extra burden Clara put upon her. "It's no good Jess, I just can't cope," she said one Saturday morning as she shoved Clara's wet sheets and nightdress into the washing machine. "I'm not cut out for this nursing lark. I've lost count of the times I've been up and down those stairs to your mother today, and this is the second lot of sheets she's peed on."

140

Jesse patted Joan's shoulder sympathetically. "Would you like a cup of tea?" he asked. Joan threw washing powder on top of the sheets and slammed down the lid of the washing machine. "What I want is a blinkin' holiday, not a cup of tea. This house is so *big*. A nice new bungalow would be easier to manage and it would be a lot cheaper to run."

"We've been through this before Joan. You know I can't sell Marbal House while mother is alive." Jesse said. "I wouldn't want to anyway. This is my home – nowhere else would feel right." He switched on the kettle, knowing that if he made a pot of tea, Joan would drink a cup of it.

"It's easy for you to say you don't want to live anywhere else, when *you* don't have to do the cleaning. Just like you to refuse to consider putting Clara into a nursing home when you're not the one who has to look after her." Joan lit a cigarette and waved it towards Lizzie who sat at the kitchen table writing out the weekend shopping list. "Put Zal disinfectant down. Get the pine one."

Lizzie sighed. "I've only got two arms y'know. I'm not a blinkin' octopus. How am I s'posed to carry all this lot back from town?" Jesse and Joan ignored her, both knowing Clover would be carrying more than her fair share of the shopping back up the hill. Joan took the cup Jesse offered her and sat down heavily at the table. "I mean it, Jess. I feel worn out. Even if I had more time for myself, I wouldn't have the energy to do anything with it." Jesse stirred his tea and wondered what he could do to make life easier for Joan. She certainly looked tired. The skin around her eyes was a bruised, yellow colour. Her hair was lank and showed grey at the roots. "I could take a couple of hours off next week for you to go to the hairdressers," he suggested, "if you'd like to."

"What if Clara needed to be taken to the bathroom? No it's not practical. I have to be here – on call, like the blinkin' nurse I'm not."

"No, you're not much good at nursing really." Lizzie scraped back her chair and stood up. "You're too heavy handed and whenever I've been sick you've started honking as well. That's off puttin' to a patient, that is."

141

"You're not being very helpful, Lizzie," Jesse murmured. "Your poor mother is doing her best."

"So am I," Lizzie said, "I've got all this shopping to do, when I should be sittin' in a café drinking expresso's and listenin' to the juke box like other girls of my age. And you'd better give me five pounds for this lot 'cos there's loads." Joan took the money from her purse and handed it over. "Bring back the change. I think you've over-estimated by a couple of pounds at least." She nodded towards the shopping list.

"Did I ask you to write down jellies? We need jellies. It's about the only thing Clara will eat."

"Yes, you said jellies. Poor Grandma, she needs a proper nurse." Lizzie said gravely. Joan wasn't sure whether Lizzie was deliberately trying to goad her, or was just being insensitive. It was always hard to tell with Lizzie. Either way, the remark niggled her. "I *know* she needs a proper nurse," she replied irritably. "Tell me something I *don't* bleedin' know."

"Well if you *know*," Lizzie mimicked as she flounced out of the room, "why don't you bleedin' well get one?"

"Don't you talk to me like that," Joan snapped in the direction of Lizzie's departed figure. "Bloody kid." She looked across at Jesse for backup. "You should say something to her. If I'd spoken like that in front of my dad he'd have-"

"Times change." Jesse said placidly. "And I don't suppose you'd have taken offence if you weren't feeling so tired – besides Lizzie's right. She's come up with the answer. We'll hire a live-in nurse. Why didn't *we* think of that?"

"I did," Joan said, "but I didn't think you could afford it."

"Shouldn't cost that much." Jesse said. I'll pick up a copy of The Lady on my way back to the studio, and we'll place an advertisement."

Joan was disappointed with the response she received from her carefully worded advertisement. She had anticipated a plethora of applicants but in fact there were only four who seemed remotely suitable. She carefully arranged for them to be interviewed on the same day so that she could make a decision without further delay.

142

The ten o'clock appointment arrived an hour late and had a high pitched irritating laugh that made even Clara in her bed open her eyes and wince. The twelve o'clock appointment looked almost as frail as her intended patient and was completely breathless by the time she'd reached the top of the stairs. When the doorbell rang to herald the arrival of the two o'clock appointment, Joan sent Lizzie to answer the door. "This should be Nurse Morris. Show her into the study Lizzie while I finish my cigarette. If she's as old as the last one, tell her she's too late - and she can take that how she likes."

Lizzie opened the door and gazed impassively at the third applicant, a woman wearing a navy blue, belted raincoat. She looked old in Lizzie's eyes, but not as old as the last one. "Hello, I'm Nurse Morris. I've got an appointment with Mrs. Marbal. Your mother would that be? She smiled at Lizzie. Lizzie nodded and opened the door wider. Nurse Morris stepped into the hallway and looked around her.

"She won't be long. You can wait for her in the study." Lizzie said. Nurse Morris turned to the right and stood outside the study door, waiting with a smile for Lizzie to open it.

"How did you know which room was the study?" Lizzie asked and chewed on a strand of her hair.

"I know lots of things," Nurse Morris said mysteriously. "I know for instance that your name is Elizabeth and your dad's name is Jesse." She put out her hand and gently eased the strand of hair from Lizzie's mouth. "That's a bad habit," she murmured. "Worse than biting your nails." Lizzie frowned at her. "Actually my name's Lizzie. No-one ever calls me Elizabeth." She opened the study door. Nurse Morris followed her in.

"Someone did," Nurse Morris said. "Someone always called you Elizabeth." And then she suddenly laughed at Lizzie's puzzled look. "I'm sorry Lizzie, I shouldn't tease you. I'm an old friend of the family, you see – that's why I know so much. Go and tell Joan. Tell her Violet's here."

Lizzie trotted down the kitchen steps. "What's this one like?" Joan asked, stubbing out her cigarette. "She's weird," Lizzie wrinkled her nose to emphasize how weird. "Anyway you know her – she said her name was Violet."

"Violet? There's only one Violet I –" Joan began, and then slowly rose to her feet. "What else did she say to you?" Joan kept her head down, addressing the ashtray on the table and not Lizzie in case Lizzie should detect the panic she felt. Violet Parker. She must have married, but why hadn't she said who she really was in her application letter? What was she playing at? God, if Violet told Lizzie the truth it would destroy her, and Jess. Lizzie was shrugging. "She didn't say anything much. Who is she, anyway?"

"She used to work for Grandma," Joan said, while inside her head a voice was screaming, who is she? Your natural mother, that's who. Lizzie sighed, suddenly bored. "I wish I'd saved my pocket money. I could've gone to the pictures this afternoon and seen that new James Bond film."

"Yes that's a good idea," Joan said quickly. She took her purse from the worktop. Better that Lizzie should be out of the way until she got rid of Violet. "Here, I'll pay for you and Clover to go."

"Are you sure?" Lizzie eyed Joan with suspicion. Joan wasn't usually generous. In fact she was usually very stingy about giving Lizzie money once she'd spent her weekly allowance. But Joan was smiling and nodding. "Course I'm sure. You haven't done much this half term except help me out. Go on – if you hurry you'll make the matinee." She patted Lizzie's arm, and kissed her cheek, then hurried up the steps into the hall and across to the study. "Bloody hell," Lizzie muttered looking down at the money Joan had pushed into her hand. Then she fetched her jacket and hurried off to Clover's house.

Violet was standing in front of Jesse's desk when Joan rushed into the study. She turned and smiled at Joan, her hand outstretched. "Hello Joan. It's been a long time since I last saw you." Joan ignored the offered hand. "What the hell are you doing here Violet?" she snapped. Violet looked annoyed at being slighted and clasped her hands tightly together. "We've got an appointment," she said with defiance. "I'd decided to come back home – back to my roots so when I saw you needed someone to nurse Mrs. Marbal, I thought well, who better than me? After all I grew up in this house. I'm practically family. I'm sure Mrs. Marbal would prefer to be looked after by me than by a complete stranger."

Joan shook her head hardly able to believe Violet's audacity. "My God, Violet you've changed since you put on a nurses uniform. Given you confidence has it? Well I suppose if anyone needed it you did - but you have no right coming here. You know full well that you were never to come to this house again. And as for expecting to be allowed to live under the same roof as Lizzie, well it's just preposterous – ."

"Why?" Violet asked innocently. "I've got very good references and I'm a fully qualified S.E.N. with geriatric experience, as I said in my letter."

"You didn't sign yourself as Violet Parker though, did you? No – because you knew full well Jess and I would never allow you to come into contact with Lizzie."

"But I'm not Violet Parker anymore. I'm Violet Morris – Mrs. Morris. You're afraid I might say something, aren't you? Tell Lizzie who I really am? Well let's face it Joan if I wanted to do that, I could easily enough. I could hang around outside her school, write her a letter, phone her," Violet shrugged. "You couldn't stop me if that's what I wanted. But I don't. Of course I've often thought about Elizabeth and I would like to get to know her a bit, but – well I gave her away a long time ago didn't I? Like I said, I've decided to come back to my roots and I've no intention of leaving. I'm afraid you'll just have to trust me Joan." Joan folded her arms and looked intently at Violet, hoping to gauge from her expression some hint of what was going on in her mind. Joan saw a round, placid looking face, the face of the Violet she remembered, only older of course, and there was something different about her eyes and her mouth. The softness had disappeared; the innocent rather vacant expression had been replaced with a harder, self-assured look.

"What I need is a live-in job for a few months, until I find a place of my own, just what you're offering, really. And I'd like to look after Mrs. Marbal again, especially with her health failing. I don't see why that should be a problem. So perhaps you and Jesse would think about it. I'm sure you'll come to realise it would be for the best." Violet smiled but there was a purposeful look in her eyes and Joan thought she detected the implication of a threat in her tone.

"I think you'd better leave now," she said. She suddenly felt confused and drained and wished Jess was with her.

"I'd like to see Mrs. Marbal first, if you don't mind." Violet said. "You *don't* mind do you Joan?

Joan sighed. "I suppose there'd be no harm in it. But I don't trust you Violet. I have to say I'm not happy about any of this."

"You have to trust me," Violet said. "You look really tired Joan. You need a rest and I'm here to help you out. We'll be helping each other out won't we? A mutual arrangement just like we did – before." Joan didn't answer. She opened the study door and led the way upstairs. "If you're married, where's your husband?" she said, over her shoulder to Violet.

"I don't know and I don't care. We're divorced, and before you ask, no, we didn't have children. He was in the navy." Violet added, as a final piece of information . She followed Joan into Clara's bedroom and stood beside the bed and held Clara's hand.

"You've got a visitor," Joan said, in a loud expressionless voice. Clara opened her eyes and looked at Joan and then at Violet. After a moment she said," I know you don't I?" Violet nodded. "It's me, Violet. I used to look after you and Jesse a long time ago." She smiled at Clara. "I expect I've changed a good bit since then."

"You're Millie's girl." Clara said. "How is Millie?"

"Fancy her remembering that," Joan muttered. "Millie died fifteen years ago, Clara," she added in the loud voice she used to ensure Clara could hear her.

"Oh dear I am sorry." Clara slipped her hand out from under Violet's and patted her on the arm. "So you've come back to look after me, have you? I didn't like the other ones very much."

"Would you like me to take care of you?" Violet asked artfully.

"That would be very nice dear," Clara said closing her eyes. "Good servants are so difficult to get these days." Joan smiled in spite of herself and Violet stood up very straight but said nothing.

146

"So what do we do, Jess?" Joan flopped back in her armchair and took the glass Jesse handed her. She had waited until after dinner, when Lizzie and Clover were listening to records in Lizzie's bedroom, before telling Jesse of Violet's arrival and relating to him all she could remember of their conversation. After the initial surprise, Jesse was quiet and then became almost phlegmatic. "There's isn't anything we can do about her coming back. We can't stop her from returning to her hometown. We have to trust her not to say anything – that's the only thing we *can* do. There's no point in getting uptight about it. I'm sure she'll keep quiet, after all she's got no proof that she's -" he hesitated, not wanting to use the phrase Lizzie's mother "- anything to do with Lizzie, has she? And why come back as respectable Nurse Morris just to cause a scandal?"

"That's just it, I don't trust her," Joan said. "Why *has* she come back?"

"Curiosity I expect," Jesse said. "She wants to see how Lizzie turned out." He looked down into his glass of blood red Beaujolais, swilling it round before taking a large gulp. "And the fourth applicant – what was she like?"

"She phoned to cancel".

"So Violet is our only option then."

Joan frowned. "You're not seriously suggesting we allow her back into the household, are you?"

"Well yes, I am," Jesse said. "I can't imagine she would be vindictive enough to tell Lizzie the truth, not after all this time. And if that's her intent, he thought, I'd sooner she did it here, that hang around outside Lizzie's school or some other location. "And let's face it, you need help Joan before your own health suffers."

Joan sank back into the cushion and closed her eyes. "On your own head be it then," she said. Some wickedness within her was thinking that it wouldn't hurt Violet to see that being a parent wasn't all joy. Jesse finished his drink. Some wickedness within him was thinking that it would be interesting to see Violet again, to have her around the house. "I'll have speak to Violet before we make a final decision," he said. "I'll let her know that if she so much as hints at anything to Lizzie I'll –"

"Kill her," Joan said firmly. And so it was that Agnes' grandmother was reinstated at Marbal House.

Chapter 9

Violet wore her hair in a beehive style, back-brushed for volume and held in place by copious hairgrips and a liberal dose of hair lacquer. She accentuated her eyes with black mascara and with eyeliner drawn like tadpole tails across her eyelids. She used pale glistening lipsticks that made her lips look as if she had just passed her tongue across them. Jesse had stipulated from the onset that she should not wear her uniform but informal clothing when she took care of Clara. Violet obliged and wore full skirts with a wide black patent belt and tight, tucked in sweaters. Lizzie thought she looked like Elsie Tanner from Coronation Street, mutton dressed as lamb, as her grandmother used to say. Joan thought that Violet hadn't looked so tarty when she'd turned up for the interview. Jesse thought she looked seductive - and wished he didn't. He calculated that Violet was forty-three or four and silently wondered that she could look more attractive now than in her twenties.

Violet thought that Joan had aged considerable in the past fourteen years. Her complexion was sallow and her top lip was permanently crimped from constant smoking. Her eyelids had begun to sag and judging from the shapelessness of her, so had pretty much everything else. With her morning cough and her evening drinks, Violet suspected that Joan's lungs and liver were not as healthy as they should be. Violet thought Jesse's grey temples heightened his distinguished look. She thought his mouth was still the most attractive she'd ever seen – off screen. He still walked with a straight-backed, purposeful stride that accentuated his height of six feet plus. There were lines around his eyes, as thin as pencil strokes that Violet found endearing. They softened his expression, and in unguarded moments made him look vulnerable. She would have liked to trace the pencil strokes with her finger tips, eased away his stress. She was sure he was stressed. She was sure her presence stressed him. And as for Elizabeth...Elizabeth, the tiny, fretful baby she had given away was gone without trace, metamorphosed into Lizzie, a gangly

149

teenager with a spotty forehead and a surly look that did nothing to enhance her unremarkable features. Violet was disappointed.

Violet had nurtured a romantic notion that there would have been an instant bond between herself and her daughter; or at least pleasure at being in each other's company, or at very least an exchange of gentle smiles that in time would have led to more. As it was, Lizzie treated her with the same disdain that she seemed to treat everyone. There was no getting through to her. Even given the fact that Lizzie was at an awkward stage of puberty, Violet concluded there was something odd about her – several odd things about her in fact. When she thought Lizzie was just downright self-centred she did something unselfish, like sit with Clara to give Violet a break. When she thought Lizzie was unbearably untidy, she surprised her by giving the house a thorough clean and polish. She shopped for Joan and sometimes washed the dishes and did the ironing and whenever she did these tasks she did them scrupulously, examining front and back of cutlery and crockery as she pulled them out of hot soapy water, and dried them until they were polished; and yet she would butter bread with a dropped knife without bothering to wash it first. She took remarkable care over the ironing, aligning hems with precision before pressing out every crease. She would weave the tip of the iron between buttons, sprinkle water over starched collars and cuffs before flattening away every little wrinkle and yet she could wear a grubby and creased blouse with apparent disregard of its condition. Lizzie was an anomaly. She didn't add up.

This then was the child Violet had wept for, pondered and wondered about, and even when she was expecting another baby, could not even for a day, forget. Had she not cruelly miscarried at fourteen weeks, perhaps the memory of Elizabeth would have dimmed with the second baby's birth. She blamed her husband Frank for the miscarriage. If he hadn't been away at sea she would have been saved from shovelling the snow that blocked her from the garage doors. The miscarriage was more

150

painful than Elizabeth's birth and again Violet had no husband present to help her through her ordeal. Frank was never there when she needed him. In the end she stopped needing him. She'd never loved him, not really. Not the way she loved Jesse.

Of course Elizabeth had been Violet's reason for returning. Once she was divorced from Frank, the urge to return to Cornwall and the small market town that she had been desperate to leave grew stronger. It was by chance that Violet had glanced through a copy of The Lady, left on the coffee table in the staff room where she worked. When she saw the advertisement Joan had placed and read the familiar name of Marbal, Violet felt her pulses race, her heart thump. This was a gift from the gods, this was a sign that she was meant to go back where she belonged. And it had been so easy to get back into Marbal House. They were afraid, Jesse and Joan, afraid of what she might say to Lizzie. There was no need. Not yet. One day, of course, Lizzie would have to be told the truth. But not yet. Violet would do nothing to alienate herself from Jesse. He wanted her, she knew that and Violet who had worshipped him all her life was prepared to wait a few more years. Then he would be hers and she would wear a ring that didn't turn green and didn't cost seven shillings and six pence from Woolworth. She could wait, just a few more years.

It was a hot June the year Violet came back. There was no breeze from the air that came into the bedroom windows at night. Cotton sheets were soon body heat warm, bed covers could be, and nightclothes were, dispensed with. One night after some noise had awoken him Jesse found it impossible to get back to sleep. His pillow felt lumpy and damp with perspiration. On his side of the bed, the sheet had loosened from the mattress and formed into crumpled ridges. Beside him Joan lay with her arms above her head her legs spread-eagled, her mouth open emitting short, rasping snores. Jesse gave up trying to sleep, got out of bed and pulled on his pyjama trousers and dressing gown. He went downstairs to the kitchen and splashed his face with cold water at the kitchen sink. He poured himself a glass of water and sat down at the kitchen table. He picked up a packet of Joan's cigarettes turning it and tapping it against the table-top. He half wished he smoked cigarettes. It would be good to light up one now, throw back his head and inhale deeply. He put down the packet and lifted his glass of water. The kitchen door had opened. Violet walked in, carrying a glass jug. "I've come to get some ice for Mrs. Marbal," she said calmly. "I take it you couldn't sleep either."

"No." Jesse watched her as she moved across to the fridge. She wore a long, cotton housecoat that under the light was almost transparent. When she opened wide the fridge door, the light from it accentuated the outline of her breasts and the large dark circles of her nipples. As she turned to face him his eyes wandered from the ice cube tray she held aloft, to another dark region beneath her housecoat that he remembered well.

"It is *hot*, isn't it?" Violet lifted the hair from the back of her neck and then let it fall again slowly. She'd seen these languid movements in loads of films and always thought how seductive they looked. She hoped Jesse thought so too. "Would you like some ice in that, Jesse?" She nodded towards his glass and then moved over to the sink and turned on the cold tap to loosen the ice cubes. "Yes, alright." Jesse pushed his glass across the bleached wood table towards her. "How's my mother?"

The situation he found himself in, alone in the middle of the night with the woman he had impregnated nearly sixteen years ago, seemed bizarre. She'd been in exile all of that time and now here they were practically naked and alone together. They were bonded by a deep secret, a secret that he could not allude to. He could not ask her what she thought of Lizzie, or how she had coped over the years, or why her marriage had gone wrong. These and others were questions that he wanted to know the answers to, yet to ask her would be too familiar and might precipitate him knowing more than would be good for either of them. Violet's housecoat, the palest blue, he saw now as she stood opposite him and slipped ice from the tray into his drink, had no buttons. It was wrapped across her held in place by a belt of a deeper shade of blue. A thin belt that wasn't doing its job

152

properly.   The housecoat gaped under the forward thrust of Violet's bosom. She has the deepest, darkest cleavage I've ever seen, Jesse thought, as the ice cubes chinked and tinkled against his glass. Violet was telling him that his mother wasn't too good. The heat, she said, was making Mrs. Marbal restless. Then Violet picked up his glass, took a sip, and walked round the table to stand before him. He took the glass with one hand, and touched the rounded lapel of her housecoat with the other. Her nipples, he noticed, hardened as soon as the palm of his hand made contact with the exposed soft swell of her breast. "Violet," he said, putting down his glass and standing in front of her, "you're coming adrift."

"So I am," she replied without looking down. She put her arms around Jesse's neck and pushed herself against him. She pulled his head down towards her and kissed his lips, impatient for them to part so that she could flick her tongue in and out of his mouth.

Jesse fervently reciprocated, pushing his tongue into her mouth while his hands squeezed and kneaded her buttocks. She groaned softly, because she felt this was the right time to let the pent up noises of desire escape from her lips, and moved her hands down from Jesse's neck to the belt around her waist. As she began to loosen the slipknot, Jesse covered her hands with his.   "No," he said, taking one last look before pulling her housecoat back into place. "You bewitch me, Violet – but no." Her eyes had become soft, doe-like, the way he remembered them. "We both know, don't we, that this isn't –"

"The time or the place?" She smiled at him. He smiled back. "Something like that."

"You'd like to though, wouldn't you?"

"Yes I'd like to," Jesse answered truthfully. Oh how he would like to. He would like to take pleasure from her body the way he had before, only now he wasn't quite as selfish. He briefly stroked her cheek then picked up his glass of water from the table and walked away from her, away from temptation.   Violet, still smiling, watched him leave. She knew it. He wanted her. He had always wanted her. She tipped the ice cubes into the jug of water, watching them bounce and settle on the surface. Time didn't matter; the passion between them was still there. She took the

153

jug up to Clara's room. Strange that the last time she and Jesse became close, it was, like now, under the shadow of death. And there would be yet another death, she thought serenely. Only with Joan's death, all would be resolved.

Violet pressed a cold flannel against Clara's hot temple. "Then," she said softly, "with poor Joan gone, Jesse and I can reach our climax, so to speak." Clara's eyelids fluttered under the flannel. "All will be resolved," Violet murmured. Had she known Macbeth, she may have considered that her thoughts held the same prophetic ring as the three witches. And she would have been right.

Jesse undressed and gently pulled his side of the sheet taut before climbing back into bed. Joan, whom he supposed to be sleeping, surprised him by turning her head towards him. "You've been downstairs with Violet, haven't you?" she said. "I heard her follow you."

"I went down for a glass of water. Violet came down for ice. Pure coincidence. What's the matter Joan?" He laughed lightly although his pulse was still racing from what he could have experienced and had turned down. " Don't you trust me?"

"I don't trust her, Violet. What was she wearing?"

"What was she wearing? " He laughed again. "Strange question, but not a lot."

"I bet she wasn't." Jesse turned on his side to face her. Even from just the moonlight shining wispy pale through the window he could see her expression was anxious. " I wasn't wearing much either, come to that. Who is, on nights like this? If you were so suspicious, why didn't you come downstairs and see for yourself what we were doing?" He sounded casual while thinking it was a bloody good thing she hadn't witnessed him peering inside Violet's housecoat or being on the receiving end of her passionate kisses.

"Actually, I was just about to - then I heard you coming back upstairs." Joan said.

Thank God for will power, Jesse thought dryly, or conscience or whatever else it was that made me leave when I did. "You don't

154

have to worry Joan. Trust me." He traced his fingers down across her stomach, towards her opened legs. "What exactly was she wearing?" Joan said.

"Some sort of dressing gown thing that came down to her ankles. I didn't take much notice," he added, lying because he knew he had to. It was ice blue, cool and light to touch. So different from the quaint, lace trimmed floral number she used to wear. Jesse smiled. In the past, all of it was history. He turned his full attention towards his wife. "Now that we're both wide awake do you feel like - a session?" He felt her quiver beneath his touch and knew that an answer wasn't necessary. Soon the creaking of the bed synchronised with the flop, plop sound of their stomachs making rhythmic contact. Jesse's taught muscles bounced off Joan's flabbier abdomen. A film of slippery sweat coated both their bodies. Joan freed her leg and wrapped them around Jesse's, their signal that she wanted him to turn over so that she could be on top. He had been rampant before he reached her, she knew that, and she wanted to finish the job she suspected Violet had started, and finish it in a way Jesse would not forget in a hurry.

When their last ecstatic tremors had passed, Joan slid hot and exhausted from Jesse, and lay in a heap beside him. He stroked her hair, wet with perspiration and told her how much he loved her. She believed him. She also knew that he lusted after Violet's body. But he had resisted her tonight, and thank God he had. Violet was a viper; she needed to be watched closely. "The next time you want a glass of water in the night," she said to Jesse, "tell me and I'll get it." Jesse stopped stroking her hair. "What made you say that?" he asked.

"I don't want you to be alone with Violet."

"You're worrying over nothing," he said. " But I don't mind waking you up to fetch me a glass of water – particularly if it ends up the way it did tonight" He turned onto his side, away from her, facing the window, the way he always slept. " It was bloody wonderful – *you're* bloody wonderful."

155

There's life in the old dog yet, Joan thought wryly. Jesse was already slipping into sleep and suddenly a feeling of sadness and loneliness came over her. She shouldn't have felt the need to prove anything to Jess, least of all how good she could be in bed – not after all the years they'd been together. Everything always came back to Violet.

She'd taken Violet's child and would be haunted because of it for the rest of her life. After having sex, Joan usually felt a soporific euphoria and floated on it into sleep, but not tonight. She was hot and sticky and had an empty feeling inside her. She felt tears prickle beneath her eyelids. A strong urge to be with her own flesh and blood overcame her and out of nowhere she heard her voice cry reedy and wavering, "I want my sister." And then the tears began to trickle down her cheeks, so heavily she had to gulp to hold them back. Jesse opened his eyes and twisted round to face her. "Hey, what on earth's the matter? This isn't like you Joan." He put his arm around her and pulled her close to him. "I want to see my sister again," Joan sniffed. "She's all I've got."

"No she isn't – you've got me and Lizzie."

"But I want Muriel."

Jesse was silent. He couldn't possibly afford to go to America – not until after his mother had died. It seemed mercenary while his mother was still alive to start making plans for spending whatever inheritance he had coming to him but he'd never seen Joan this upset before and wanted to console her, whatever it took. There would surely be enough money coming his way to finance the trip and if that was what Joan wanted, then so be. "Alright," he said. "When - when we've got through this, we'll go to America. You, Lizzie and I. We'll go and visit your sister."

Joan stopped crying. She felt like a spoilt child now. She'd cried and got something she wanted. She couldn't remember that ever happening before. Now she felt rather silly, yet this was laced with another emotion that she hadn't felt for a long time – a fluttering of excitement. "Are you sure, Jess?" she whispered.

"If it's what you want – and if it means I can get some sleep." His light-hearted tone belied the tiredness he felt. In a few hours he'd have to drag himself out of bed and go to work. He felt relief as

Joan's body began to relax, her back against his chest, her legs drawn up with his legs nestling behind them. He wondered what had made her so emotional. Hormones probably. Women were unpredictable creatures. His heavy eyelids closed and before long he was dreaming of Joan. Joan with brown eyes and with a cleavage so vast and velvety that a man could bury his head in it and suffocate.

By the end of the month Clara was dead. Violet left Marbal House shortly after the funeral. She began a new job on the geriatric ward at St. Luke's hospital. From her divorce settlement, she had enough money to put a deposit down on a small bungalow. Joan was dismayed. She had hoped, although she realised it was a foolish hope, that Violet would go away again. Now it was clear she was back for good. But there was the excitement of the visit to New York, and by the end of the summer Jesse had kept his promise. His inheritance amounted disappointingly to the contents of Marbal House and five hundred pounds in premium bonds. Clara had long since sold the properties Albert had left her and had happily spent the money over the years on holidays and whatever else took her fancy. She had left her remaining two thousand pounds to Lizzie. Jesse sold Clara's jewellery, apart from the emerald earrings, to finance the America trip and to pay off his overdraft. Clover had once told Jesse the story of the emerald earrings and he decided that he would keep them for Lizzie. His princess should have them on her twenty- first birthday.

New York was larger, brasher and more cosmopolitan than Lizzie had imagined. It was not the America of her dreams, it was even better. Everything enthralled her from the yellow cabs to the towering glass and metal skyscrapers. And she swore she'd seen Gregory Peck in a burger bar just off Third Avenue. She let her Aunt Muriel know in no uncertain terms that this was only her first visit - she would be back. Aunt Muriel told her that she would be counting the days.

Chapter 10

In September of 1966, Lizzie who had turned seventeen that May, left home taking Clover with her. Clover had wanted to go to university, but Clover's mother said that five G.C.E.'s and three A levels were enough for anyone and it was high time my girl to put them to good use and get a job. Clover cried and pleaded and Lizzie hatched a plan. She had just completed a two-year commercial course at the local Technical College, and her next step towards America was to become a fashion buyer. Aunt Muriel had said so. She'd told Lizzie to learn shorthand and typing because that was something a girl could always fall back on. Then, she said, get yourself some experience in the fashion world. After that, if she still wanted to and Joan and Jesse didn't object, Lizzie could come over to New York and work for her and Uncle Chuck. Lizzie definitely still wanted to. It was the thought of going to America that had made her get up at six o'clock every morning and take the old steam train to Camborne Tec. America was the incentive to try and make sense of the thick and thin lines, dots and curves that was shorthand and to stay awake during civics lectures and to put up with the biting sarcasm of her accountancy teacher.

Jesse was proud of Lizzie for completing her course and said she could come and work for him in the photography studio, but Lizzie had other plans. She explained to her father that she wanted to be a fashion buyer, and to do that she needed to go away to a big city where there were departmental stores and Clover was coming with her. London would be the best place for them to go, Lizzie said. Jesse put his foot down. She was far too young he told her. She had no idea of the dangers there were for young girls in London, or any other city, come to that. Joan however, felt it would be a good idea for Lizzie to leave home, not least because it would take her out of Violet's reach. Violet had been acting strangely for months. She would turn up at the studio or at Marbal House, just a social visit she would say, just to see how they all were. Joan pointed out to Jesse that if Lizzie went away for a while, perhaps Violet would give them some peace. As she also pointed out to Jesse, Lizzie had her inheritance money behind her and would be legally entitled to leave home when she was eighteen, with or without their consent, so why not let her go now? They'd save themselves months of tantrums, sulks and whinging hell. In the end, Jesse backed down but a compromise had to be made. London was out of the question. Clover suggested Exeter because of the university there and as she hadn't given up the hope of getting a degree one day the thought of living near a university appealed to her. Of course Exeter was where Violet had trained to be a nurse and Jesse hadn't been back there since the day he brought Lizzie home to Marbal House. He had been there several times before however, and he liked the place. It seemed safe as cities went, clean, and with its cathedral and colleges, rather charming. Joan said optimistically, that perhaps Lizzie would find herself a decent undergraduate there, settle down and forget all about that America nonsense.

Lizzie may have won her parents over, but Clover still had her own mother to deal with. Clover had been forced to work in the Co-op since leaving school and her mother wasn't at all happy one Monday night, lamb stew night, when Clover came home and said she was going to share a flat with Lizzie in Exeter. Her mother said oh no she wasn't, so she could get that idea out of her head right away. An argument ensued. Clover told her mother that she was ruining her life and that she hadn't slogged away at school for six years to end up working in the bloody Co-op. Her mother had slapped her across her cheek and told her she'd best get up to her room if she knew what was good for her, using language like that in this house. Clover, bawling fled upstairs. She'd have to enlist her Granny's support. Clover's granny had loved her dearly ever since she'd passed the eleven-plus when that Marbal maid, as Clover's Granny called Lizzie, had failed it. Clover was the only person in the family who had ever shown an academic bent. Granny told everyone that Clover was 'some brainy,' and had felt Clover's decline from the Upper Sixth to the

159

Co-op cheese counter almost as keenly as Clover had herself. In her opinion, Clover should have been allowed to go to university and read books, or literature as Clover called it, like she wanted. Granny therefore would be a worthy ally. Granny however, turned out to be worthy but ineffectual. As a last desperate measure, Joan and Jesse agreed to visit Clover's mother to try and win her round. When she opened the door to them, Clover's mother was at first fuming that Clover hadn't told her the Marbals were coming over. Not that the house wasn't tidy enough for visitors, it was always immaculate, but visitors weren't encouraged and when visiting was inevitable, Clover's mother liked plenty of time to psych herself up for it. Eventually though, with Joan heaping praise on, and admiration for Clover and with Jesse doing the same but directed at the mother rather than the daughter, they managed to charm her into agreement. An ecstatic Clover could go to Exeter with Lizzie after all. When the time came, Clover's mother even condescended to drive up to Exeter with the Marbals and look over the flat the girls were to share. Of course it wasn't right. It was dirty, and there was nowhere to hang out your washing and it would cost a fortune to heat in winter and Clover needn't think she could come running back home once she realised what a mistake she'd made. She'd made her bed and she knew what she could do with it.

Joan was pleased that Clover would be around to take care of Lizzie; however, before Lizzie left for Exeter, Joan decided it would be wise to talk to her regarding the dangers of unprotected sex. Lizzie said, "Yeah, yeah, I know all that stuff, we did it in Mrs. Peter's class at school." In truth, Mrs. Peter's had been too embarrassed to say anything other than open your biology book to page thirty one girls, and read it quietly. But there were Cosmopolitan magazines and peers to fill you in on what sex was all about and Lizzie planned, once she was away from home, to lie about her age and get prescribed The Pill. "I'm not *stupid*," she said with a scowl, concluding Joan's little talk with her. "Of course I'm not going to get pregnant when I go to Exeter." And then she promptly did.

Clover found employment in a little bookshop which she really rather liked, not least because of Marcus, who owned it. It didn't take long for her to fall madly in love with Marcus, even though he was married and twice her age and Lizzie thought he was a drip. Lizzie, driven by her own American dream, had walked into the largest departmental store on the high street and asked to see the manager. "Which manager?" The Perfumery assistant enquired. "We have several." Lizzie told her she didn't mind which manager, as long as she had something to do with fashion. After a long wait she was shown to an office where a portly man surveyed her from his side of the desk. He didn't invite Lizzie to sit down, but she did so anyway, and promptly asked him for a job – as a fashion buyer. When he had stopped laughing, the manager asked Lizzie her age and then facetiously her qualifications. Lizzie proudly told him about her Commerce Course Certificate, and her R.S.A.'s adding that she'd always wanted to be a fashion buyer and had moved all the way from Cornwall so that she could work in a big store, like his. The manager mistaking Lizzie's dreamy naivety for plucky enthusiasm, said he *would* give her work – as a shop assistant in the fashion department. He would see how she got on and then maybe if she was doing well enough, he might consider training her as a buyer. That was good enough for Lizzie. She was in. She was however disappointed when it transpired that she would not be working on the ground floor in the boutique department where there was a Biba counter and lots of Mary Quant, but on the First Floor Ladies Fashion where no self- respecting teenager would dream of entering. Furthermore, she had to wear a uniform of navy blue knee length skirt, navy and white spotted blouse, flesh coloured tights and black shoes.

On Lizzie's first day at work Mrs. Melton, the department supervisor, pointed out to her the recherché' of Jaeger, Belino, Vyella and Berketex. These clothes with their fussy linings and over-sewn seams Lizzie recognised as having the same labels that Grandma's clothes had, and which Lizzie and her mother had stuffed into carrier bags and quickly deposited at the local charity shop. These clothes, according to Mrs. Melton, were exquisite. But then, what did Mrs. Melton know? Mrs. Melton had pearl toned hair and wore lipstick the colour of raspberry jam and had small balls of muscles in her skinny calves from wearing spindly high heels all her working life. Furthermore, Mrs. Melton had an unpleasant whiff of mothballs and underarm perspiration about her and underneath her diamante trim upswept glasses, was a liberal smearing of blue eye shadow, making her eyelids very similar to that of a budgie's. Lizzie decided she couldn't take seriously anything Mrs. Melton said, not even learning to correctly gauge the size of customers. "Whatever you do," Mrs Melton said, tapping her Biro against the receipts book, "don't ask a customer if they're a size sixteen when they're a size fourteen." She gave Lizzie a budgie blink. "Customers get terribly offended if you assume they're a size larger than they actually are." Lizzie decided she wouldn't assume anything. She'd just ask.

Lizzie walked to work each morning, with her blue skirt turned over three times at the waistband to shorten it. She strode, rather than walked, her long legs taking her at full speed along the pavement from Heavitree Road to the centre of town. On her way she passed a building site where a couple of new shops and flats were being constructed. It was here that she encountered her first wolf whistle. Lizzie was surprised and pleased and turned to see who had whistled at her. He stood on the scaffolding and grinned down at her. He wore a pair of cut down jeans and a dark blue tee shirt. His arms and legs were muscular and brown from working out of doors. Lizzie thought he looked quite hunky and smiled back. The following day he whistled again, only this time some of the other builders joined in with catcalls. Look at the legs on that! You can wrap them pins round me any time you like darlin' and another less flattering, I bet you can sing like a canary, 'cos you've got legs like one. Lizzie had no trouble in ignoring them; she just looked at the lad with the brown muscles and waved. By the end of the week, he had asked her out, or to be precise, had told her the name of a night club he would be at on Saturday evening and said perhaps he might see her there.

Without parental disproval, or indeed Mrs. Melton's, Lizzie was free to wear a pair of false eyelashes and a skirt as short as she wished. She wore her long straight hair down, and lacquered it until her fringe stuck to her forehead. She was pleased with her newly purchased pair of white PVC knee high boots bought with staff discount from the ground floor boutique and when she viewed herself in her bedroom mirror, thought she bore a striking resemblance to Cathy McGowan.

"Lizzie," Clover said cautiously, "when you bend over, I can see your knickers."

"Well that's a relief," Lizzie replied, "because I wasn't sure if I'd remembered to put them on."

"Seriously," Clover said, frowning, "I think that skirt is a bit too short." Lizzie sighed. "Oh God, Clover, you're worse than my mother. Have another glass of cider and shut up."

"Well I do sort of feel responsible for you."

"Why 'cos you're eighteen and older than me?"

"No, because your mother asked me to look after you. So did your dad actually. Come to think of it, so did that Nurse Violet person."

Lizzie scowled. "Cheeky bitch. What's it got to do with her?" She sat on the end of the bed and peered at herself in the mirror. "I do *look* eighteen don't I? It would be awful if I couldn't get into this club place."

Clover put her head to one side and brushed her fair hair vigorously. "They'll probably let you in, but I'm not sure about me."

"He'll think I've stood him up if they won't let me in." Lizzie said. Clover rather hoped they wouldn't be allowed into the club. She wasn't at all sure that Lizzie's parents would appreciate their daughter meeting up with a casual labourer – particularly as she didn't even know his name.

To Clover's dismay they got passed the bouncers at the door without any problem. "I expect they think we're under-graduates," she whispered to Lizzie. Being mistaken for a student was as much as she could hope for. She and Lizzie paid to leave their

163

jackets with the cloakroom attendant, and Clover nervously followed Lizzie as she marched into a room where live music blared out, and mirrored balls dangling from the ceiling threw sequins of light over the dancers beneath. Lizzie scanned the dance floor and the tables dotted along its perimeter, but most of the scene was in a hazy gloom. "I can't see him," she yelled above the din to Clover. "I'm not surprised," Clover yelled back. She felt self -conscious standing there, clutching at her handbag. Apart from her and Lizzie, everyone seemed to be partnered off, or with a group of friends. "Why don't we go to the bar, and get a drink?"

It was marginally quieter at the bar. Clover furtively slipped her purse out of her handbag, feeling all eyes were upon her, pitying her because she had to go up to the bar and buy her own drinks. She'd never bought drinks at a bar before and had never been to a night-club. So far, it was an experience she wasn't enjoying very much. "What do you want to drink?" she asked Lizzie. Lizzie shrugged. "I dunno. We've started on cider so maybe we should stick with it."
"I don't really like cider," Clover said. "We could try a Cinzano – with lemonade."
"You decide," Lizzie said. "I'll see if I can find us a table."
"No!" Clover's eyes were large with apprehension. "Don't leave me on my own."
She leaned closer to the bar counter and tried to engage the attention of a bar attendant. Eventually, after several people had been served before her, Clover waved her purse aloft. "Excuse me, I think I'm next!" She called. The closest attendant swivelled on his heels to face her. "Yes, love?"
"Two Cinzano's, please."
"Ice. Lemon?"
"Umm yes – oh, and lemonade."
"Lemonade? With it or in a bottle?"
"Pardon?"
While this exchange was taking place, Lizzie continued to look around her for the lad with brown muscles. Just as Clover

164

flustered and embarrassed, handed Lizzie her glass, she spotted him. He'd obviously seen her first, and was smiling at her from the other end of the bar. She smiled back and waved at him and called out hi. He edged around the people standing at the bar, making his way across to her. "You made it then," he said. "Shall we go and sit down?"

Clover traipsed behind as they picked their way to a table that had four seats with only two occupied. Lizzie sat down, and he was just about to, when he realized Clover was with them.

"Oh I'm sorry," he said. "I didn't know you were coming over as well. Here, have this chair. I'll get another one." Clover sat down with a sulky thud. "I feel like a wallflower," she hissed ay Lizzie. "I wish I'd never come."

He soon returned with a chair and to Clover's horror, a friend. "This is Dougie," he said. Dougie was over-weight and acned. He smiled at Clover. "Fancy a dance?" he said. Clover was too polite and inexperienced to refuse. She gulped at her drink and found herself walking towards the crowded dance floor.

Lizzie turned to the lad with brown muscles, which were now hidden beneath a black, pin striped shirt. "I don't know your name," he said to her. "Lizzie," she answered. "So, what's yours?"

"Declan," he replied. "I'm called Declan."

Chapter 11

Sister Bernadette ended her walk around the convent garden by stopping by the grotto of Our Lady. A small jet of water rose and fell with a pleasant tinkling splash around the Virgin's feet. Sister Bernadette looked at the grotto in an abstract way born out of familiarity, and then looked closer. A small browned leaf had stuck to the Virgin Mary's crotch, giving the statuette a most distasteful appearance. Sister Bernadette reckoned the offending leaf was a cotoneaster horizontalis and was contemplating finding a twig to brush it off, when she heard Sister Ann calling her name. Sister Bernadette winced. Sister Ann had an unpleasant knack of getting inside Sister Bernadette's head. She could still hear her voice, still see her face hours after a conversation with her had ended. Sister Ann was that sort of person and so Sister Bernadette did her best not to enter into discourse with her if at all possible. She heard Sister Ann boom out her name again. "Sister Bernadette. You have a visitor!" Sister Bernadette half turned towards her. "Then send my visitor out here to me."
"You're not coming inside then?"
"No. I have to find a twig."
"You have to find a *what*, sister?" Sister Bernadette didn't answer. She looked down at her feet, amongst the clumps of frost hard grass for a suitable knocking off implement. Sister Ann stomped her way back to the edge of the drive, and seconds later Sister Bernadette heard heavy footsteps behind her and then the words, "Hello Aunt Bernadette." Instantly she knew. Her frame stiffened and she wondered how she could have been so stupid, so narrow in her thinking. 'Dear Aunt Bernadette…' why had she never once considered that a nephew and not a niece could have written the note pinned to Agnes' cot? "If you've come for Agnes, you're thirty years too late," she said, not turning to face him.
"I realize that, but I've come all the same." And then she did turn towards him. "Thank God you're poor mother isn't alive to witness your shame, Declan O'Connell." She crossed herself and looked at her nephew, the man who had abandoned his baby on her doorstep. He looked gaunt, his hair was thinning, his over-coat

166

was ill fitting. He did not have the look of a prosperous man, which pleased Sister Bernadette, because he hadn't deserved to prosper. "What brings you here now?" she asked coldly.

"I want to see Agnes. I want to tell her why we abandoned her. Y'see we were no more than kids ourselves, her mother and me, and it seemed like it was the only way out at the time. I always meant to come back though. Really I did."

"So why didn't you?"

Declan patted the pockets of his overcoat and brought out a packet a cigarettes. "Do you mind if I smoke?" Sister Bernadette drew herself up as tall as she could and tucked in her chin the way Mother Superior used to. "Do I mind if you smoke? I would prefer to see you in flames for your sins, but no doubt that will happen soon enough." Declan gave a crooked smile, not sure whether she was jesting with him, and lit his cigarette. "I didn't come back because I was afraid. I thought it would be all over the newspapers. I thought I'd be arrested and end up in prison." Sister Bernadette looked down at the grass and prodded a tuft with her toecap. "It. was kept out of the papers. At first we thought the mother would come back for Agnes, and by the time it was obvious she wasn't, Miss Trellis had decided Agnes was -," she looked up from the grass, and directly at Declan, "sent by an angel. But no, it was the devil had deposited her. And now you want to see her you say? Make everything all right. You'll have a job doing that, I can tell you." Declan drew nervously on his cigarette. "Why? She's not …she's not dead is she?"

"No. She's not dead."

"So you'll tell me where I can find her then?"

"I will. She lives at a place called Marbal House, but we have to talk first you and I, and then I'll have to warn Agnes that you plan to visit her." Declan was staring at Sister Bernadette, his forehead creased with incredulity. "Did you say Marbal House? God that's amazing. Marbal House is where her mother grew up. Lizzie Marbal, is Agnes' mother- and you say that's where Agnes lives?"

"A coincidence maybe but on the other hand it was the only place in town at the time offering bed-sit accommodation And if Agnes hadn't gone to the dentist for a root filling the day he'd decided to let the attic, she wouldn't be living there now." Declan looked puzzled.

"She lives in the attic? I assumed she owned the house and lived there with her husband and kids maybe." He shivered. "Can we go somewhere and talk, Aunt Bernadette? It's chilly out here."

Sister Bernadette tucked her hands into her sleeves and led the way across the grass over the gravel drive to a small chapel in the grounds. Declan stubbed out his cigarette as Sister Bernadette pushed open the door. The air inside the chapel was not much warmer than the air outside it. It smelt like all churches Declan had ever known, which wasn't many. Candles and dust, and damp.

Sister Bernadette lit a candle, crossed herself and then knelt at the alter rail, her hands clasped, her eyes tight shut. Declan did the same, although he lacked his aunt's knack for spiritual communication. I'm sorry Mother, he tried, I'm sorry for what I did to baby Agnes. Forgive me Mother. I'm sorry Mother. After a while his knees began to ache. He didn't want to stand up before Sister Bernadette was finished, but his arthritis got the better of him, and he stiffly got to his feet and rubbed at his knees. His movements seemed to bring an end to Sister Bernadette's prayer. She too rose stiffly, and then walked passed him to sit at the back of the chapel. When Declan was seated next to her she said, "So how did you do it? How did you leave her?"

"It wasn't easy," Declan began, "When I said goodbye to her, she was sleeping in her cot and I kissed her cheek, with tears coming down my own. And then –"

"I'm not interested in your whinging," Sister Bernadette said tartly. "I meant how did you manage to leave her in the porch without being seen?"

"Ah, right." Declan's clasped hands dangled limply between his knees. He sighed. "Well I'd borrowed a van off a mate to drive down here. We were living in Exeter, y'see. I gave Agnes her bottle and then I left very early in the morning. The movement of the van seemed to settle her and for once she just lay there in her cot sleeping. It was barely light when I arrived. There was no one around. You were probably all at prayer or something. I took Agnes out of the van. It was a Bedford three seater, you know, with the long seat in the front?" Sister Bernadette tutted impatiently. "I fail to see the significance of the seating arrangements Declan."

"It was only that I didn't want you to think I'd had her in the back of the van. She was up there beside me the whole journey. Anyway I carried the cot down the drive to the porch. And I....I placed her there." Declan, who hadn't visited this scene in his memory for many years could suddenly hear the rooks in the trees, see the lacy shadows over Agnes as she slept, feel his own salty tears on her tiny, ball of a cheek. "And then I ran. I ran up the drive and into the van. And I cried all the way back to Devon."

"And where was the mother in all this – Lily, or whatever you called her."

"Lizzie. She was waiting for me to return, cases packed, practically dancing with excitement she was. We flew out to New York the very next day." And for a while, Declan thought, I put Agnes right out of my mind, just as Lizzie had told me to do. He felt uncomfortable now, and tapped the soles of shoes fretfully on the scuffed floorboards. He wanted a cup of coffee, a cigarette.

"Could we go somewhere else to talk, Aunt Bernadette? Somewhere more congenial?"

"No we could not," Sister Bernadette replied frostily. "If I'm to hear your confessions, where could be a more fitting a place to do so?" Declan closed his eyes wearily. "What more is it you want me to tell you, Aunt Bernadette?"

Sister Bernadette wriggled to a more comfortable position on her seat. "Everything Declan. I've waited over thirty years to have the mystery of Agnes solved. And now I want to hear *everything*."

Chapter 12

Six weeks after the night Lizzie first had sex with Declan, she thought she might be pregnant. After two months she told him she definitely was. "My God, Lizzie," he said aghast. "I thought you were on the Pill."

"The doctor wouldn't give it to me. He asked me if I was married and I said no. He asked me if I was engaged and I said no. Then I asked him if I could have the Pill anyway and he said no. He said -."

"Never mind what he said," Declan snapped. "The point is if you weren't on the Pill you should have told me."

"I did," Lizzie said. "I told you weeks ago we should use those condom, things- and we have done."

"I mean right at the beginning Lizzie. That's when you should have told me. There wasn't much point in using a bloody condom when you were already pregnant, was there?" Declan sat on the edge of the bed and felt sick. "What are we going to do now?" he groaned. "God this is a nightmare."

"I'll have an abortion," Lizzie said. She sat up in bed and placed her pillow against the headboard and nestled into it.

"You don't want to keep it then?"

"Don't be stupid." Lizzie glowered at him. "I want to go to America, that's what I want – not a baby." Declan began to feel less sick, less trapped. He twisted round to look at Lizzie. She had switched on her transistor radio, and was swaying her head in time to the music. "I got you, babe", she sang in her off key voice.

"How?" Declan said. "How will you get an abortion?"

"I don't know," Lizzie said. "I think you can get them in London, but it costs a lot of money. I'll ask Clover, she knows everything."

"She knows you're pregnant then?"

Lizzie nodded. "I've told her not to say a word to anyone when we go home at Christmas. My parents would kill me – and you. Besides they wouldn't let me come back here. They wouldn't trust me; they wouldn't let me out of their sight. It would be awful."

"So where will you get the money from, for the abortion?" Declan stood up and began to dress.

"I don't have much. I've got a bit but I was saving it for America."
Lizzie sighed. "This is all a bit of a bloody nuisance really."
"A nuisance you call it?" It's a bloody catastrophe." Declan brushed back his hair and pushed up the casement window.
"I'd better get going before it gets light enough for that witch landlady to see me leave. It rained in the night," he said. "The ground is really muddy underneath this window."
"Think yourself lucky we're on the ground floor." Lizzie said. Declan picked up his jacket. The way I'm feeling right now I could fling meself off the roof. Look, will you try and find out some information about abortion?" He hesitated. "I mean if you're sure that's what you want to do."
"I told you, I don't want a baby. I never want to have a baby."
She was making it so easy Declan began to feel guilty. "Only it is a human life we're talking about," he murmured.
"No it's not. It's just cells and stuff. Now go on if you're going. It's freezing with that window open."
Declan climbed over the window-sill. "I'll see you tonight in The Bull. Don't forget to ask Clover about you know what." He dropped down onto squelchy ground fronted by a laurel bush, the perfect cover for creeping stealthily to the garden wall. He slid over the wall and began to run. The air was fresh and felt good. He slowed down to a trot and took in deep breaths and then he began to walk. An underlying feeling of unease began to grow within him. It wasn't just that Lizzie was pregnant. It was her casual attitude towards it. He should be grateful, he supposed, that Lizzie didn't want to have the baby; God knows he wasn't ready to settle down and be a father. He was only twenty after all, just starting out. All the same she seemed so unconcerned, not so much cold as – well, indifferent. And that wasn't natural, was it?

Clover, who was mortified by Lizzie's pregnancy and blamed herself for not keeping a closer eye on her, looked into the matter of abortion. The thought of abortion repulsed her, yet on the other hand, if it was done quickly no-one need be any the wiser and hers and Lizzie's reputations would stay intact. Clover also comforted herself with the sure knowledge that Lizzie would have made a dreadful mother anyhow and that Irish git of a boyfriend would be equally dreadful as a father, always assuming he stayed around that long. All in all, in Clover's opinion, it was probably crueller to allow the embryo to develop than it would be to abort it.

Clover reported back to Lizzie that to have an abortion she would need at least one psychiatric report to say that she wasn't fit enough to be a mother, adding that in Lizzie's case that probably wouldn't be too much of a problem. But Lizzie was horrified at the thought. "I'm not going to a psychiatrist!" she yelled. "They'll never let me into America if it's on record somewhere that I'm a nutter." Anyway, how the hell do you get to see a psychiatrist? I mean where do they hang out?" Clover told her that anything was possible if you paid for it. And that was another thing. Once she'd got the psychiatrist's report and found a willing doctor, and Harley Street was probably her best bet, the abortion would probably cost around one hundred and eighty to two hundred pounds, plus travel expenses and possibly overnight accommodation. Lizzie groaned and said that it was all too much for her, too difficult to sort out and perhaps she'd better tell mother after all. She would ask her mother not to let her father know. Keep it a little secret between the two of them. Perhaps she would give her the money for the abortion. At least she could organise it for her. "I'll talk to my mum when I go home at Christmas,"
Lizzie told Declan, and that seemed to please him. Clover was less pleased. "It will spoil everything," she wailed at Lizzie. "And just when I'm getting on so well with Marcus."
"He's married," Lizzie said. "And he's old enough to be your dad."

Before going home for Christmas, Lizzie had her hair cut in a fashionable Vidal Sassoon geometric style. Joan thought it looked great but Jesse wasn't keen on it. His little princess was all grown up. Cutting her hair short and sharp symbolised the demise of his little girl. Lizzie was a young woman now, lounging over the sofa arm in her black leggings and Mary Quant sweater, her eyelashes coated with layers of black mascara and her lipstick

172

so pale it was almost white. Lizzie had grown up and Jesse wasn't ready for it.

The moment for Lizzie to have a quiet word with Joan, didn't present itself. For one thing, Joan was unwell. She had bronchitis, she said, not that it stopped her from smoking. The day after Boxing Day, the day before Lizzie was due to return to Exeter, she almost told Joan she was pregnant, and might have done so if Violet hadn't turned up. She said she was passing and called in to wish them the compliments of the season. Joan groaned which brought on a coughing fit and Jesse asked Violet if she would like a sherry. Violet accepted. She couldn't help noticing that the room was a mess. Pine needles all over the carpet, date stones stuck to the bottom of a dirty ashtray, balls of screwed up wrappers in with the sweets, empty shells on top of the nuts. She couldn't help but make comparisons with her own lounge in her little bungalow; an artificial tree that made no mess, neat piles of kumquats and filberts and pistachios in sparkling crystal bowls – and no-one to appreciate it but the cat. Joan however, wasn't looking at all well. Bronchitis did she call it? Well Violet had seen her up at the hospital waiting in out-patients for Mr Coles, the thoracic man, and Violet doubted Joan's coughing and pallid complexion were due to bronchitis. With a bit of luck, Jesse would spend next Christmas in more orderly surroundings, such as he was used to and no more than he deserved. She should feel sorry for Joan really, but how could you have sympathy for a woman who was smoking and drinking herself to death? She looked dreadful, but she only had herself to blame.

Violet outstayed her welcome, which as far as Joan was concerned would have been achieved before the first sherry. Violet had brought Lizzie a Christmas present, a diary and pen in a presentation box. Lizzie couldn't fail to notice that Violet bringing her a gift had seemed to irk Joan. Even after Violet eventually left, the atmosphere at Marbal House was tense. Joan went to bed early, saying she hoped they didn't mind, but she really wasn't feeling too well. Jesse said an early night was a good idea because she needed to get rid of that cough by New

Year's Eve. He told Lizzie that he and Joan were going to the Photographic Association dinner and dance in Bodmin on New Year's Eve, and that Joan had been looking forward to it for weeks. After giving her this piece of information to which he received no response, Jesse didn't quite know how to communicate with his changed Lizzie. He felt awkward with her, and she seemed distant and bored. Eventually he decided to switch on the television and they watched the Val Doonigan Christmas Special, and then went up to bed themselves. Lizzie wished Violet hadn't turned up. She didn't want her poxy pen set and now there wouldn't be a chance to talk with Joan. Lizzie fortunately wasn't to know that if she had told Joan she was pregnant, everything would have turned out differently.

Declan phoned his mother over the Christmas holiday. She asked him if he still had that good job in Birmingham or was it Liverpool? He said it was Manchester and he was doing fine. He asked his mother about the rest of the family, and she updated him on his brother and sisters and then she said her sister Bernadette was teaching now, at a convent school in Cornwall. When she said the name of the town, which Declan recognised as being Lizzie's home town, his mouth went dry and he had a terrible sensation of being trapped in a net, a big butterfly net. He could feel it over his head and shoulders, pinning down his arms. He blurted out to his mother that he was saving up to go to America, and she laughed and said to be sure and send a postcard when he got there. As soon as he came out of the phone box he lit a cigarette. What if Lizzie had told her mother and it was already all over the town – would it have reached the ears of Aunt Bernadette yet? Did she already know that her nephew had got a girl called Lizzie Marbal pregnant? He smiled at the absurdity of the notion. How could she know? Lizzie wasn't a Catholic and Aunt Bernadette had probably never heard of the Marbals. Besides, no member of his family would ever suspect him, because they thought he worked in a factory in Manchester. Even so it was a weird coincidence, sinister almost, that Lizzie's family lived in the same town as his Aunt Bernadette.

Declan was angry when Lizzie said she hadn't told her mother she was pregnant. It was New Year's Eve and they were on their way to a party thrown by Marcus and his wife. Clover hadn't really wanted Declan to tag along but he assumed he was invited and was now striding ahead with Lizzie, making Clover run at a trot to keep up with them. "Why the hell didn't you tell your mother? You promised you would."

"I told you. She wasn't well."

"Do we have to go over all this tonight?" Clover said. She hoped Marcus would approve of her friends. He'd told her to bring them – well Lizzie anyway.

"Yes we bloody well do," Declan snapped. "You'll do it now," he said, and grabbed hold of Lizzie's arm. They were alongside a telephone box. He heaved the door open with his free hand and pushed Lizzie inside.

"Hang on a minute," she said. "It's not that easy."

"No it's not." Clover said. "She can't just phone up and say, Happy New Year mum, by the way I'm pregnant."

"She's got to say something," Declan said. "Time is ticking on. She'll be too late to have an abortion if she doesn't hurry and get it sorted out."

"True." Clover said. "Why don't you ask her to come up at the weekend Lizzie? Tell her there's something you need to talk to her about"

"What if dad answers the phone?"

"Just dial the bloody number." Declan jammed the door open with his foot and blew onto his cold hands. Clover stamped around in a little circle trying to get warmth into her feet. Lizzie leaned against the side of the phone box and listened to the burr of the phone. She could picture the black phone on the hall table and imagined Joan rising from her chair by the fire and going put into the hall to answer it.

"Let it ring." Joan said. Jesse had just locked the front door. Joan stood beside him in a fur coat that had once belonged to Clara.

Joan had her hair done and had spent a long time over her make up. Jesse had already told her that she looked bloody lovely, and as he looked at her now, a gold lame' evening bag clutched against the fur coat, her feet in delicate high gold sandals, he had an urge to kiss her. Instead he smiled. "I ought to answer it," he said. "It might be Lizzie."

Joan laughed. "That's the last person it'll be. Lizzie never phones. Come on let's go. I'm getting cold." Jesse handed her the car keys. "You go and start the engine. I'll have to answer it."

The burr burr reverberated in Lizzie's ear. And then she remembered. "They're not in. Dad told me they were going to some photography thing tonight. They must have left." She replaced the receiver just at the moment Jesse reached the phone. Lizzie shrugged at Declan. "Bloody parents," she said. "They're never there when you want them, are they?"

"Well?" Joan said.

"I don't know who it was. It rang off just as I got there." Jesse settled into the passenger seat. "No doubt if it's important whoever it was will phone again tomorrow."

"No doubt," Joan said, and released the hand brake.

They both agreed it was the best night out they'd had in a long time. Jesse put his arm around Joan's waist and they ran together from the hotel steps out towards the car park, leaving behind the warmth and light and sounds of jaded revelry. Their eyes squinted against the cold sleet and they huddled close as Jesse went through his overcoat pockets for the car keys. "Oh hang on," Joan said, "I've still got them. I may as well drive back – I've had less to drink than you." She took the keys from her gold lame' handbag and unlocked the car doors. They talked about the other guests, their friends and acquaintances, as they headed out of Bodmin, on their journey home. They laughed over those who had drunk too much and made fools of themselves, decided who looked better and who looked worse since they had last seen them. "In my opinion," Jesse said, "you were the most attractive woman there." Joan laughed and pressed down her gold

176

sandaled foot to accelerate around a bend in the road. "God, you must be drunk," she said. Jesse looked at her and smiled. "Only a bit he said, "yet not too drunk to see the New Year in with a bang, if you're up to it."

"Oh I'm up to it," Joan said, and looked across and smiled back at him. A smile was still on Jesse's lips as he turned to face the road. The lights of the oncoming vehicle dazzled him. He heard Joan gasp as she pulled hard on the steering wheel but he knew she'd lost it, and then he heard the shattering crash of impact and then the awful sound of silence.

Violet was thinking about taking her break when the ambulance tore across the hospital car park, its blue light flashing through the window of the ward she was on. Her ward sister, Sister Mary, was fairly new at the hospital but had already gained a reputation for strictness and adhering rigidly to the rules. She was only young and would have been quite pretty if she smiled occasionally or hadn't been a nun and had worn a bit of make-up. Violet wondered if it was worth asking Sister Mary if she could take her break now as the ward was so quiet. She'd probably say no. She'd probably make her wait another ten minutes. Violet decided to ask anyway. Sister Mary told her to check on Mrs Rickard first. She said she was sure she'd heard her calling out. She had. Mrs Rickard wanted a drink and then a bedpan. Violet emptied out the bedpan in the sluice and was about to re-enter the ward when she saw a nurse she knew from accident and emergency. "You've been busy tonight," Violet said. "What was the ambulance case- road accident or drunken brawl?"

"Bad accident. Seems it was a head on collision. They've taken one driver to Truro Hospital. The other one was dead on arrival. Poor woman, so close to home too. Mrs Marbal – you know, the Marbals with the photography studio?" Violet paled. She felt chilled "Joan? You mean Joan's dead? Oh my God." The bedpan nearly slipped from Violet's hands. She grabbed it tighter, clutched it to her as she asked, "Was there anyone else in the car with her?"

177

"Her husband," the nurse said. "He's just been taken up to Trelawney Ward. "Hey, are you alright Vi? Are they close friends of yours?" Violet nodded. "Very close. Do me a favour and tell Sister Mary I've taken my break will you? I've got to go to Jesse." She thrust the bedpan at the nurse and hurried to Trelawney. Her heart beat fast and her mind whirled. Joan was dead ...My God. She had often fantasised about Joan being out of the way so that she could have Jesse, but now that it had actually happened Violet felt almost responsible. And yet strangely powerful. Jesse needed her now; she would look after him. She had to concentrate all her thoughts on him, and Lizzie of course.

Jessie was in a side room. Violet saw him through the glass paned door. A nurse was adjusting the saline drip attached to his arm. Violet pushed the door open. Jesse's eyes were shut, his face gashed and streaked with dry blood. The nurse turned as Violet entered. "Morris," she said, "would you go and make sure the duty doctor has been sent for? I'm concerned with –"
"You go." Violet said. "I'll stay with him. He's a friend of mine."
"Is he? Alright you stay with him then. I won't be long." The nurse smiled at Violet and gently touched her arm as she left the room. Violet stood for a second looking at Jesse and then, while knowing she could be dismissed for it, climbed beside him on the bed and slipped her arm beneath his head to cradle him. He made a low groan and opened his mouth to speak. "It's all right Jesse," Violet crooned. "I'm here now." She pushed a lock of blood streaked hair away from his face and lightly kissed his forehead. She saw the trace of a smile on his lips and she smiled too, with a warm feeling of contentment. "I'm glad you're here," he said, so quietly that Violet could scarcely hear him. But she had heard. Her smile deepened. He wanted her, he had always wanted her. He made an effort to move his hand. Violet locked her fingers in his. "You won't leave me again?" Jesse murmured.
"No my darling", she replied softly. "I'll never leave you." She felt Jesse relax against her. "I knew," he whispered. "I knew you'd come back to me, Ruby. I've missed you." Violet stopped stroking his hair. She looked down at his face, bloodied, bruised and

178

peaceful. "Who," she asked, "is Ruby?" As she looked at him she knew he was beyond answering. She lowered his head onto the pillow, stood up and straightened his sheet and then put her hand to her mouth and wailed like the creature in pain that she was.

Chapter 13

The parish church was packed for the double funeral. Lizzie had phoned Muriel and she came across from America to take care of the arrangements. At the funeral Lizzie wore a black PVC coat and her white boots. Clover wore a Jaeger coat that Mrs. Melton had given to her for Lizzie. Clover had personally gone to the store to tell Mrs. Melton the tragic news. She might have thought it was some sort of sick joke if Clover hadn't looked so red eyed and ashen faced. Mrs.Melton clasped her be-ringed hands to her mouth and gasped "Both parents? Oh no, how awful. The poor girl. Is there anything I can do? Actually, yes, I think there is." And then she'd fetched the black Jaeger coat from the rail, saying that it was only a size ten, and even though Jaeger were cut on the generous side, the department didn't have much call for size ten, not like the boutique downstairs where everyone was trying to look like Twiggy. Even in the sale, she doubted they would shift it, she said, and to be quite honest, to her eye, the collar didn't sit quite right but that was only *her* – it was so minor a fault no-one else would notice it. Clover knew Lizzie wouldn't wear the coat, but Mrs. Melton was folding it and wrapping it in tissue paper with quick, accustomed movements and had slipped it into a large Sale bag before Clover could think of anything to say other than thank you.

Declan drove the three of them down from Exeter in his mate's van. They stayed at Marbal House, all of them sleeping in Lizzie's bedroom because Clover wanted to be on hand to comfort Lizzie and because she didn't fancy sleeping in a room on her own while there was still such a strong presence of Jesse and Joan in the house. As soon as Muriel arrived Lizzie perked up, comforted to have her aunt with her and willing to let her sort out the solicitor and undertaker and make arrangements with the vicar.

Aunt Muriel held Lizzie's hand as they walked behind the two sets of coffin bearers into the church and passed the pews full of family friends and local businessmen and locals who never missed a good funeral. Violet felt her rightful place was in the front row, next to Lizzie and Muriel, but Clover took that place and next to her, Declan. Violet made do by wedging herself in the pew behind, where Clover's mother and granny sat, the mother with a stony face and a powerful voice when it came to the hymns, the granny crying and dabbing at her eyes with her handkerchief throughout the service. Afterwards, they went back to Marbal House where Muriel had arranged a buffet for the mourners.

Violet had only one thought in mind now that Jesse was gone. It was partly revenge because with one word he had shattered her belief that he had always loved her. If only he hadn't mentioned the name Ruby, if only he hadn't mentioned any name, she could have cherished her old dream after he died, and got comfort from it. But now she realised how deluded she had been all these years, just a play -thing for Jesse to pick up and put down, or rather, fondle when he wanted to. Lizzie was still hers though, nothing could change that and the sooner Lizzie knew the truth the better. It might help her to know that she still had a real mother – only one parent to mourn. On the other hand it might not, but it would help Violet. She wanted Lizzie to know who she really was. Too bad that Jesse and Joan never wanted Lizzie to find out, because Violet didn't have to do what they wanted any more. They'd ruined her life, really.

Violet had toyed with idea of telling Lizzie right after the funeral, but in the event decided against it. For one thing, she hadn't banked on Muriel being around all the time and for another Lizzie scarcely looked at her, let alone spoke to her and so Violet lost her nerve. She quite liked the idea of standing up in a roomful of mourners and telling Lizzie that Joan wasn't her real mother. But realistically the role of Bad Fairy would have to wait for a more appropriate time. Muriel *did* speak to Violet. She made a point of telling Violet that it was nice of her to come. She said she understood that Violet used to be a servant to Clara as well as Joan and Jesse, and that Violet's parents had also been employed as servants at Marbal House, and didn't Violet come

181

back to nurse Clara during her last few weeks? My, what dedication, Muriel said, adding that it just went to show what wonderful employers the Marbals must have been. And then her eyes misted over and she said she still couldn't believe her darling sister Joan was gone, and dear Jesse too, and that we never knew did we, when our time was up? Muriel rankled Violet with her servant and masters talk and Violet would like to have given her a few revelations about her darling sister Joan and indeed Clara Marbal, who had felt the need several times in her last weeks to confide in Violet that she'd been a cold wife because she'd never loved Albert and found sex with him repugnant, although she had quite enjoyed it with Hester, but by and large could have lived without sex altogether. She would also like to have told Muriel that she, Violet had given birth to Jesse's child, so she was a bit more than a servant, thank you very much and he wasn't quite the gentleman he'd seemed to be. What she did say, just to get Muriel thinking, was, "Jesse and I were very close – like brother and sister when we were young. We both grew up together in this house, you see. He's always been here for me - an integral part of my life. As I said, we were *very* close right up to the end. I don't know how I shall cope without him." Muriel's pencilled eyebrows arched and then she asked Violet to excuse her, because she wanted to thank the vicar before he left. Violet inwardly smiled. She'd speak to Lizzie just as soon as Muriel went back to America.

Muriel wanted to take Lizzie with her when she left. She thought Lizzie had been incredibly brave throughout her double tragedy, but of course she realised it wouldn't be practical for Lizzie to join her in America until all the legality had been completed. Lizzie agreed, knowing it wouldn't be practical until she'd sorted out some business of her own. Jesse had made a will leaving everything to either Lizzie or Joan, depending upon who died first. Once Marbal House was sold along with Jesse's studio, Lizzie would be financially well set up and by June she would have sorted out her personal problem, one way or another. It was mutually agreed that Lizzie would join Muriel and Chuck in mid-summer.

At the time of the funeral Declan had no work on because of the bad weather and Marcus had told Clover that she could take a couple of weeks off to be with Lizzie, adding that he would miss her. Once Muriel had left, Lizzie began the marathon task of clearing out Marbal House. She was ruthless and would have been more so if Clover hadn't persuaded her to call in a reputable auctioneer from Par who was delighted with the treasures he found at Marbal House, most of which had belonged to Clara. The antique ornaments and furniture were soon collected and carted off in the auctioneer's van leaving rooms with a hollow, cold feel which Clover found depressing but Lizzie appeared unaffected by. In fact the faster she could see empty spaces the better she liked it. "There's so much stuff in this house," she said as Declan and Clover piled Jesse's books into a tea chest. "We'll never get rid of it all." She scooped an armful of Joan's old magazines off the bookcase and into a cardboard box. "You can make a bonfire with this lot Declan," she said kicking the tea chest. "And as soon as you've cleared the bookcase, put it in the study with the other stuff, then this room will be nearly empty."
"Not the books," Clover said. "You can't burn the books."
"I can," Lizzie said.
"Please don't," Clover begged. "We could put them in the van and take them back to Exeter. There are lots of second-hand bookshops that would have them." She looked at Declan for support.
"Alright," he said, "I'll take them out to the van so they won't be in the way – but don't put any more in that tea chest, I'll never lift it. And talking of lifting," he added to Lizzie. "You shouldn't be carrying that box."
"Why?" she asked. "Because I might have a miscarriage? Huh, as if I'd be that lucky. You'd think," she went on bitterly," that I'd have had one already with all the stress I've been through." Clover looked up from the book she'd been leafing through. "You do

realise," she said gently, "that you've left it too late to have an abortion."

"Just as well, I suppose," Declan said. "Abortion is a sin."

"Who says?" Lizzie snapped.

"The nuns for one."

"We'll give it to the nuns then." Lizzie said. Declan smiled wryly, thinking Lizzie was joking, but Lizzie never joked. Lizzie was about to tell him of the convent orphanage nearby, when the doorbell rang. Later she was glad that she hadn't mentioned it in front of Clover because leaving the child at the orphanage had to be a secret that even Clover mustn't know about. "Shall I get the door?" Declan said. Lizzie sighed. "If it's that bloody vicar again tell him to sod off." Clover winced. Declan opened the front door. It wasn't the vicar, it was Violet, and so he let her in. Violet stood in the room where only weeks before there had a Christmas tree and Jesse had handed her a sherry. Now there were ugly pale patches of carpet that had been covered by furniture; furniture that she had spent years cleaning but now it had all gone. Her mother had cleaned this room; her father had mended the window frames. She and Jesse had done jigsaws together in front of the fire, when Clara was away. This room, like all the other rooms at Marbal House held memories. Lizzie threw down a magazine and stared at her. Why the hell had Declan let *her* in? "Did you want something, Violet?" Lizzie said. "Only as you can see we're rather busy."

"Yes, I can see," Violet said. "Perhaps I can help?"

"We can manage." Lizzie said.

"At least let me make you all a coffee then." Violet tried to smile although her stomach churned with mixed emotions. Lizzie was selling up, going away. If she didn't tell her soon it would be too late. Lizzie would leave without knowing the truth and that would never do.

Clover was about to say that a coffee would be lovely, but Lizzie spoke first. "Look Violet, if there's nothing you want, would you please go?" Violet's resolve strengthened. Lizzie was like the rest of them, talking down to her, treating her like a servant. She knew she was setting herself on a dangerous course, just as she had when she'd told Joan she was pregnant. Then, as now, there could be no turning back no matter what the consequences. "As a matter of fact there was something I wanted," she said quietly.

"What then?" Lizzie looked around her. "An ashtray? Oh no you don't smoke do you? There's a box in the hall that's going to the charity shop. Have a look through that if you want something." Violet bit her top lip in agitation and then said, "Lizzie I know you've been through a lot but there's no need to be rude to me. I haven't come here to rummage through your junk. What I want is to talk to you. There's something I need to tell you, in private."

"I don't think so Violet," Lizzie said. "There's nothing you can tell me that I wouldn't want Clover and Declan to hear, so whatever it is, carry on."

"Perhaps we should leave you alone," Clover said scrabbling to her feet. She had been kneeling by the tea chest with a book in her hand, squirming at Lizzie's brusqueness towards Violet. She would never dare to be that rude. Lizzie now shot her such a withering look that Clover slowly knelt down again. Declan folded his arms, intrigued. "What I have to say is extremely private," Violet said, "but I'm prepared to tell you in front of your friends, if that's what you want."

Lizzie turned her back on Violet, picked up a book from the bookcase and made a play of studying its cover. Violet took a deep breath. "Alright then. What I have to tell you is that Jesse – your father and I, had an affair." The room had become so quiet that Violet could hear Lizzie's fingertips as they moved over the book's dust jacket. Then Lizzie slowly turned to face Violet. "You're mad," she said. "Completely bonkers. My dad wouldn't have an affair with you. He felt sorry for you. He told me that once, when I asked him why you kept hanging around. He said he felt sorry for you because you had no family of your own. And this is the thanks he gets for being kind to an old servant. Lies, nasty malicious lies when he's not here to defend himself."

"Oh no, I'm certainly not lying," Violet said stoutly. She didn't doubt that Jesse had said he felt sorry for her. Pitied her. She'd never wanted his pity. "We did have an affair – and you were the result of it. Joan wasn't your birth mother, I am." Clover gasped,

Declan frowned, crossed his arms and rocked back on his heels. Lizzie turned white, her eyes lit up with temper. "You stupid, spiteful, old fool," she yelled. "Get out of here before I call the police and have you arrested for libel!"

"Slander," Clover whispered.

"A blood test would prove it." Violet said doggedly.

"A blood test?" Lizzie gave a sarcastic laugh. " I've got a birth certificate if I wanted proof. Not that I need proof to know someone like you couldn't be my mother. I'm not your daughter you jealous, deluded old bitch. So go on, what are you waiting for? Get the hell out of here and never come back!"

Violet flushed. "Don't worry, I am going," she said. "I've ruined my life because of you Marbals. So high and mighty you think you are, but you're not. Joan was an alcoholic, Clara was a lesbian and Jesse was a cheat. And as for you," she said pointing to Lizzie. "I don't want you anyway. You're right," she added, tears forming ready to drop," you're not my daughter. My Elizabeth wouldn't treat me like this. I don't know what they've done to you, but – but I want her back. I want my baby back." She turned, with as much dignity as she could, and as she had done eighteen years earlier, ran sobbing out into the street. "Black as black," Lizzie sang loudly after her, "I want my baby back, grey as grey since you went away from me!"

"Stop it Lizzie," Clover yelled leaping to her feet. "That's really cruel."

"Cruel?" Lizzie shouted back. "She's the cruel one. As if I didn't have enough grief to deal with without her making up dreadful lies."

"But why would Violet want to lie about being your mother?" Declan said unwisely. "What if she wasn't lying – what if she was telling the truth?"

"Don't you ever say that again!" Lizzie hurled the book she was holding at Declan, who neatly caught it with one hand. "You say that again and I'll kill you. I'll kill either of you if you ever mention any of this again!"

"Alright, alright," Declan held up his hands in a gesture of submission. "I'm sorry."

"Why don't you go and have a lie down?" Clover said gently. She had never seen Lizzie so full of emotion before, and was beginning to feel shaky herself.

"I don't need to lie down." Lizzie snapped. "There's far too much to be done, so let's get on with it. The sooner we get out of this bloody place the better. And you," she said glaring at Declan, "can get a bonfire lit instead of standing around like a gormless idiot. I'm going to sort out the study." She left the room slamming the door behind her. Declan looked at Clover and shrugged. "Jesus," he said, "and I thought my family was weird. "What do you make of it all?" Clover brushed the dust off her skirt from where she'd been kneeling and spoke in a low voice in case Lizzie was listening. "Violet's gone crazy. She admitted Lizzie wasn't her daughter, didn't she? I don't know what made her say all that stuff about her and Jesse. Maybe she always fancied him - perhaps she lost a child of her own once or something. I just wish I hadn't heard any of it. Lizzie's right – we mustn't mention it again. It wouldn't be fair on Jesse and Joan. They were lovely people that much I do know." Declan, realising he wasn't going to get anything of interest out of Clover, picked up a cardboard box and went out to the garden to start a bonfire.

Clover walked over to the window and stared out at the bare branches of the cherry trees, and the winter dormant borders that Joan had always taken pride in. The garden would be bursting with colour in the spring with pink cherry blossom spread like confetti over the drive and along the pavement outside. Clover pensively bit her bottom lip. The Marbals had treated her like one of the family; they *had* been lovely people, but that wasn't all she knew. She was sure Violet had been telling the truth as soon as she said Clara had been a lesbian, because Lizzie had told Clover that Christmas Muriel and Chuck had stayed at Marbal House. Lizzie had come downstairs to fetch her Girl Annual and had overheard the grown-ups talking about lesbians and Queen Victoria and then Clara had said that once she'd had an affair with a woman. Lizzie had been puzzled. She'd asked Clover to find out what lesbians were. Clover turned her back on the window

187

and sighed. If that part of Violet's outburst was true, then perhaps so was the rest. Only that didn't bear contemplating because if Joan wasn't Lizzie's natural mother, then Muriel was no relation to her either and to acknowledge that would break Lizzie's heart. Clover decided to go into the study to make sure Lizzie was alright.

Lizzie was clearing out the drawers of Jesse's desk. She flourished her birth certificate at Clover as she walked in and slapped it down on the desktop. "Name of mother, Joan Enid Marbal. That Morris woman ought to be locked up." Clover smiled weakly. "Put her out of your mind," she said. There was nothing more she could say without the risk of saying the wrong thing and setting Lizzie off again. "Do you want me to help in here?" she asked, "or would you rather be on your own?"
"Why would I want to be on my own?" Lizzie asked.
"Well," Clover said hesitantly, knowing she had already said the wrong thing. She tried to choose her next words carefully and without mentioning the doubt Violet had cast over Joan being Lizzie's natural mother. "I know Violet's mad, but even so having to hear all those allegations must have been awful for you."
"I thought you said I should put her out of my mind."
"I did but that's easier said than done, isn't it?"
"No." Lizzie said. "It's not - so if you want to be useful instead of standing there talking rubbish, you could empty out all the stuff in the filing cabinet. Muriel said I should give it to the accountant to sort out so it needs to be boxed." Lizzie began fishing around in the desk drawers again. The topic of Violet was closed.

Clover took out a handful of files and dropped them into the nearest cardboard box. "Gran said she'd bring pasties over at lunchtime," she said trying to lighten the atmosphere. Even in the early months of pregnancy, Lizzie had liked her food. Lizzie didn't answer. She had found a small black box at the back of one of the desk drawers. She pushed the hinged lid open with her thumb, read a note lying inside the box, screwed the piece of paper tightly in the palm of her hand and then slammed the lid

188

back down. "Here," she said to Clover. "You can have this."
Clover turned and took the box from Lizzie's outstretched hand. It
was a box she thought she recognised. She opened it and
gasped. "Oh Lizzie, it's Clara's emerald earrings. I couldn't
possibly accept them. They're far too valuable."
"I thought you liked them." Lizzie said tersely.
"I *do*!" Clover said. "I've always loved them. How could I not?
They're so beautiful." She took an earring from the box and held it
up. "Just look how they catch the light. They're so – so exquisite."
"You sound like Mrs. Melton," Lizzie said without humour.
"Everything's exquisite with her. Take them. I don't want them."
"I don't know what to say," Clover mumbled. "But if you're sure, I'll
keep them for you. Maybe one day you'll want to have them back.
"

"I won't," Lizzie said. "Keep them." She felt the note scratching the
skin under her tightly clenched fingers. *For my Princess on the
occasion of her 21st birthday.* She briefly wondered when her
father had taken the earrings from the safe and written the note.
Perhaps the night of the accident. Perhaps he'd been in a hurry
and forgotten to put them back. Not that it mattered. What did a
pair of earrings matter? Deep in her heart she knew he had
deceived her. They had all deceived her. That was all that
mattered.

Chapter 14

Sister Bernadette poured herself another cup of tea. She and Declan had moved out of the church into her sitting room. Declan's story was longer than she thought it would be and she had reached a point in it when the coldness of the church and the stiffness of her joints had forced her to seek physical comfort. While Declan was outside smoking a cigarette, Sister Bernadette contemplated all he had told her. The knowledge of Agnes' parentage and how she came to be left at the convent had not given Sister Bernadette the peace and relief that she'd hoped for. Indeed, knowing for sure that a member of her own family had been one of the protagonists, proved to be worse than not knowing. Sister Bernadette sipped her tea and began to mull over the details. Clover had turned out to be a disappointment. Sister Bernadette had quite liked the sound of her, until Declan told her that Marcus had left his wife for Clover and the pair of them had gone to live in either Bournemouth or Brighton, he wasn't sure. Clover had written shortly after the move to say that her mother had found out about her and Marcus and had disowned her. Clover had said that was no great loss. She wrote again once, but Lizzie never replied and when she and Declan moved to another flat, pretending to be a married couple they lost all contact with Clover. Declan said he had no idea how things turned out for her.

Declan came back into the room. He sat down and took the cup of tea Sister Bernadette offered him. "Lizzie had a terrible time of it when Agnes was born," he said. "And then her stitches turned septic."
Sister Bernadette winced. "When I said I wanted to know everything Declan, I didn't mean *everything*."
"No – but it could explain why there was no maternal bonding. Lizzie was too poorly to look after the baby. She had no contact with her, you see. The nurses cared for Agnes and it was several weeks before the pair of them were allowed out of hospital. By then, there was no chance of bonding – if there had ever been. I looked after Agnes 'cos Lizzie would have nothing to do with her. I

190

was supposed to've taken Agnes to the orphanage. That was the plan. But I couldn't do that. I knew you were here, so that's why I left her at the convent. Lizzie never knew," he added softly. "I never told her about you, or where I'd left Agnes."

Sister Bernadette thought Declan was beginning to sound a bit emotional, as well he might, nevertheless she was sure she couldn't cope with a grown man's tears, so tried to make him forget about Agnes for a while and talk about Lizzie. "Lizzie doesn't know you're here then? She's not with you obviously."

Declan made a hah sound that was half scornful half laugh. "I haven't seen Lizzie in over thirty years. She only took me to America with her so that I'd be safely out of the way and keep me mouth shut. She didn't want me anymore than she wanted Agnes. I knew that, but I wasn't going to miss out on a chance of a lifetime was I? She was my ticket to America and that was good enough for me. It wasn't long before we went our separate ways. I got married you know. I've two grown sons ...somewhere."

"Somewhere? Don't tell me you abandoned them at a convent too." Sister Bernadette said dryly.

"Ah no. They abandoned me more like. No more than I deserved, I know that. The devil drink, Aunt Bernadette. Working in Murphy's Wine Bar was grand until I started drinking as much as I was serving." Declan put down his cup and briskly rubbed his hands together as if brushing away the past. "But that was a long time ago. Things are different now. I'm back now and I went to make things up with Agnes." Sister Bernadette smiled sadly. "You've left it too late for that I'm afraid. I can't be sure she'll even want to see you Declan."

"Will you talk to her?" Declan said earnestly, "Try and make things right so I can see her?"

"I will." Sister Bernadette said. "I'll try but I can promise nothing."

Declan stood up. "I'm staying at the Volesworth Arms," he said. "When you've spoken to Agnes would you phone me to tell me what she says? If she'll agree to it, I'll call at Marbal House tonight – about seven o'clock. Would you tell her that? Maybe she'll let me take her out for dinner." Sister Bernadette got up from her chair. "I think you're rushing it Declan. I've no idea how

191

Agnes will respond when I tell her about you turning up out of the blue, but I suspect it won't be favourably. If I were you I'd leave it for a while before you start making plans to meet up with her - never mind anything else."

"I can't do that, Aunt Bernadette," Declan said. "I've lost too much time already. Just ask her for me. Course, if she won't see me yet, well then I'll have to wait."

As soon as Sister Bernadette had sorted out the business with the leaf and the Virgin Mary, she set out for Marbal House. She used her key for the downstairs door, and tried to rehearse what she would say as she walked along the corridor to the door leading to Agnes' flat. She just couldn't decide the best way to tell Agnes about Declan and as she knocked on Agnes' door, decided her best policy was to leave it to divine intervention. The Good Lord would put the right words into her mouth. Sister Bernadette knocked on the door again. There was a pause and then Agnes in an irritated voice demanded, "What? Who is it?"

"It's me – Sister Bernadette. Can I come in for a while Agnes?" Agnes opened the door a fraction. "I wasn't expecting you," she said, in a less than friendly tone.

"No, and I wouldn't be botherin' you Agnes, if it wasn't important. May I come in?" Sister Bernadette smiled benignly.

Agnes opened the door wider to let her through. Sister Bernadette knew from experience that if she waited to be asked to sit down, she'd be standing throughout, and so sat on one of the chairs by the electric fire which, mercifully, was switched on.

"Look," Agnes said, suddenly less hostile, "I bought meself a telly since you were here last." She nodded towards the portable television placed on a table next to the fire escape door, and went across to it and switched it on. She stood in front of it, for a moment oblivious of Sister Bernadette, her attention now directed at The Tweenies singing and twirling.

"That's grand," Sister Bernadette said weakly. "Grand company for you, but would you mind switching it off now Agnes, because I need to talk to you without distraction." Agnes compromised by turning down the volume and reluctantly came to sit opposite

Sister Bernadette. Agnes sat straight backed, her ankles and knees close together, her hands folded in her lap, the way the nuns had taught her. Now that Sister Bernadette knew who Agnes' father was, she searched her features for any likeness to Declan. She imagined she could see some similarities. They both had small, blue eyes and there was a something about the way they both set their mouths. Tight lipped. In fact now she thought about it, Agnes had a slight look of Kathleen, Declan's mother about her. "Well now Agnes, and how have you be keeping?" Sister Bernadette said by way of easing into the news she had come with it. But Agnes was keen to get back to The Tweenies and had no time for niceties. "I'm alright," she said, adding bluntly, "so what did you come for?"

Sister Bernadette said a silent prayer and then the words, "I had a surprise visitor today Agnes. A nephew of mine called. Declan came to see me all the way from America," sprang from her lips. Agnes looked unimpressed. Sister Bernadette surged on. "Agnes, you'll know I've often wondered who it was left you at the convent when you were a baby?"

Agnes nodded. Sister Bernadette cleared her throat. The Good Lord wasn't helping her out as much as she'd hoped. "Can you guess why Declan came to see me, Agnes?"

Agnes shrugged. "I dunno," she said.

"He had something he wanted to tell me." Sister Bernadette said.

"I 'spect he did," Agnes said, "if he'd come all the way from America."

"Can you not guess what it was, Agnes?"

"Not really, no." Agnes said, sounding disinterested. Sister Bernadette had a distinct feeling that the Good Lord had decided not to intervene after all. She was on her own then and as subtlety didn't seem to be working she may as well come straight out with it. "He came to tell me that he was the one who left you at the convent. It's my nephew Declan who's your father Agnes, and he wants to see you, if you'll let him" Sister Bernadette waited nervously for Agnes' reaction. Agnes seemed to sit even more rigidly, her small eyes opened a fraction wider, her hands so tightly clasped that her knuckles turned white. She stared at Sister Bernadette without speaking.

"Are you alright child?" Sister Bernadette said softly. "I know it's a terrible shock for you, sure it is, but would you say *something*. Tell me what it is you're thinking."

"What did he want to come back now for?" Agnes said in a cold voice. "Bloody cheek comin' back now, if you ask me."

"I am asking you Agnes. You're the important one and you don't have to see him if you don't want to." Sister Bernadette leaned forward and would have given Agnes a comforting pat on the knee but knew Agnes didn't like to be touched and so curtailed her tactile urges. "Why don't we have a nice cup of tea?" she asked instead. "And maybe I could tell you how it was you came to be left at the convent – if you want to hear it that is. And something else, Agnes. Remember how you once told me that this place feels like home to you? Well Marbal House is your home Agnes. At least it was your mother's home. Now isn't that amazing? Would you like me to tell you about that?"

A flicker of interest passed over Agnes' features. "I was alright as I was," she said tersely. "But now that you know, I'll have to know won't I?" Sister Bernadette looked bemused. "I don't quite follow, Agnes," she said frowning. Agnes sighed impatiently and stood up. "I can't have you knowin' stuff about me that I don't know. It would've been better if nobody knew nothin'." She checked the kettle for water, added more to it, and switched it on. "But now you know, I'll have to know, won't I?" Sister Bernadette decided it was best to agree to this logic, and began.

Throughout Sister Bernadette's retelling of Declan's story, Agnes remained silent. Sometimes she stood up and paced around the room, her arms folded, her face grim. At times her eyes glinted with anger. Sometimes she sat passively and stared into space. When Sister Bernadette had finished talking, Agnes surprised her by saying, "So he wants to come here at seven, does he? Tell 'im to come then."

"Are you sure you want Declan to come?"

"He might as well, seeing as how he's come all the way from America."

"Will it make it easier for you if I come with him?"

Agnes shook her head. "No. Give him the keys. He can come on his own."

"If you're sure that's what you want."

Agnes looked at the immaculate space around her. "I've got to tidy up now," she said. Sister Bernadette took the hint and stood ready to depart. Once she was gone, Agnes appeased her nerves by filling a bucket with hot, soapy water and disinfectant. She scrubbed and rubbed every available surface, then put on her coat, unlocked the door to the fire escape stairs and began to scrub them.

When Declan knew that Agnes had agreed to see him, he became nervous and excited. He took a bath, shaved, applied Brut liberally, put on clean underwear, a fresh shirt and his only suit. He smoothed his thinning hair into place, buffed up his shoes and went down to the Volesworth Arms Lounge Bar for a double whisky and water and as many cigarettes as he could smoke until his glass was empty. Agnes changed her orange bri-nylon polo neck sweater for a lime green one, combed the ends of her hair and pushed her Kirby grips up tighter, then she settled down to watch television.

At a quarter to seven Declan, sucking a mouthful of Tic-Tacs, left the Volesworth Arms and headed out of the town and up the hill to Marbal House. He wished he'd thought earlier of taking a present for Agnes, but what could you give to a thirty two year old daughter you'd abandoned when she was four weeks old? A bouquet was hardly adequate. Perhaps he should have bought a bottle of wine; they could have shared it to help break the ice, make them feel more relaxed and at ease with each other. He tried to imagine how Agnes was feeling at the prospect of meeting him. A bit angry probably and nervous, but he hoped she was feeling a smidgen of excitement too. Declan put his hands in his pockets. It was a cold night, already frosty and he was glad he'd had the whiskey to warm him up. As he neared Marbal House he tried to picture how Agnes would look. He wondered whether she had turned out to look like Lizzie.

Agnes opened the door to her father. He was gangly and grey and smelled strongly of the three things she hated most, after-shave, cigarettes and alcohol. She took a step back. "Agnes," Declan said, smiling, "you've no idea how pleased I am that you've agreed to see me." He was in truth a trifle disappointed at his first sight of Agnes. She was plain and her short, lanky, pinned back hair made her look like a skivvy. Her vile jumper clashed hideously with her washed out complexion. She was skinny as Lizzie had been and Lizzie had been no beauty yet she'd had something – a self-containment, which was both arrogant and intriguing. Agnes seemed plain dull. Plain and dull, if he was to believe his first impression. Declan walked into the cold room that had a pervading smell of disinfectant blended with bleach. The television had been left on with the volume turned down but he was still aware of spasmodic canned laughter and a flickering of colour which drew his eyes towards the screen, no matter how hard he tried to resist it. He wished Agnes would turn it off. "You've been here before, haven't you? Agnes said, speaking for the first time. She made it sound like an accusation. Then she pointed to a chair and told him he could sit down if he wanted. Declan, feeling edgy and not elated as he'd thought he would, sat and took another look at the room.

"I have been here," he said. "It looked a lot different then." It had been piled with junk mostly, and Clara's unsold paintings. Declan had come across a few treasures though, glass shaded oil lamps, old cameras, a trunk of Edwardian clothes and a load of toys that had been Jesse's when he was a boy. Declan had particularly liked a wooden Noah's Ark complete with its pairs of animals, all wrapped in tissue paper and as good as the day they were made. Lizzie had told him to take it to the charity shop, but he'd kept it for years and eventually gave it to his own sons to play with. They'd lost the animals and broke the ark in no time. Declan looked up at Agnes who stood with her arms folded, staring at him. "Won't you sit down too, Agnes?" he said. "We've got such a lot to say to each other." Agnes perched on the edge of the free chair. "Sister Bernadette told me everythin' so there's not that much to say." She sniffed. "You must've had a lot of money when you dumped me, seein' as you owned this place."

"Not me Agnes. Marbal House belonged to your mother, Lizzie." He felt even more ill at ease.

He knew what she was getting at. If Lizzie owned Marbal House they could have afforded to keep her if they'd chosen to. "Did...did the nuns not treat you kindly?" he asked.

Agnes shrugged. "They were alright."

"Not like a proper family though, was it?"

"Dunno. Never had one." Agnes stood up. "You can have a cup of coffee if you like, then you'll have to go. I've got things to do." Declan looked startled. "Have I got to go so soon? I was hoping we'd spend time chatting, getting' to know each other a bit. There's such a lot I want to find out. I know it was unforgivable, what we did to you, but I never stopped thinking about you Agnes, honest to God I didn't." He gave a hollow, nervous laugh. "I didn't think I'd find you again. I thought you'd be long gone from here – married with your own kids."

"I'm happy on me own." Agnes said. "I don't need no-one. Do you want a coffee or no?"

"I will, if it's not too much trouble." He watched Agnes as she turned and went into the little kitchen area, spooning instant coffee into mugs, adding sugar to both although he didn't take it. Her movements were small and jerky. Her greasy hair hung lifelessly over the collar of her jumper. His spirits sank. He shouldn't have come, it had been a mistake. He didn't want to know his daughter had turned out like this. Agnes returned with the coffee and set his down on the table. She remained standing to drink hers and constantly stared at him over the brim of her mug. "Who chose my name?" she asked suddenly.

Declan looked at her, surprised by the question. "Your name? I chose it," he said, sounding almost pleased with himself. "I thought it should be somethin' saintly seeing as –" He stopped himself from saying, seeing as I was going to take you to a

197

convent, and thought Jesus, how bad would that have sounded? "Do you like your name then, Agnes?" he said.

"No I think it's 'orrible," she said.

Declan sighed with disappointment. "Well now, isn't that a shame, seeing how it's the only thing I've ever given you." He couldn't drink the coffee, what with the sugar and a vague taste of bleach and the fact that he knew full well she'd never allow him to have a cigarette with it. He put it down and stood up. "Look Agnes," he said. "It's probably right that I go now. It's all been a bit of a shock, for you, hasn't it, me turning up like this? Perhaps we could get together again in a day or two – maybe go out for dinner or somethin'."

"I don't eat out," Agnes said. "You never know what the kitchens are like."

"Well – somethin' else then. Maybe I could take you out and buy you somethin' really nice. Some new clothes perhaps?"

Agnes tilted her head slightly. "You've got my keys," she said. You can leave them on the table."

"Ah right, so I have." Declan took the keys from his pocket and dropped them next to the coffee mug. He looked at her, unsure of what to do next. Should he put his arms around her and kiss her goodbye? Should he shake her hand? But Agnes resolved the situation by moving away from him, towards the television table. She pulled back the curtain at the side of it. "You can go out this way," she said. "Down the fire escape." She switched on an outside light and opened the door, letting in a blast of cold air. Declan moved towards it. "Well good-bye then Agnes, for now." he said and automatically held out his hand. Agnes looked at it, and briefly rested her fingers against his, and then she shut and locked the door behind him, brushed her hand off against her skirt, switched off the lights, fetched her coffee, turned up the television and settled down to watch Eastenders.

Long after Eastenders had finished, Agnes heard voices, one male and solemn, one female and excited, coming from the bottom of the fire escape. She stood very still for a moment, and then decided it was time to get ready for bed. She bleached and rinsed the cups, put them away, straightened the chairs and put on her favourite night attire – a pair of baggy pyjama trousers and a top printed with a winking owl on a branch; the owl so large it covered her flat chest. Agnes was about to remove her hairgrips, when she heard a loud knocking on her front door. She suspected it might be a police officer, and she was right. Agnes peered at him from behind the door she'd partially opened. "What d'you want?" she asked.

"I believe you had a visitor earlier this evening," the officer said. Agnes nodded.

"Would you mind if I came in for a moment? It's about your visitor, a Mr. Declan O'Connell, would that be right Miss...?" The officer waited for Agnes to offer her surname but as she only gave him a blank stare, he added tersely. "Could I have your name, miss – all of it."

"Agnes," she said. "Agnes Logan and that's all of it". She opened the door wide enough for the officer to enter. He stared at her winking owl for a second and then told her that Declan was dead. He told her that the woman in the downstairs flat had thought she'd heard a prowler and had called the police and that when he'd arrived to investigate, he'd found a man crumpled at the foot of the fire escape.

The officer told Agnes that he'd called an ambulance, but by the time the ambulance arrived, it was too late. Declan's neck had been broken by the fall. The ambulance was sent away, the coroner notified and a doctor called to sign the death certificate. Mr. O' Connell's body was now with Hendley undertakers. "His passport was in his wallet," the police officer added, "That's how we were able to identify him." He looked at Agnes' blank face and wondered whether she was simple or in shock. "Were you related to Mr.O' Connell?" he said, thinking that if she was, Agnes might tell him in what way. Then he remembered that Agnes only seemed to respond to direct questions. "Was he an uncle? Your dad? A friend?"

Agnes didn't want to say it, but she had to. "He was my dad," she said quietly.

199

She was in shock, then, the officer decided. "I'm sorry love. Why don't you sit down?" He waited until Agnes was sitting, her knees tight together under the baggy trousers, then he said, "You didn't hear anything this evening? Your dad falling, or the ambulance – or anything?" Agnes shook her head. "I had the telly on." She wished the officer would go away, but he sat down opposite her and asked if there was anyone he could contact for her. She thought for a moment and then said, "Sister Bernadette."

"Your sister, Bernadette?"

" She's not my sister," Agnes said, tutting with irritation. "She's -" Agnes suddenly realised that if Declan was Sister Bernadette's nephew, they were related after all, which was neat really, because she'd been given Sister Bernadette's surname. "She's my auntie now...I think."

"O.K. love, so where will I find your auntie?" The officer suppressed a sigh and tried to sound gentle. Agnes was beginning to exasperate him. She wasn't reacting right, and he wasn't entirely convinced now that it was due to shock, neither was he entirely convinced it was because she was a sandwich short of a picnic. In fact he didn't know what to make of Agnes. One thing he was sure of though, that there was a poor bugger lying with a broken neck in Henley's morgue with a daughter who didn't give a toss. The officer scrutinised Agnes' impassive face. "Did you two have a bit of a fall out, tonight? He watched her, waiting for a flicker of emotion. Agnes stared back. "How could we?" she said. "I haven't seen her."

"No – not Bernadette. Your dad. How were things between you when he left?"

"We were alright." Agnes didn't want to think about Declan being in her flat, she didn't want to remember anything about him being there. She wished the police officer would stop staring at her and just go away. And he thought he detected a slight uneasiness about Agnes. Her relationship with her father was a line to be pursued, but not now. He'd have a chat with the Bernadette woman first.

"So Agnes, and where might I find your Auntie Bernadette?"

"At the convent of course," Agnes said stoutly. "Where else would she be at this hour? So don't you go disturbin' the nuns at this time of night. You can tell her to come round in the morning - if she wants."

The police officer didn't argue. He stood up and asked Agnes to show him the door to the fire escape. She pulled back the curtain and the officer unlocked the door and stood on the platform step, looking down into a pool of darkness. He walked back into the room and locked the door again. "Had your dad gone down those steps before?" he asked.

Agnes shrugged. "I dunno. He might have done, when he used to live 'ere."

"Why didn't he leave by the main stairs tonight?" Agnes felt a bit queasy. She didn't like all these questions or the way the policeman stared at her. "He was in a hurry and this way's quickest. He said 'e had to meet someone, but I think he wanted to have another drink," She pushed at her hair grips until they dug into her scalp.

"He'd been drinking then, had he?"

Agnes nodded. "I could smell it on him. Couldn't you smell it?" The police officer didn't answer. He took out a notebook and wrote something down. "Shame your dad was in such a hurry," he said, as he put his biro away. "Because he never got to where he was going anyway, did he? Now if he'd left by the front door .. ah well." The police officer gave Agnes a rueful look and tried to keep his eyes from wandering back to the hideous owl. "Right, we'll leave it there for now and I'll make sure this Sister Bernadette is notified first thing tomorrow." Along with C.I.D. he decided.

In the morning a WPC broke the news of Declan's death to Sister Bernadette, and then drove her to Agnes' flat. Sister Bernadette searched Agnes" face for some kind of emotion but couldn't find any. The WPC took a statement from Agnes and, before he left, said that the coroner would almost certainly record Declan's demise as death by misadventure; yet Sister Bernadette had, as indeed had the police officer, an uneasy feeling that her nephew's death had not been entirely accidental. She looked down the length of the fire escape, to the black asphalt below where Declan's twisted body had been found. She said a silent prayer for his soul, and walked back into the flat.

Could it be that Agnes doused the steps of the fire escape knowing full well that by the evening they would be iced over and treacherous, she wondered? Had Agnes switched off the lights because of her thrifty nature, or because she wanted to plunge Declan into unexpected darkness? Had the television really drowned the sound of his scream as he slipped and fell? The girl in the downstairs flat had heard him. Sister Bernadette looked across at Agnes who was busy rubbing away at an unblemished work-top. "Wasn't this a tragic way for it all to end Agnes?" Sister Bernadette said, with a sigh.
"It was an accident."
"Ah, so you keep saying. But you *did* pour water over those steps last night, didn't you now Agnes? I can still smell the bleach."
"I like to keep them clean." Agnes said defensively. "There's no law against keepin' your steps clean, is there?"
"Well now, there could be, under the circumstances." Sister Bernadette sat down. "Would you stop that cleaning Agnes, and come and tell me about last night?"
Agnes reluctantly put down her dishcloth and stood, arms folded, in front of Sister Bernadette. "We talked a bit. He didn't stay long. He said he'd come again another day – take me out to buy some clothes. Bit late for all that. He should have stayed in America." Agnes sniffed. "Then I opened the door for him."
"Knowing that the steps would be frozen and dangerous?"
"I didn't think."
Sister Bernadette sighed. "Well now, Agnes," she said, "I believe this was one time when you *did* think. You wanted to harm Declan, right enough. Course, he could've got away with a broken ankle. You weren't to know it would be his neck that got broken. But you hoped now, didn't you Agnes?"
Agnes looked defiant "It was an -"
"An accident, so you keep saying."
"You can't prove no different."

Sister Bernadette stood up to leave "You're right enough there, Agnes," she said, and smiled, a sad smile.

"If you're goin' you'll need these." Agnes reached behind her and picked up the keys to her flat from where Declan had dropped them. Sister Bernadette looked at the keys lying in the palm of Agnes' hand, and shook her head. "No Agnes," she said. "I don't believe I will be needing them."

Sister Bernadette walked away from Marbal House for the last time. She knew that she had done as much as she could do for Agnes and prayed God would forgive her that it hadn't been enough.

Agnes put her foot on the pedal bin and dropped the keys inside. She held her hand under the hot tap until the water had scorched away the key's contamination. Scoured of Declan and indeed Sister Bernadette, Agnes felt a sense of contentment. She would be left alone now and that was the way she liked it. Tomorrow was Friday. The consultants would be doing their rounds. Agnes smiled briefly at the thought of the thorough cleaning job she would do on her ward.